A SCARLETT OLEANDER NOVEL

TRADED
&
Teased

LIZ HIGHLAND

Liz Highland

To my brats.

You know what you want and you go after it. Don't ever stop.
Daddy will understand.

Content Considerations

This is an adult erotic romance. It will include material intended for those mature enough to read about such things as graphic sex, violence, and criminal activity. If you wish to avoid spoilers, you can skip these, but don't say I didn't warn you.

This book contains heavy kink, but it is not a manual for BDSM. It discusses negotiations and aftercare, but please remember Risk-Aware Consensual Kink (RACK) if you are interested in setting up your own dynamic. Additionally, note that the characters in this book frequently act without taking proper precautions or preparation. For more information about kink and how to play in the best environment and headspace, visit www.kink101.com.

Things to consider before reading are as follows:

- Sex club owner MMC and activities
- Discussions and acts of sex work
- Don consigliere MMC
- Sex worker FMC
- Morally gray MCs
- Virgin trope
- Age Gap

- MMF romance
- Mafia and criminal activity with violence (including gun violence)
- Murder and discussions of past murder
- Kidnapping and hostage situations
- Abusive father (emotional and verbal, with some physical at the end)
- Touch her and die
- She needs protection
- OTT Alphaholes
- Forbidden romance, e.g., Dad's best friend/godfather and boss/employee
- Alcohol use
- Queer sex, including FF and MM
- Dom/sub dynamics, with Master/slave play (in a BDSM dynamic, not related to race)
- Daddy kink without age play
- Degradation and praise
- Humiliation and corruption kink
- Masturbation
- Saliva play
- Anal
- Oral
- Rimming
- DP/DVP
- Bondage and blindfolds
- Impact play
- Gun play (unsafe; do not replicate)
- Subservience and service kink
- Orgasm denial, edging, and orgasm torture
- Collaring
- Breath play
- Brat and brat taming
- Voyeurism and exhibitionism

- Squirting and cum eating
- Sharing

Playlist

If you're into listening to music as you read, I present to you a playlist of songs that fit the vibe of Traded & Teased. While some songs may sound like they are only between two love interests, I like to imagine that it's all three of these wild babies singing their hearts out to each other. Not that Reagan would be caught dead singing, even if he has a great voice.

For the full ham playlist experience, check it out on YouTube here: https://tinyurl.com/TradedTeasedPlaylist

- Gangsta- Kehlani
- Genius- LSD
- You Don't Own Me- Grace feat. G-Eazy
- Do You Know (What It Takes)- Robyn
- Play With Fire (feat. Yacht Money) (Extended Mix)- Sam Tinnesz
- I Dare You- The xx
- Dreamers- K.Flay
- Gasoline- Halsey
- Bubblegum Bitch- MARINA
- I Feel Like I'm Drowning- Two Feet
- Break Me Beautiful- Silk & Smoke Radio (on YouTube)
- I Want To- Rosenfeld
- High Enough- K. Flay

- chosen one- Ella Martine
- Go Fuck Yourself- Two Feet
- Love is a Bitch- Two Feet
- Run- AWOLNATION
- Can You Hold Me- NF
- sex money feeling die (slowed version)- Lykke Li
- Make Me Feel- Elvis Drew

1
The Attempt

Lila

My blood zinged, dancing in my veins with a mix of apprehension and boredom. I was so ready for tonight to be over, but there was no way I'd rather be at home. *Ugh, not with Dad's head shoved right up his ass.*

"Lila, you're needed in the Red Room. A new client has requested you specifically. He's passed the preliminaries, but let me know if anything feels off. We're having trouble getting his details from older than a few years ago."

I smiled, pulling the red lollipop out of my mouth with a satisfying pop. "*Edward*, what are you doing dragging your fine ass down here?"

Cocking a brow at the hunk that was our CEO and owner, I smirked and pulled down on the tiny harness bra that barely kept the girls in place. He glared, even if I knew he didn't mean it. No one called him that except me. It was *always* "Mr. Scarlett."

"It's a special request, *Lila*, and Elle is busy. Are you good to go out there?" Boss Man raised his brows at me, and if anyone else had said it, I'd have taken the remark for impatience.

But not Edward.

The big, scary owner of the Scarlett Oleander was really just a giant teddy bear, admittedly one who looked like he could fuck your damn brains out or break your kneecaps in equal measure, but he was also...well, sweet. He actually checked in on all the subs, even the Doms. I hadn't been working for the club for long, and that was clear from day one.

"Yes. I'm fine. I'll see you in an hour, Boss Man."

Sticking the lollipop back in my mouth, I winked at him and then walked past to exit the changing rooms. As I did, I was sure to smirk at Edward, dragging my long fingernails across his chest. Add in a hip sway for just the right about of tease, and I was so very ready to get fucked. Who cared if it was Edward filling my head when it happened, right?

I walked down the long hall of rooms, doors lined up perfectly on either side. It was familiar to me now, and even the subtle nerves I'd had when I first started were gone. It'd been like about a month, after all, and once you'd seen one cock you'd seen them all.

Well, there are a few I wouldn't mind getting a peek at. But that's about as likely as Edward relaxing.

Mr. Scarlett had been incredibly hesitant to hire me, flat-out saying no at first. He actually *knew* my dad, but with my dear, absent father's permission and Reagan on standby to keep an eye on me, it appeared that it was perfectly fine with the Famiglia de Carpinelli Don that his daughter worked at a sex club that specialized in BDSM.

I laughed to myself as I walked down to the far end, where the Red Room was located—the private chamber for the most *involved* client requests. I could still remember how Edward had looked at me: wide-eyed and slack-jawed. He did *not* want me working here, saying I was a threat to his business.

Still, I won him over when I'd lied and said this wouldn't be my first time. That eased the tension of being the cause of Dad's coronary when he put two and two together and realized that he'd basically sold my virginity to some stranger.

Sorry, Dad. I'm not letting you make any more money off me, and this'll keep you from marrying me off to some enemy famiglia.

I mean, yeah. It was a lie, but I was the only one who knew that I was still sporting my V-card at a sex club.

It was a damn miracle I was able to pull it off, but most of the time, the Johns were content to get some good smacks in, a bit of fingering, and maybe some eating me out if I was lucky. Still, I was known for one thing, and that's what the guys usually asked for.

Because no one gives a better blow job than yours truly.

Hence the lollipop. It helped with saliva. *Speaking of…*

I crunched the thing between my teeth and swallowed down the rest of the sugary pieces. The sweet cherry taste lingered on my tongue as I knocked lightly on the door to the Red Room. A deep voice answered quickly enough, a rough "come in" booming through the lacquered black wood.

Let's just hope this one isn't one of those rare "I can go twice" assholes.

Oh my god, someone is trying to kill me! What the absolute fuck? I mean, sure, my dad is like constantly under attack, but me? The hell?!

God, please let Edward know what to do.

My bare feet pounded on the floor as I ran down the hall toward his office. Jesus, I'd been working for him for four goddamn weeks, and I was running to the guy to keep me safe from one of my father's numerous fucking enemies.

The glorious beacon that was the door was right there, though, and I pushed everything into my legs, knowing that the asshole in the Red Room would be coming around from that knock to the head any damn second.

And then I heard it.

A very distinctive, very *familiar* sound gently boomed out of Edward's office. I'd know that sound anywhere, and if it weren't for the fact that it was actually quiet in the hall, I would have assumed it was coming from one of the other suites. But nope. Edward was fucking someone.

Holy shit.

As I stepped forward, curiosity gripping me, I cracked open the door. I had to know who my hot-as-hell boss was actually fucking in his office, maybe see if they were okay with a third once this whole assassination thing was over.

But when I saw him, my jaw dropped.

"Reagan?"

My godfather—my dad's bestie and the bodyguard who was supposed to be here only to keep an eye on me—was balls fucking deep in Edward's ass. In fact, Reagan's hand was wrapped around Edward's throat as he bent the owner over his own desk. Edward's hand tore away from his cock, which dripped with a sticky trail of precum, and the two of them separated so damn fast I was shocked neither of them fell over.

"I…What…" The words were gone. I was too blown away to think, at least about anything that wasn't how incredibly fucking hot that just was.

"Lila," Reagan's voice was a menacing growl, and it really should have scared the fuck out of me instead of turning me on, "the fuck are you doing in here?"

"I…" Oh, shit, I really needed to say something instead of standing there like a moron.

Edward was shoving his cock back inside his pants as Reagan did the same, and all I could do was stare at them, silently wishing they hadn't stopped so that I could enjoy the show.

Enjoy the show…enjoy the show? Why does that–Fuck!

At once, I remembered why the hell I ran to Edward's office–

the phrase being one of my favorites and utterly interrupted by a firm slap across my face that had *not* been negotiated. Neither had the gun that was pointed at me seconds later.

Shaking myself, I pointed out into the hall, the door behind me still cracked open. "He fucking pulled a gun on me! It has to be someone out to hurt my dad, right?"

"Someone–Fuck."

Reagan hurried forward, snagging a suit jacket from a rack of them near the desk. Edward apparently had backups available, but I was still having trouble thinking around the fact that I'd just seen the two of them screwing, their clothes still mostly in place, right in Edward's office. *So hot. So not the point.*

When he reached me, Reagan threw the jacket in my face. "Put that on."

I barely caught the thing, scoffing out my annoyance as Reagan shoved past. As I slipped my arms into the holes, I remembered I'd discarded the harness bra I was wearing, and the minute coverage it offered was gone. My tits had been out this whole time.

Whoops.

Edward came up to me in a flash next, his hands going to my shoulders as he lowered into my line of sight.

"Are you okay?" The words were choppy and pointed as if Edward were trying to get through to someone in shock.

I wasn't, though, not because of the killing thing at any rate. I mean, it was mostly because they'd been–Yeah, I needed to stop thinking about it.

"I'm fine. I hit the guy on the head with one of the stupid glass decoration things. He dropped like a sack. But he had a gun, and…how did he get in?"

I'd had the thought right away, but now that I voiced it to Edward, I realized how big of a deal it actually was. Someone with a mean streak had gotten into the Scarlett Oleander. That wasn't supposed to be possible.

Glaring up over me, Edward's muscles strained beneath his skin as he clenched his jaw.

"I don't know."

We met Reagan by the Red Room door after Edward had taken another five minutes to ensure I was okay. I knew it was his job and all, being the owner of the club, but I was starting to get annoyed by the pestering. My own Dad didn't "mother hen" this much, so I wasn't used to all the attention.

"There's no one here."

I looked up from the floor, my eyes tracking the intricate geometric shapes that had been created with shimmering tiles, and Reagan glared at me.

"I searched the room from top to bottom. I don't see—"

"I'm not lying!" I interrupted, my brows shooting to my hairline as I surged forward. "Why the hell would I lie about that? I know how serious it is."

Edward appeared before me, having slipped around my side to face off with me. "Are you sure it wasn't something else? A prop he wasn't supposed to have? Did you negotiate CNC?"

"No, it was not a prop. I know what a real fucking gun looks like. And no, we didn't. The guy wanted a blow job, Edward. It was damn straightforward. I pegged him as a newbie until he slapped me across the face. Which, you know, was right before he stuck a mother fucking gun in it."

Reaching for my chin, Edward turned my face to the side, eyeing my cheek that still subtly burned. I stared up at the ceiling, so over this fucking interrogation that I didn't deserve.

"It's red. "Look," Edward let go, turning to Reagan, who had folded his arms over his chest and stood in the hallway like a menacing shadow, "we'll check the camera feeds."

They work in the hallway."

"Fine." Reagan rolled his eyes, shaking his head. "But if you were fucking playing, Lila, I'm going to have a real fun talk with your father."

I just glared right back at him. I wasn't nuts. I knew a bad sitch when I was in one. Being a mafioso's daughter has a way of providing that education hard and fast. But Reagan was a grump at the best of times and a downright asshole at the worst of them. So this was hardly new.

"Can I come with?" I looked from Reagan to Edward, ensuring the glare stayed in place until I met Boss Man's eyes. "I want to see it for myself."

Edward sighed. "Yes, that's fine. And Jesus, you two. Knock it off. I swear, for being Lila's godfather, you both seem to prefer antagonizing each other."

Reagan got moving quickly, heading down the hall to where I assumed the security room was located.

"Don't pin that shit on me. Lila's been a spoiled brat since day one."

I scoffed, my jaw dropping as I furiously followed after him. "Oh, fuck you, too, asshole."

"That's enough," Edward boomed, and I clammed right the fuck up, never having heard him like that before.

Seeming to eye me as he walked past a door and then came to a stop, Reagan cocked his head. It was as if he were measuring the exchange between me and the boss for helpful hints and ways to rein in his goddaughter.

Tough luck, Reagan. I know you way too well for that. You wouldn't hurt me even if I asked you to. Not with dear old dad in the picture.

I didn't bother saying any of that, though. Reagan already knew. I already knew. Papa Carpinelli had cracked down on the law about his daughter right at the beginning. Reagan had gone from a rather "wild" consigliere–from what I'm told–to a glorified babysitter damn quick.

We both resented the fuck out of it.

"Lila," Edward's voice almost crooned behind me, and the tension that had been crowding my spine eased a bit, "I need you to step aside so I can unlock the door."

I couldn't tell if it was a flirt or if Edward just didn't know the sound of his own voice, but that seemed unlikely. *Ugh, I'm probably reading into things–again.*

Yes, it was true. Me and the dating world had never really gotten along well, which was probably why I'd ended up here and managed to hang onto my virginity despite everything. I wasn't sexually active unless I was working, and it wasn't because being on-call had taken the shine off the rose.

On the contrary, I knew what I liked now, at least much more, and my already high standards had gone way up.

"Sorry." I shimmied to the side, clutching the jacket of Edward's that I was still wearing over my bare chest.

Edward unlocked the security room, and the three of us stepped inside. Boss Man sat in the main–and only–chair while Reagan and I stood and peered over his shoulder.

"Okay, I'll pull up the footage from the hall when you went into the Red Room." Edward did his thing on the computer, quite familiar with the program that was utterly alien to me. "Here we go."

The screen displayed an overhead shot of the hall. The camera was positioned at the far end, where the Red Room was located, so the image of me appeared to be approaching the screen, getting closer to the camera. I knocked and went inside just like I remembered.

There was nothing for a few minutes, about ten or so, and then I came running out of the door. That part I remembered, too.

"He has to come out. I wouldn't make this up. I swear."

Neither of the guys was looking at me, but Edward stayed

focused on the screen without closing the program. He was at least willing to wait it out.

It felt like years, staring at that damned screen and hoping that the guy would walk out. I knew he had, too. I actually wasn't lying, and the irony of the consistent liar asking people to believe her was not lost on me.

The slut who cried wolf. Great.

But then, a dark figure stumbled out of the Red Room door, clutching his head. He weaved a bit, careening into the wall at one point. That's when I saw it.

"Wait. Go back."

Edward turned toward me. "Lila?"

"Go back to went he hit the wall and pause it." I met his eyes, pleading. "*Please.*"

"Alright." Edward hovered over the recording's progress bar, finding the frame we wanted. "Say when."

"This is fucking bullshit, Lila. If you're playing us–"

But Reagan didn't get to finish before I blurted out, "There!"

Pausing the feed, Edward caught the guy falling into the wall just in time. Because as the fucker did, his jacket had ruffled, and tucked into the interior pocket was a gun, the handle catching the light so that it reflected right into the camera.

"Well, I'll be damned." Edward leaned in, examining the footage. "He's got a gun."

Faster than Edward or I could account for, Reagan shoved the boss's chair to the side and surged forward, getting his face in the screen. He managed to knock me over in the process, and I cursed as my ankle hit the sharp edge of one of the legs on Edward's rolling chair.

The room was quiet, I rubbed my new slice, and then Reagan stepped back from the screen and bee-lined it out of the room. Edward and I were quick to follow, which kind of sucked, considering my ankle hurt and I was going barefoot at the moment.

"Reagan," Edward called out, "what are you doing?"

"He needs to know." My godfather hardly paused to look back at Edward. "Emilio's daughter was almost killed. On *my* watch. He needs to know–now."

"You want to tell my dad now?" I faltered, my eyes going everywhere before landing on Reagan. "He's going to be fucking pissed. I...I don't know."

Stepping up to me, Reagan leveled me with an icy stare. He was right in my face, and I couldn't help but tremble slightly.

"I do. We're fucking telling him."

2
The Chat

Reagan

Lila looked seconds from crying, and I just…I could not see that right now. But I couldn't back down either. So, after a moment, she nodded, remaining silent as her stare went to the floor.

"If you're leaving now to talk with him, I'll accompany you."

Edward stepped forward, a hand going to Lila's shoulder in a move to provide quiet comfort.

"And why exactly are you coming?" I glared over at him, even though I knew it wasn't Edward I was really mad at.

No, that would be me.

I was supposed to be protecting Lila–my goddaughter and charge, who had only been permitted to work there because I would be around–but instead, I got caught with my literal pants down.

Emilio was going to be furious. I'd be lucky if I made it out of that conversation alive, but it needed to be done. And if I was deleted from the Family as a result, well, I had it coming, didn't I?

I failed her. Lila was almost killed.

"Because this happened at my club." Edward's voice forced me out of my head. "Emilio's Family drama had spilled out onto *my* floor, and I won't have it. My staff is to be safe at all times. But there is only so much I can do in the face of mafia resources."

We didn't say mafia out loud in public spaces. We weren't morons, and here was Edward dropping that word even though his precious staff might hear us, which would put them all in danger.

He was serious.

"Fine." I stared off for a moment before returning my angry glare to the two of them. "We go now, and we go *quietly*. Lila, get changed."

She snapped into focus, her hazel stare coming up to mine. The confusion and overwhelm there was so fucking obvious, and she was coming down from the shock going by the way her reactions were sluggish.

"Umm, right. Okay. I'll be right back."

Turning on her heel, she sped down the hall to the changing room. It left Edward and me alone in the corridor, and I didn't want to hear what I knew he was about to say.

"We're going to have to address the…*incident* as well."

Facing away from him, I watched the changing room door for the moment Lila stepped back out.

"No, we don't." I wasn't interested in entertaining the idea of all three of us chatting about what Lila had seen; I'd been dealing with it on my own. "I've got it covered."

Edward scoffed behind me. "Sure you do, asshole. Sure you do."

Arriving at the compound with both Edward and Lila in tow was quite the affair. I could see the guys staring at us from a mile away, and they all needed to get their fucking eyes back in their damned sockets, or I was going to do it for them.

"Don't you have things to do?" I glared at Ricco as he watched me climb the massive steps up to the front door.

The guy didn't say anything, and I walked with Lila and Edward right on my heels past the threshold and inside the enormous manse.

Emilio was far from subtle, so when we got inside, I wasn't surprised to hear Edward quietly scoff. The decor screamed, "I have money," and I knew that's all that Emilio was really trying to do with it anyway. He wasn't one for minimalism, and when his wife, Mariana, had died, he redecorated the house in *his* style.

Ornate curving staircases sat on either side of the foyer, going up to the second floor, where you could get to the upper levels—and other wings—of the house. The floor was a cream marble that contrasted with their dark wood and the deep mahogany color of everything else made of wood in the entire damn house.

Light, it certainly was not.

Edward stepped to my side as we approached the stairs on the left, his gaze traveling up to the massive chandelier hanging from the ceiling.

"Subtle really isn't in Emilio's repertoire, is it?"

I couldn't help the scoff that bled into a laugh. "That's a no."

"Explain to me how it can be both gaudy and overwhelming while still feeling cold and devoid of life."

Lila laughed at that one, coming up along my other side. "You've met the man, haven't you?"

Edward smiled at her, and it was odd to be stuck in the middle of them as we walked down to the East Wing, where Emilio's office lay. Even stranger still, it felt sort of *right* to have them flanking me as they were.

My two charges. Too bad I'd gone and fucked this up royally by allowing a hitman into the club to kill Lila. He hadn't succeeded, but something told me that wasn't going to matter to the don.

We walked down the long carpeted hall, the sound of our steps so muffled that it was nearly silent. I could sense the tension radiating from my companions for the day, mirrored by my own, but Lila seemed especially off.

And, of course, she did. She'd nearly died, and now that the shock was receding somewhat, Lila was likely feeling the full force of all the fear she'd blocked out. I didn't like it. I'd always felt protective of her. And sure, that was my job, but you spend enough time around some–even someone as fantastically bratty as Lila–as you tend to start caring about their wellbeing.

The door to Emilio's office was shut, so as we approached, I wrapped my knuckles against the wood panel firmly.

"Come in."

He didn't sound to be in too horrible of a mood, though that was difficult to determine with the don, grouchy fuck that he was. And that was coming from me. King of Grumps, according to Lila.

Stepping inside, I whispered to Lila and Edward before approaching Emilio's desk.

"Let me do the talking. I know how to handle Emilio."

The two of them glanced at each other, something brewing behind their eyes, and then both of them nodded. It was off, and I didn't trust either of them as far as I could throw them.

"Reagan," Emilio eyed them, running an appraising stare over the group, "and you've brought company. Lila."

The way he gritted out her name told me he was already displeased with her arrival, which did *not* bode well for her–or any of us.

"And Mr. Scarlett. Such an interesting gang of fools is interrupting my afternoon. And to what do I owe the displeasure?"

I'd known Emilio for nearly my entire life. We grew up

in this Family together, he by blood, and I was roped into it because I wouldn't leave his side once we became friends as kids. So, when I saw him acting like this, it was a real dick-punch.

Emilio was never a "good" guy, but he wasn't like this. It felt odd, and I'd been seeing more and more of it lately. Still, there were more important things to be thinking about instead of Emilio's bad mood.

"Your daughter was nearly killed." I looked him dead in the eye. "It's fortunate that she has some semblance of self-defense training."

"At my club, I might add. And I know that I've made it clear that your 'business' is supposed to stay well away from mine aside from the payments."

Edward's voice was smooth and direct, but dammit, he wasn't supposed to be butting into this conversation.

"Lovely rug, by the way." He glanced down at the large carpet beneath our feet, the deep red and cream colors mingling as they created a traditional pattern of swirls and vaguely floral shapes. "Persian?"

I clenched my jaw, clamping down on my molars so hard that I thought they might crack. *That little brat is going to get it.*

Glaring across the room, Emilio tented his fingers as his elbows rested on his desk, the deep brown matching the entire home. The intricate, oversized details carved into the surface made the thing look unwieldy and heavy, this thick monstrosity that boasted way too fucking loudly how much money the guy made.

"Edward." Emilio eyed him, both of them utterly locked in, a silent battle raging. "Are you saying that this little mishap was *your* fault?"

Mishap? Jesus, Emilio. Lila is right here.

Risking a glance in her direction, I noticed that Lila wasn't looking up at her dad. Her eyes focused on the floor, and even though it was subtle, her bottom lip trembled slightly.

"Hardly. The security footage showed a pro. We ran the usual background check, and I even advised Lila to be cautious. Thank god, that actually worked."

The don didn't respond, and I took a step forward, putting myself more in his eyeline than Edward.

"It was Mr. Scarlett. And aside from going in that room with her," I raised my brows, knowing that Emilio was aware of my word to avoid that at all costs on Lila's demand, "there was little I was going to be able to do either. Which, frankly, pisses me off. The guy knew this was the best way at her. He had inside information."

Closing his eyes for a moment, Emilio dropped his head toward his desk. It was several moments later when he let out a sigh and then stood up, the chair he sat in squeaking loudly in the quiet room. But for each moment that I watched him come around his desk and lean back against it, Emilio wasn't reading like a father upset that his daughter had been in danger.

Something was just off, and it didn't sit right with me. Emilio had never been especially doting, and sure, I never thought he would be. Still, this was a level of apathy about Lila's near-miss that I couldn't even understand from a distant friend, let alone the girl's fucking dad.

"So," Emilio finally looked back up at the three of us, his stare zeroing in on Lila, "what I'm hearing is that my daughter took a stupid risk that I warned her about months ago. What I'm hearing is that my *fucking daughter* got herself into a goddamn mess with someone from another family because she just had to go off and stick it to her old man, sell her good for cash."

I wasn't one to have my jaw drop, but the shock of Emilio's words hit hard, and I had to force myself to swallow down the immediate rage that roared to life in my blood. Why the fuck was he talking about her like that?

Lila shifted forward, her head still down like some scared animal facing a predator.

"Dad, I–"

"You what? You thought that it would be fun to fuck strangers? You thought that because Edward knows me, it wouldn't be risky? Use your fucking brain, Lila! You were reckless, as always. You're going to wind up right where your mother is. Six feet underground. You need to remember your place, your role in this Family."

I was an asshole, and even I knew that was a low fucking blow. Flicking my eyes to Lila, I watched her eyes widen as big as saucers, a glossy coating covering them as unshed tears built up. The girl had barely been able to say two words, and Emilio clearly just wanted to scream at her.

"Emilio," I turned toward him, the urge to do something for Lila too strong to fight, "she agreed to have me on site. That wasn't being reckless. This guy had information he shouldn't. He–"

"That's enough," he cut in. "I'm not interested in excuses. I shouldn't be surprised."

He wasn't even looking at her. Emilio didn't throw one glance in Lila's direction as she stood there, taking the brunt of his words and trying not to crumble. Worse, the asshole seemed…bored–like this was all just an *inconvenience* that he shouldn't have to deal with.

"Lila never has been good at much." Pushing off the desk, Emilio turned his back on them, going back to his plush seat. "If only I'd had a son like I should have. A proper heir. Hmm, such a shame."

Floored was a polite way to put it. I couldn't think of what else to say to him, but there *was* more to this. No one gets into the Scarlett Oleander without background checks, and you don't know that, know that you have to fake a record, unless you know about the club. You don't know how to book with *Lila* unless you already know about the club.

Goddamn it.

"You're dismissed," Emilio announced. "I'll deal with it."

Before I could say another word, Lila flew out of the room, sprinting down the hall faster than I thought she was capable of. Edward glanced over at me, the look telling, and I nodded in response.

We needed to go back to the club. This wasn't over.

3
The Plan

Lila

The boom from my door slamming echoed through my room and out into the hall. I flicked over the lock, even though I knew that if my dad wanted in badly enough, he'd just use his key. But something told me Emilio Carpinelli wasn't looking for another heart-to-heart.

His point was made—in spades.

God, I've never seen him like...that.

I mean, I wasn't an idiot. Dad was *not* a cuddly teddy bear, but he usually didn't scream at me. Sure, the volume went up only a few times, but his intensity—the things he fucking said—made up for it. Hell, most of the time, Dad was content to basically ignore me. If it didn't have to do with my eventual marriage to someone from another Family—a situation that had never come up because Emilio rarely made deals, preferring to eliminate his enemies—my father was more than happy to pretend I didn't exist.

A blessing and a curse.

Still, blaming me for the incident was a new low. I knew my dad didn't see me as much, which was sort of my fault because I leaned into it. The "ditzy mob princess" persona served its purpose and allowed me a bit of freedom, really. If I couldn't be trusted with information, the Family didn't give it to me. If they believed I couldn't handle it, I didn't have to.

But I wasn't loving how it was working against me now. Dad really thought it was my fault some asshole tried to kill me. And yeah, hearing him call me a slut–without saying the actual word–was not what I'd call fun.

God, he'd been furious when I told him I'd lost my virginity. That was the only other time I'd seen him that blatantly aggressive with me. I still stood by it, though. I knew it had been the smart move. If I were "spoiled goods," I was less appealing to another Family looking to establish a treaty. Sure, I still was, but that lie had gone over so well, even I forgot sometimes.

It was about then that I realized I was still standing in front of my closed door. I hadn't moved. The deep wood panels were still staring me in the face, and it was dead silent. I hated silence. It's been way too much of a constant with my mom gone.

She was the one who always had music playing in the house–the only one who seemed to be able to temper my father and keep his more cruel side at bay.

Lord knew why she married the asshole. It clearly wasn't out of love, and not for the first time, I wondered if my mom was some bargaining chip another Family had put forth to prevent war. Maybe that was why my dad was in no hurry to do the same; the rewards hadn't outweighed the costs.

With a deep breath, I finally turned around, scanning my room for something to do next. I was never good at planning things out, so it seemed as likely as anything else that I'd find the answer amongst my fluffy duvet and plethora of pillows.

The sound of pattering feet on the wood floor started abruptly and got louder as they approached me from the large walk-in closet to my left.

I got my hands up just in time to keep Ludo from crashing into me. "Hi, buddy. D'you miss, momma?"

Ludo's short tail wagged nonstop as he bounced up and down, jumping up enough to lick me across the face. I scratched him behind the ears, manipulating the pointy little devils so he almost looked like an alien. When I finally knocked him down–and he actually stayed–I pointed to the bed, wearing my "stern" face.

"Go lie down."

The Doberman quickly obeyed, hopping up onto my bed and then turning around to lie down facing me. His tail still wagged incessantly, and I couldn't help but smile.

"I'm getting changed. Stay."

Whining a little, Ludo remained on the bed because he was a good boy, and I knew I could leave him in my room and trust him not to get into anything. I'd taken the time with the trainer to be there for every moment, and the two of us just got each other.

He was my baby, and the only other person I trusted around him was Reagan. Though, that asshole made enough jokes about the dog peeing in my bed so frequently that I installed a doggie door in the closet that went down to a dog run in the back using a little ramp.

Sometimes, having money really was nice–even if it was dirty.

Padding into my closet, I was about to take off my harness bra when I remembered that I was still wearing Edward's jacket. The look definitely didn't help my situation with Dad. But fuck him. It still wasn't my fault that some guy got into the SO and tried to kill me.

Reagan thinks something is up there. He's never been wrong, either.

Shaking myself–decidedly not dwelling on that right now–I undid the three buttons that sat a little too low on my petite frame. Edward's jacket slipped off, and I tossed it in the hamper in the corner. The housekeeper would launder it and give it right back, so Edward would have his expensive suit back in order in no time.

Unless I keep it...

The tiny boyshorts, which barely covered my ass, and fishnets were next. Those I didn't bother tossing in the laundry. Nope, they went straight to the trash in my bathroom, which was right off my closet instead of my bedroom proper. I hadn't understood the design at first, but now I loved it.

Because the thing was, I could get undressed, deposit my clothes in the hamper, and walk straight to the shower. On the flip side, I could shower, snag a towel, and then go right into my closet for clothes. Truly, whoever had thought of it was a genius.

And that was the plan. Hop under the spray for a minute to rinse off the residue from the club, and then grab some PJs so that I could be nice and comfy for the evening. It was still pretty early, all things considered, but I wasn't leaving this room. I'd be ordering from the kitchen and throwing on some shitty romcom or something.

My classic, post-bad day routine.

Naked, I slipped into the bathroom, turning the shower on full fucking blast. In this puppy, that meant super warm with all the wall jets on and the downpour spout on overhead. I wanted to be essentially power-washed at this point. Today needed to get off my skin.

It felt incredible, with torrents of water running all over me, as if I were in a waterfall. After a few minutes, I switched it to just the overhead nozzle and stepped to the side to grab my shampoo. It wasn't supposed to be wash day yet, but my curls would manage.

After lathering up, I scrubbed my scalp with my nails and rinsed before applying the conditioner and repeating the process. Only this time, I combed it through from roots to ends and let it sit.

"Ugh, so much better."

When I finished, I switched everything off and stepped out. As I took the towel off the rack near the shower door, I gazed across my bathroom. It was so different from the rest of the house. After Mom passed away, Dad remodeled the entire house, except for my rooms. He'd tried, don't get me wrong, but it was one of the few fights I'd actually one.

Probably because my dad was sick of dealing with it.

I wrapped an oversized, fluffy black towel around me and used my twisty towel on my hair. Managing curls was a thing, and if it weren't for a few tricks I'd learned over the years, like this microfiber towel, I'd still be living in frizz city–or straightening it.

The horror.

I walked to the closet, getting my pajamas–the massive tee I loved to wear with a faded Mickey Mouse on it and a pair of underwear. I was a simple girl when it came down to it. But then it was back to the bathroom because you didn't just dry and go with 3A curly hair. No, thank you.

So, about a million years later, I was ready to get in bed with Ludo and enjoy some crappy movies. He was delighted to have me in the bed at last, and I ruffled him up, kissing his cold, little nose before grabbing the landline phone that only dialed inside the house. It looked like one of those antique designs from the 50s, but it was clearly a reproduction. I still loved it, though.

"Popcorn, a bottle of merlot, and some quesadillas, please."

"Right away, Lila."

I wasn't sure who'd answered, but it didn't matter. I was getting my comfort food, and visual entertainment was next. And if I were still up after all that, the musical entertainment would be next.

Playing CDs always made me feel better, and I had a little collection of them–stuff from the 90s and 2000s. No one had CDs or records anymore, but I did. And all my favorites were even compiled into mixed playlists, burned onto CDs thanks to the guys in the Family who still owned computers with the correct disk drives to make them.

Sure, Spotify and YouTube were amazing, but there was something about the tangible business of popping in one of my favorite CDs into the stereo and getting lost in the music, the methodical Pavlovian response of relaxing whenever I put on *Robyn Is Here* and listening to the entire thing from start to finish when I was feeling ways about life.

It didn't take long for someone to bring up my food. I had the guy leave it at the door before I got up and snagged it. Ludo accompanied me, of course, but he didn't beg for any of the snacks. He knew he'd get some of the popcorn anyway.

"Time for movie mode."

The nice thing about having cream walls, which were still decked out with vintage luxury touches like ornate filigree but way more minimal than Dad's, was that they would look like whatever color you shined on them. So, I switched the color-changing lights on my end tables and in the black chandelier to red.

Everything in the room was either cream or black, from floor to ceiling. The bed frame, nightstands, curtains, paintings, and even the small decorative pieces were black. The ceilings, walls, sheets, and the design woven into the black rug were cream. Adjusting the lighting transformed the room from a classy, old-world traditional space to a decadent and sensual one.

I adored my room.

My TV lifted from inside a large dresser-looking piece across from me, and I pulled up Netflix. Ludo snuggled in next to me, happily munching on the bit of popcorn I'd given him. He'd make sure not a single crumb was missed.

"Okay, what do we watch?" Ludo was no help in deciding, as usual. "Ugh, fine. How about…okay, yeah. Here. A Netflix original. It's bound to be cheesy and wonderful."

I hit play and set about chugging that bottle of wine. A good buzz would make this even better. Once my head was fuzzy, memories of today's events would disappear.

But something nagged at me.

Dad had been so concerned about me "playing my role." I knew he was still planning on marrying me off. I didn't know when that would be or to whom it would be. I couldn't go through with that. I didn't want to get married, stuck in this life all the more.

That was the reason I started working at the Scarlett Oleander. I wanted my life to be mine. I knew I could make a complete break for it until my dad was dead. Morbid, yeah, but also very accurate.

I can't get fucking married. Ugh, the virginity thing should have quashed all this.

Taking a hearty swig, I slumped back into my pillows. Ludo perked up, noting my unhappiness, and I idly rubbed him between the ears. But my mind was still churning. I needed a way out of any possible marriage. My "purpose" be damned.

I really thought the sex thing would have been enough, but apparently, Dad was determined. What would make him really see me as too damaged to pawn off? Memories of all the times I'd truly angered him surfaced like a body you didn't want to be found.

Accidentally–except very deliberately–backing the car into a pole, sneaking into his study when I was eleven, kissing that ridiculously cute guy he hired to be his new runner…

"That's it!" I shot forward, startling Ludo. "Sorry, buddy."

Soothing him with some pets, I sipped some more wine and started munching on the popcorn like it was going out of style.

The idea was churning, puzzle pieces falling into place as I thought about just how I'd go about it. No doubt, my plan was *not* an easy one.

However, it had merit–quite a bit, even.

And that was the most important thing right now. I needed something that would work, and screwing my father's consigliere and his most annoying business contract just *had* to work.

It's just a bonus that I've been dying to anyway.

4
The Tension Release

Reagan

I was surprised my ass didn't hurt from the door closing behind us so fast. Emilio would never offer the advice to "not let it hit me," and I was ready to pop a fucking gasket at this point.

"What the fuck is wrong with him? Can't he see that there's more going on?" I paced outside the don's door, unable to keep still. "That guy had information. It was the only way he was able to get into the club. And Emilio–ugh! It's like he's not even concerned!"

A hand landed on my shoulder, squeezing. I turned around to see Edward, his brows raised. He met my eyes with that patient expression of his.

"Reagan, this isn't the place." He regarded me, his stare narrowing. "I agree with you, but we should discuss this… elsewhere."

I knew he was right. Hell, I usually would have suggested it. I didn't understand what had made me lose my temper so quickly. I wasn't that guy. Handling myself in a crisis was a point of pride.

The fuck is wrong with me?

Nodding, I relaxed–if by force–and gestured with my head down the hall. "My room."

Edward eased up, nodding once back at me, and then I led the way to my bedroom, ready to lock myself up behind a closed door in a room that I regularly checked for bugs.

It was a short enough walk down the hall, the wooden banister running along the side the only thing keeping a person from tumbling off the edge and down into the foyer. My room was across that massive hole, directly in line with Lila's. I knew she was upset, and part of me wanted to check on her.

Still, I had no information. There was no point in meeting with Lila if I couldn't provide some clarity or new data to go off of. When I had something about the thug, I'd go talk with her.

"Here."

I stopped in front of my door, reaching into my pocket to snag my key. Unlocking the room, I held the door open for Edward, and then we both breathed a sigh of relief as I closed things back up and made sure that *no one* was getting in.

"Is the room secure?"

Walking to the back corner where I kept a wet bar, I stripped off my suit jacket and tossed it on the one extra chair I had in the room. *Drink first.*

Snagging a crystal decanter from the bar, I took a stout rocks glass and poured myself a couple of fingers of whiskey. I threw a gulp back, relishing the way it burned down my throat, and then exhaled hard.

Nodding at Edward, I gestured with my glass still in hand. "Yeah. The door only has one key, and I check for bugs anyway. In fact…"

I finished off the rest of my liquor and made a quick sweep around the room, checking in the usual and unusual spots for any wires or listening devices.

"Yeah, we're good."

Loosening his tie, which Edward had only bothered to straighten again when it was clear we'd be leaving the club, he walked over to the bar and mirrored my need for whiskey. Pouring himself some, I noted the hefty amount before he slogged back at least half and sighed.

"Today has been..." He considered, never one to choose his words rashly. "...not fun. Well, it was quite fun for a bit, but then...Ugh, I'm very ready for this to all be over. But I know it's just begun."

I scoffed, cocking my head as I took another swig. "Yeah, we're nowhere near done with this shit. I know there's something fishy going on with all this, and I'm not about to rest until I find whoever that was and beat his brains in."

"You always have been one for the direct approach," Edward smirked, but it slipped away as his stare veered off, those cogs in his head turning. "I don't like that someone knew about how extensive our background checks are. And I like it even less that someone knew Lila was working there. We use a stage name for her, and I've never publicized that I have a *mafia princess* working for me."

"Jesus, I fucking hope not." I ran a hand through my hair, tugging at the roots as if the pressure would relieve the coming migraine. "Dammit. I know it wasn't the club, not directly. But if you think a member of your staff could be compromised, or maybe there was a hole in your firewall that it took a real pro to find. I don't know."

Edward approached me, his stare set directly to my eyes, and the way those hazel eyes of his penetrated deep into me left me feeling exposed...vulnerable.

"Look, I'm aware you're upset. I know Lila is your charge, and you take the responsibility to heart. But don't beat yourself up about this. You can see how it took someone with real know-how to make this work. They got one past you, and they got one past me, which I, of course, intend to rectify as soon as possible. I can assure you that if I find out anyone on my staff had anything to do with this...Well, you can have them, baby."

A brow shot up, and I narrowed my eyes at Edward. That was a first. He'd called me a "pet name," and while I couldn't exactly say I hated it, this was only supposed to be about sex. We had a working relationship, yeah, but we weren't dating. It was fucking.

"Watch it." I glared, but I couldn't stop the corner of my mouth from ticking up in a smirk. "Though the idea of getting to relieve some tension doesn't sound too horrible."

Sauntering even closer, Edward clinked his glass against mine. As he swallowed what remained of his whiskey, I watched his throat bob, reminded of how well he took me down. But we weren't at the club, it wasn't after hours, and this was my fucking house, for god's sake.

It wasn't going to happen.

"You and Emilio seem to be on the outs." I raised my brows at Edward as he set his glass down on my nightstand. "Trust me, I've noticed the complaints. Today certainly proved the growing animosity as well. Care to tell me about what's upsetting you so much?"

As I stood there, not really willing to answer his question, Edward went for my tie, loosening the fabric so that he could slide it free from my neck.

"Edward," I warned, "this isn't the time."

"So, stop me." He just held my stare, the defiant little brat that he was.

His fingers worked open the top few buttons of my shirt, shifting to my left wrist and then right as he undid the cuffs and helped me to roll up my sleeves.

"This isn't what I meant. I was talking about blowing off some steam on the asshole who attacked Lila."

"All in good time, I'm sure." Edward reached for my belt, dragging the end out of my belt loops in one slow pull. "In the meantime…"

The leather of my belt thwapped against me, and I groaned lightly, annoyance not discomfort, making me clench my jaw. Still…if this was going to happen, I might as well enjoy it.

And be honest with yourself. You've been wanting to finish what you started in the office since it got interrupted.

The memory of said interruption peaked in my head, and dammit, that's not what I needed. But I couldn't fight it away, particularly not when my belt was being undone, my zipper sure to follow.

That had been the first time I'd seen any part of Lila that she didn't regularly display. It was hardly the time to be appreciative–potential murder and all–but *fuck*. Her fucking tits had been spectacular, the best I'd ever seen. And I'd seen my fair share, being something of a playboy when I was younger.

She was a petite little thing, but Lila's breasts were perfectly round, perky, and blessed with the epitome of great nipples. These tiny buds perched at the tip of her breast, *aching* to be touched.

My cock twitched behind my fly, and Edward looked up at me with a smirk. "Excited already?"

I was, and it wasn't just the thoughts of Lila. Those I could push away, but the idea of shoving myself all the way down Edward's throat, making him choke on my cock, those I was going to see made reality.

"Did I ask you to speak," I reached for his chin, tipping it up toward me, "*slave*?"

A satisfied groan bled from him, and I knew Edward was hard beneath his slacks, even if I couldn't see it. With a grin that was equal parts happy to please and ready to defy me, Edward pinched the tab of my zipped between his teeth and pulled it down.

The bulge of my erection pressed through the hole the downed zipper created. When Edward reached up for the button, I grabbed his hand.

"Ah ah. I'll be staying dressed, pretty boy. We have things to do when we're finished."

Plus, I also loved staying clothed while I forced Edward to drop his slacks. Power dynamic play was always a win for me. My sweet slave smiled, snarky to the last, and then reached inside my pants, going for the little button that kept my briefs closed.

When he found it, Edward was quick to flip it open and yanked my cock free. A hiss left me as I briefly scraped over my zipper, and I eyed Edward hard.

"Naughty boy." I pressed my tongue to my molars, contemplating for just a moment. "And you spoke out of turn in Emilio's office. I think someone deserves a punishment."

We'd chatted more about our "rules" over the past few weeks, and before today, both of us had been pretty good at adhering to them. But fucking in Edward's office was a big step over the line–one that we both agreed to at the moment, however.

One of the rules that I'd insisted on, though–both in and out of the bedroom–was that Edward was supposed to listen to me when I gave a direct order. Sure, his defiance had also been negotiated, but so had the punishments.

So here we are.

"I regret nothing," Edward shot back, and I knew he didn't.

My boy enjoyed his punishments even when I thought I was being fairly strict. Perhaps it was time to up things a notch.

"You will." I gestured with my head to the drawer on my nightstand. "Open it up."

Eyeing me, Edward hesitated for just a moment before crawling over and opening the drawer. He stopped there because malicious compliance was his love language, not that we *loved* each other.

"Reach inside and find the gag."

His jaw dropped. "Why do you have a gag in here?"

"Shh. Don't question me." I pointed. "Go get it, slave, then bring it back to me."

Giving me just a hint of attitude, Edward did as told, fetching the unique gag and bringing it back. A lightbulb had gone off in his head when he saw it, and as he knelt before me again, he sucked in a deep breath through his nose, readying himself.

"Open up." I smiled when Edward glared, but again, like a good slave, he opened his mouth for me. "Good boy."

I fitted the ring gag into his mouth, the metal keeping his jaws apart for me. Securing it around the back of his head, I watched happily as drool began to gather along the bars. All the better to lube things up.

"Now, since you can't talk," I actually snickered, tickled by my own sadism, "I'll look for those fingers. But I want you to know that since this is a punishment, I need to see the three fingers raised twice before I'll honor them. Just like we talked about. Nod to show you understand."

Not one speck of defiance lost, Edward nodded.

"Excellent. Now," I stroked my cock, positioning it at Edward's mouth, "I believe you have a job to do."

Just as his eyes flicked to my shaft, I stuffed it into his mouth. I wasn't gentle or slow. I hit the back of Edward's throat hard and held his face to my hips as I bottomed out. He sucked in breaths of air, fighting the need to push me away, to relieve the ache, by gripping my pants tight enough to turn his knuckles white.

He felt incredible, his throat hugging me so wonderfully, and I groaned low, the noise turning into a growl as I took the back of Edward's head and forced him to start bobbing up and down.

"That's it, slave. Take your master's cock."

Moving just as ordered, Edward matched the pace I demanded of him, his eyes squeezing shut and watering. *So very pretty.*

The rim of the metal coasted over me just enough as I mercilessly fucked Edward's mouth. It provided this new sensation that I adored. I'd yet to use this toy, waiting for the opportunity to bring it with me to the club for one of our "after-hours" sessions.

But then, a very specific sound pulled my attention down to Edward's hands, and I caught him unzipping his pants.

"No." I kicked his hand away just as he freed himself. "You're not getting any attention until I say so."

Edward glared, practically growling as I shoved my dick all the way inside and then held his head to my hips again.

"But you can leave that drippy dick out. I do enjoy watching it bounce for me as I fuck you."

Balling his hands into fists, Edward pushed them into the top of his bent knees as he waited for his air supply to return fully. Breathing through the nose like this could only do so much, but I was feeling particularly cruel right now, so instead of returning it, I went for something else that had been on the to-do list.

When he looked up at me, silently questioning, I locked eyes with him and smacked the back of his head, forcing myself just that little bit deeper. Edward reeled, his hands flying up to my hips and grabbing fistfuls of my pants.

"You're going to be a good boy now, aren't you? You've learned your lesson?"

Edward glared up a me, unwilling to be broken that easily. *Fine by me, slave.*

I whacked his head several more times, jerking my cock in and out of his mouth hard and quick with each one. He was going to explode or relent soon.

On the last one, Edward held up three fingers, and I paused. "Do you have something you'd like to say to me?"

Slipping free, I allowed him to nod. As he did, sticky trails of saliva dripped from his mouth, little strings connecting me to him. His breath was a ragged disaster as well. God, I loved it.

When he was breathing steady again, Edward glared up at me, gesturing at his mouth like I was going to remove the gag so he could talk. *Absolutely not.*

"Not necessary. You can nod and use hand gestures." I leaned forward with my hips, dragging the tip of my dick across his lips and then smacking the side of his face with it. "Go on."

My sweet CEO was so very worked up, but this was exactly what we both wanted. Edward got to release the reins a bit, and I was able to come down from the anger I knew was going to make me do something I regretted. *Win-win.*

Rolling his eyes closed, Edward sucked in another breath through his nose and then held my stare. He pointed to his mouth, then put his hands together in front of his chest, one atop the other.

"You're sorry for speaking out of turn?"

He nodded and then gestured to my erection, repeating that same hand gesture.

"And you're sorry for scraping me against my zipper?" Another nod. "Good. Make me forget the sting. And maybe…"

Lining myself up with the ring in the gag again, I began to slide my cock into Edward's mouth–slow but entirely, right up until I hit the back of his throat, the head of my dick testing his gag reflex.

"…I'll be nice and reward you."

The promise of something good was enough to get Edward moving on his own. He took my length entirely, bobbing his head up and down for me, so we worked together in a perfect rhythm. He channeled every bit of skill he had, giving me the best damn blow job yet.

My balls pulled up tight, my shaft throbbing, and I emptied

myself down his throat.

Edging–even if it hadn't been on purpose this last time–had a way of making me come more than usual, too. So the release was several moments long, my cum streaming into Edward's mouth in thick ropes.

He tried to pull back, the amount testing his limits. But I seized Edward's head, pinning him to my hips again and forcing him to take every last drop. A cough tried to break free, but it was muffled and did nothing to stop my spend from filling his throat.

When I was done–at least with that first one–I slid myself free, and Edward collapsed to the carpet, gasping. He'd done well, though, so I reached around his head and unbuckled the gag. It clattered to the floor, and nearly as fast, the words Edward couldn't say came flying out of his mouth.

"You fucking bastard." He struggled for breath, swallowing over and over; just the sight was enough to get my dick hardening again. "Ugh, asshole."

Chuckling, I waited for Edward to lift himself back up, his pretty cock still jutting out of his pants and rock fucking hard.

"Looks like you loved it."

He glared, but he didn't deny it. "Was I *good* enough for you?"

"My little brat," I smoothed my hand over his hair–gentle but then taking hold of his locks, "you were very good. Are you saying you deserve more than your Master's cum as a meal?"

Edward's dick twitched, leaping wonderfully as my words shot to the center of him. He nodded with my hand still gripping his hair, and after a moment, he slowly reached down toward him. He wasn't touching, not quite. What Edward did was loop a finger through the desperate precum that dripped from his cock and then licked it off his skin.

"Still hungry," his eyes burned into mine, "Master."

I couldn't help but laugh. The way Edward teased and bratted was a damn delight. I was nothing if not an asshole, though, so my slave was going to have to earn it just a tad more.

"Very well." I walked away from him, crossing the room so that I stood next to the bar. "Crawl over here and make me a drink. I'd like a whiskey while I fuck that ass of yours."

Eyes flaring for only a second, Edward visibly weighed the pros and cons of just obeying me or resisting. I could tell he was truly desperate for it when he didn't say a word, just got on his hands and knees and made his way to me.

Once he'd reached the bar, I nodded that he could stand. Edward faced the bar then, and I stood behind him, reaching around to his pants and getting his belt and button undone. His zipper was next, and then Edward's pants dropped to the floor, his belt clattering against the wood.

"Stroke yourself, slave. And use the free hand to pour my whiskey."

Edward sucked in a heated breath through his nose. I could tell he was fighting the urge to be defiant. But he did, his hand going to his shaft and stroking so nicely as the other fumbled for the glass decanter.

"You spill a single drop, and that's another punishment."

He nodded. *This is too much fucking fun.*

I stepped to the side of him slightly. I wanted to see his face while he fought to pour a clean glass of whiskey as he masturbated. And I was *not* disappointed by what I saw.

Edward chewed on his lip as he concentrated, his thumb brushing over his little hole as it wept for me. The whiskey had a screw-top lid as well, and he glared over briefly as he tried to get it off with just one hand.

"Come on. Figure it out."

Gripping the base of the bottle, Edward's large hand just barely wrapping around the glass, he brought the top to his mouth and used his teeth to unscrew it.

"Good boy. See, that mouth is good for so many things."

Another delicious glare came my way, and I slapped Edward's ass. The whiskey nearly spilled. And I noticed his strokes had slowed.

"Faster, slave. Don't let that cock get soft."

Picking up his speed, Edward growled, the aggravated sound so lovely to my ears. I patted his ass again, several quick strokes that he had to account for. But after a few moments, I had a couple of fingers of whiskey in a glass, and Edward's dick was swollen and red at the tip.

Perfection.

"Master." Edward handed me the glass, and I took it, sipping down a large gulp. "Is there anything else I–"

"Keep stroking and bend over the bar."

It was a bit tall to be a comfortable setup for him, but fuck if I cared. I pushed Edward's head toward the bartop, and he hissed as it clunked against the decanter, moving the thing to the side until his cheek hit the marble.

"You fucking–"

"Ah, ah, ah. No more talking. Unless you're begging me to come, I don't want to hear it."

Edward dug his fingers into the surface of the bar, his eyes squeezing shut as his jaw muscles flexed. I loved seeing him so worked up. Best of all, he'd been good and never stopped stroking. After our interruption, he was undoubtedly close to exploding at this point.

Circling around behind him, I ran my fingers up and down Edward's ass, reaching around to his dick and coating my digits in the glistening strings slipping down his shaft. I smoothed it over his hole, but inspiration struck, and I chuckled sadistically.

"Are you ready, slave? Do you want me inside you?"

"Yes, dammit." The words came out through gritted teeth,

and I grinned.

"Very well."

I took a sip of my whiskey, enjoying the taste of the twenty-year-old scotch, but then I lowered my mouth and let the stream of liquid gently leave my lips, coating Edward's asshole with the stuff.

He bucked, nearly knocking the bar right over, and just as his hips leveled, I thrust myself in. Glorious groans and muffled cries bled from him as I rammed my cock all the way into his ass, bottoming out.

"That's my good boy." I pressed forward a hair longer and then relaxed, blissfully sheathed inside him. "Now, fuck me."

It took Edward several seconds to adjust, to come down from the shock, but he did, and then he was rocking himself back and forth so that my erection speared him over and over. He fought with himself to keep stroking, the filthy sounds getting louder.

"Keep that voice down, slave. Don't want to wake the neighbors."

I took another sip of whiskey, focusing on the taste as Edward fucked me, the feeling of being hugged by his tight ass exquisite. Our pace quickened, my hips naturally pistoning as the pleasure ratcheted higher and higher.

"I'm going to come. I can't…Ugh…"

Edward was trying to fight it back. Such a good boy, but I wanted his release. I wanted to feel his ass clamp down on me as he came.

"Come for me, slave." I fisted his hair with my free hand. "Paint that fucking bar with your cum."

Thrusting hard, Edward cried out. "Fuck!"

And he fell apart for me, a near-endless stream of thick cum gushing out of him and covering the front of my bar. It went on, his ass squeezing me, and I felt the tingle begin again in my own shaft.

Tossing back the last dregs of the whiskey, I threw the glass on my bed, where it landed safely, and gripped Edward's hips, giving him everything I had. It forced more cries from him, the sound of his cum hitting the bar once more, and I careened over that edge as well, pumping his ass full.

The energy of the room came down, and when I was good and spent, I slipped free of Edward's ass. He stumbled, his mind likely gone after all that, and he sank down to the floor on one knee.

"Oh, look at that. You're the perfect height." I shoved Edward's head forward, smushing his face into his spend. "Clean it up, slave."

Groaning, Edward did as told, his tongue dragging through all that creamy white. When it was all but gone, Edward sat back on his heels and sighed.

I stared down at him, admiring the destroyed look on his face, the way he couldn't open his eyes.

"Still hungry?"

Edward shook his head. "Hmm, stuffed."

5
The Contact

Edward

"So," I looked over at Reagan, who was lying beside me in his bed as we caught our breath, "I'm still curious about what you've been seeing from Emilio."

He glanced at me, that patented Reagan glare working over his expression that had been so…well, about as "peaceful" as the man could get.

"You're still on about that?"

"I think it's pertinent." I scooted so that I was lying on my side, holding my head up with my hand as I planted my elbow in a pillow, "and I know you do, too. You wouldn't be so up your ass about it if it weren't."

"Ugh, you're insufferable."

As Reagan sat up, groaning in an exaggerated huff, I had to laugh. He was such a grump, and even though I'd never tell him as much, it was actually kind of adorable.

"Yes, I've heard that quite a bit. But it doesn't change the fact that I'm right. Now spill."

Glaring again, he stared at me for a while before finally giving up and sighing. "Fine, fine."

He stood up from the bed, rearranging his clothes into proper order as he spoke.

"He's been...off. I know. Not exactly helpful, but I don't have proof of anything. It's just a feeling. I've known the guy for years. He's been my oldest friend since we were stupid fucking kids. All I can say is that he's been...crueler. And if our line of work, that's saying a lot."

The cogs in my mind whirred, trying to pull together pieces of this puzzle from wherever they were scattered. There had been a change in demeanor that I'd noticed as well, and there was that sudden change to our deal when Reagan and I had first met.

"I understand, and what's more, I fully support following your instincts. You've known the man for so long that if something feels off..."

I paused, letting him finish.

Reagan faced me, nodding. "It probably is."

Nodding back, I similarly stood and straightened up. We needed to look a bit more "presentable" if we were going to leave his room without issue. Still, there was a part of me that wondered about Reagan's chances of not hearing about this little detour from some of the other men in the house.

It didn't seem like taking private conversations in his room was the norm for Reagan. Though he was an incredible liar, considering how little the outside world knew about him.

"I need more information. But getting that without alerting anyone in the Family is going to be hard." Reagan rubbed his fingers over his beard, staring down at the floor. "I'll have to go outside them, but finding a–"

"I know someone. A hacker I've used in the past to ensure the club's background check procedures can be thorough."

Glancing up at him, Reagan's brows rose to his hairline before knitting back together. "Do you trust him? This isn't something to dick around about. Plus, if he's found out, it could get him killed."

"Lavar is quite skilled, and I do trust him. The money will

be right, and he's a self-professed 'fighter for the little guy.' He won't mind sticking his neck out if it means sticking it to the mob."

Reagan scoffed. "Ha, well, okay then. Go talk to him."

As I walked past, Reagan grabbed hold of my tie, yanking me to a stop right in front of him. The pain zinged through my throat, going straight to my cock. As he raked his eyes over my face, I could see that ever-burning fire in his eyes sparkle brighter.

"Do not go out the front. Follow the hall as it continues to the back of the house. There's a framed portrait, eight by four feet. Pull it open and step through. The passage will take you to the back." He pressed my car keys into my palm. "And don't turn your headlights on until you're off the property."

Wrapping my fingers around the back of his neck, I pulled Reagan forward. I nipped at his bottom lip before kissing him, brushing my leg over his crotch.

"Anything you say," I nipped that lip one more time, "Master."

Before he could say anything else, I slipped through the door and took off. *See you later, baby.*

***

"Drake," I stopped him where he stood in the hall, gesturing with my head at the ceiling, "have we heard back from the security team about the additional cameras?"

The guy nodded, turning toward me as I let go of his arm. "Yes, they're ordering the cameras you requested today. Should be here in forty-eight. And they are researching the best way to install metal detectors that aren't visible."

"Perfect. Thank you." I bobbed my head in a nod, knowing I needed to get back to my office to answer emails as well. "Alright, we see that the staff have their updated handbooks delivered and goes through them. I know how likely they are to actually read them. Have Terese conduct the next round of mid-employment background checks as soon as possible, and have Carmen conduct mental health check-ups on everyone. No exceptions. It's mandatory for employment. Understood?"

Drake nodded once, his expression serious and composed. "Of course. I'll see it's all done. Also, you have a call on line two. I was actually looking for you."

"Oh?" I cocked a brow, wondering who would be calling so early. The club wasn't even open yet.

"Yes, sir. A Lavar? He wouldn't provide a last name."

Scoffing through a laugh, I rolled my eyes. "Ah, yes. Thank you. I'll take it in my office."

"Of course, Sir. I'll radio Evergreen to send it over."

"Perfect." I headed down the hall, calling out over my shoulder. "Get me those results ASAP!"

As I hurried to my office, I unbuttoned my jacket, knowing I'd be in my office for a minute if Lavar were calling. Opening things up, I quickly stepped inside and shut the door again, locking it for good measure.

Interruptions had been a bit too frequent as of late, even if there had just been the one time.

I sat down at my desk, pulled open my laptop, and then grabbed the phone receiver. There would be no speakerphone today.

"Lavar, thanks for waiting."

"Your hold music sucks." The guy has always been a rather blunt one. "You good to chat on this line?"

"Yes. I've had it double-checked." I thought back to the conversation I had with Reagan this morning, where he detailed how to check for a wiretap.

"Perf. So, your dude, Mr. Carpinelli," there was the sound of typing in the background like Lavar was going through the information again as he sat at his computer, "is into some serious shit. I know mob and all, but damn. He's got his fingers in several pies."

Furrowing my brow, I pulled up the encrypted note-taking software I'd installed on the computer and began typing myself.

"What do you mean?"

"I was able to pull up some paper trails and online discussions between Carpinelli and several parties. Two in particular, though." There's a pause, and Lavar hums, either thinking or…

"I swear to god, Lavar, if you're fucking while talking to me again, I'm going to hang up, and you won't get your finder's fee."

There's a tiny whimper, and I roll my eyes. *Oh, for fuck's sake.*

"You're aware I can't say no, Edward. Rules are rules." In the background of the call, I hear a distant voice–darker and deeper than Lavar's–and I know it has to be his partner, Kendrix. "Focus, princess. Your client is waiting."

I was aware that Lavar and Kendrix had a 24/7 dominant-submissive relationship, and I wasn't really all that upset. Their situation was intense, and one I couldn't see working for me right now, but I understood it.

Still, I was frustrated with this nonsense and how it affected my club. I wanted those around me to take it equally as seriously, which I could understand was asking a lot. I just didn't want to care about that at present.

"Yes, I am indeed waiting." Lavar hissed, and I ignored him, channeling the dominant side of myself that I hadn't been using much since I started fucking Reagan. I did miss it, being a true switch. "So get with the storytelling, fucker."

"He's got emails and text threads that I could access because the thing was linked to his laptop. Considering he's part of the mob, I really expected more from him. Ugh, umm, he should really know better."

"I don't fucking care about your methods, Lavar. What did

you find?"

There was another pause, and I tapped a pen on my desk, getting rather impatient.

"Umm, he's been chatting with someone, screen name rvtrip69@gmail.com, email is attached to the phone number he's been texting, too. It's pretty vague, which, umm, makes sense considering, you know, mob. But–Jesus, Kendrix!"

The phone dropped at that point, and it was several moments before I got back on the line with Lavar. And as much as I hated to admit it, I had to struggle to keep myself from breaking out into a fit of laughter.

"Please, god, tell me you're finished. *I* didn't request edging today."

"Whoops," there was mild guilt in Lavar's tone, but only just like he was putting it there because he knew he should be, "sorry about that. Umm, yes, so they have sent a few messages to each other in various forms that reference stock and getting more of it, re-upping their supply, but it doesn't seem to be his usual drug or arms dealing based on how cordoned off these messages were, an upcoming purchase market, and a so far unknown string of numbers that could be coordinates or dates or both, I guess. Maybe dates and phone numbers. I'm working on it."

Lavar had a habit of regurgitating everything in his mind as he thought about it. You got used to it the more you worked with him, but I could tell that his mind worked differently.

Of course, I was one to talk.

I was highly fastidious about my work and home life, excluding whatever the fuck was going on with Reagan, and my anxiety was much higher than the typical person's. Which, of course, had a lot to do with the type A aspects of my personality. I liked control–a lot.

You know, until I didn't, until I was willing to let it go, for the right person.

"Thank you for that, Lavar. I'll look for the next update, which, perhaps, you could just email me at the private account. It's on a secure server, and I'd like to avoid conversations that get...a little personal, hmm?"

"Sure, whatever you're cool with, Scarlett." Lavar was one of the few people I knew who I permitted to call me by my last name. "As long as I get paid."

Ah, yes, Lavar's most highly prioritized aspect of the job.

"I'll have the first portion wired to you. I want to know the IP address and name of whom he's communicating with, and any clues about what they are discussing. Understood?"

"I got you. Just give me time. These assholes are slippery, and I'll need to dig harder than usual."

"Fine." I adjusted in my chair, ready for a bit more concrete good news–such as hearing the renewed background checks were well underway and going well–and closed out the encrypted note program as I finished summarizing the call. "Just send me whatever you have by the end of the day tomorrow, and then I'll release an appropriate portion of the escrowed funds."

"Ugh, you sound like my awful mother." Lavar groaned, likely rolling his eyes on the other end of the line; he was a handful of years younger than me and certainly *not* type A. "Well, foster, but whatever. I'll hit you with the details when I've got 'em. Later."

Lavar hung up, and I rested the receiver back in the cradle. The relationship between that admittedly brilliant man and his partner–whom I had only ever heard in the background like today, really had to be something.

Because putting up with his "lifestyle" required a particular type of person.

When I ran my eyes over the notes I'd taken, a few things stood out, and moreover, I knew I had to discuss what I'd learned with Reagan. He was due in with Lila in about an hour, which would give me the opportunity to kill two birds with one stone: check in on my employee and fill in my–

"Well, I suppose he's just my Master."

I shrugged to myself, something itching in my mind at the thought of Reagan's kink compared to what I'd almost called him, even if it was just in my head.

Keep a lid on it, Edward. He's not *your boyfriend.*

6
The Flirtation

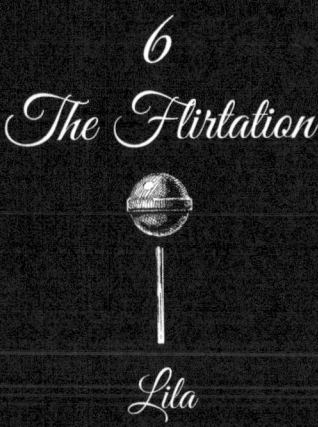

Lila

My lips were tingling when I closed the door behind me. The guy knew to wait a few minutes before coming out, which was sort of a godsend because now that everything was said and done, I wasn't really feeling like chatting.

Not that I was a big talker once a John's tank was empty anyway.

I scoffed. Edward hated it when I called them johns. They were "clients." But come on, who were we kidding? I was getting paid to perform sexual or submissive tasks; usually both in one go. I was a sex worker, and they were johns.

And goddamn, I wanted to know what the real thing was like.

Hell of an interesting life I had, huh? I was still a virgin. I'd done basically everything else, and it was all done under the pretense of being a submissive at the Scarlett Oleander. I'd never done anything because it sounded fun, never had a fun romp with a guy or gal or enbi because *I* wanted to.

And I'd chosen this. This had been *my* decision–because of my father, I might add.

Emilio Carpinelli was crystal damn clear on the handful of rules that he enforced with me. One, no dating or sex. I was to remain a virgin until I was married off. Two, no touching any of the guys in the Family. They were all especially off-limits. And three, I listened to what he said at all times.

The truth was I was shit at all of them.

I'd tried to date, but that had been a massive bust. I tried to flirt with the guys in the Family—a combination of boredom and curiosity—another bust. And listening to everything he said was a big no. I pushed back–a lot.

He was less than appreciative.

Why is it that after BJs is the time I get all existential? Ugh.

Still, all that was why I started working at the Scarlett Oleander. I was sick of listening to my father at the expense of my own happiness, and even if I wasn't going to push it too hard, this mafia princess needed to rebel. I was pretty late to the "teen angst" party at twenty-seven, but it wasn't like I had any type of life before I hit twenty-one.

It took me this long to find my spine, and using it had been pretty damn fun.

And after yesterday...

Yeah, it was time to up things a notch. Dad clearly didn't care about my well-being as much as he cared about the Family image, so fuck him all the way to hell and back. I'd already broken the virginity rule–to him, at least–so it was time to break a few more, right?

Right.

Starting with Reagan. We'd see where it went after that. That was the plan, anyway. The plan I'd cooked up after half a bottle of wine and too much "rom-com" action on the TV, but still. Come morning, my plan still sounded as good as any to give Dad the old middle finger and keep myself from being married off to some equally shitty guy.

Cuz make no bones about it. I know my dad isn't a "good"

person.

Now, if only the butterflies in my stomach would get the message.

I sighed, walking the long hallway with its red walls. It was time for a break between "clients," and I needed to level out. As far as attractive patrons, I was used to some pretty good-looking people, but I had to admit that nothing turned my crank quite as much as my godfather and boss.

As I rounded the corner into the dressing room, I ran smack dab into Reagan.

"Oof!"

I stumbled backward, Reagan catching me by the elbow and yanking me to my feet. As he righted me, I got a good, hard look at the straining muscles beneath his suit, and my heart skipped in my chest. Smiling, I met his eyes, my breath a little more shallow than I cared to admit.

"Well, speak of the devil."

He cocked a brow, that dark arch making me warm as the expression I knew so well from Reagan bloomed over his face. *Dammit, why does he have to be so fucking hot? All tailored suit and trimmed beard. Asshole just has to make the sexiest annoyed face I've ever seen. Ugh, I'm so screwed. At least...hopefully.*

"Excuse me?"

Shrugging, I waved him off, playing cool. "Never mind. What's up?"

Glowering at me like I was a moron, Reagan crossed his arms over his chest. "I'm checking on you. We discussed this. You come to me after every session."

I nodded, an exaggerated motion with my brows raising because I completely didn't remember.

"Riiight. Yes, I have come to check in with you. It was fine. Totally normal." I turned over my shoulder, looking back at the room I'd just left, where the guy was coming out, a security guard there to show him out. "See, there he goes."

Reagan glared at me, his head dropping to the side. "Lila, could you at least try to pretend like you care about your own life? You were nearly killed yesterday."

"Important part being 'almost,'" I quipped, pointing up at him and putting on a little smirk. "I'm fine. And I *do* care about my safety. I was just distracted, okay?"

"By what? A cock."

I nearly choked on my spit but saved myself by scoffing instead. "Jesus, no. There's a lot to process with Dad. He was…well, he was just lovely yesterday, wasn't he? I'm just still thinking about it, is all."

Reagan nodded, seeming to take the words at face value and accept them. It wasn't a lie, not really. I was thinking about my father, and how to stick it to him. Which, indeed, speaking of–this probably was the best time to enact the first step.

Time to get my flirt on with Reagan. My body heated. *Goody.*

"Can we at least go to the dressing room so I can sit down?" I looked up at him, the asshole being about a foot taller than me, and smiled sweetly.

"Fine." Reagan swept his arm backward toward the door behind him, pushing it open. "When is your next client?"

Sliding past him, I got a bit closer than needed. "I do not know, Reagan. I'm waiting on eggshells just like you."

He cleared his throat roughly as I brushed against him, and then my overbearing godfather stepped inside after me. As I sat on the blush banquette bench against the far wall, covered in soft red velvet, I ran my hands across the fabric slowly. Reagan didn't sit, instead choosing to stand in front of me like some fucking shield or something.

God help me. Does this man ever take a break? Oh, wait. Yeah, he does–with Edward.

The thought had my core burning, the memories of seeing the perma-grump giving it to my boss enough to have me wet in seconds. I could watch that shit all damn day, and being a part of it would be even better.

"You gonna stand there or come sit down?" I raised my brows at Reagan. "Come on. It's weird to have you just towering over me."

"I'm good, Lila. Just take your break."

It was like talking to a brick fucking wall. Sighing, I slid forward on the bench, remembering that I was still in uniform. I had a black bra and panties on, little cuffs secured to my wrists and ankles. They could be hooked up to any of the beds or furniture in the joint. A collar was wrapped around my neck, this one with a long metal leash that the last guy had requested.

The only thing I had on over the bra and panties was a thin silk robe, also black, and I hadn't bothered to tie it closed.

Looking up through my lashes at Reagan, I put my hands in front of my chest–a little pleading gesture. He glared down at me, the muscles in his jaw working as he clenched them.

"Please," I kept my voice low and breathy, "come sit by me?"

Reagan sucked in a breath through his nose. He was still standing there with his arms folded over his chest, and in this position, it really did look like he could yank me forward and demand head right then and there.

If I could only be so lucky.

"Lila," he growled, "what are you doing?"

We both knew the answer to that question, and it really was stupid to ask me. But I loved to push Reagan's buttons, and dammit, I knew he enjoyed it when I did it, too. So...

"What? I'm just asking you to come sit by me." I purposefully flicked my eyes down to his crotch–imagining that zipper coming down–and then back up. "Is there something else you were thinking about?"

I swear, just as I snuck another little glance, Reagan's cock twitched. My mouth fucking watered, and I clenched my thighs together on reflex. He was so damned hot. I wanted him to just grab me and fuck me already. I wanted to do all these submissive things I'd learned about from the club for *him*.

Picturing me on my knees for him, taking everything my "Daddy" had to give, was a fantasy I'd entertained a few times, and fuck, it was flaring bright as hell now.

A rumble escaped Reagan's lips from deep in his chest, and I was melting. Heat waves knew nothing about getting a girl to strip compared to this furious, intrigued glare from Reagan.

Please, Reagan...just say the damn word, and I will swallow every inch of your cock like that.

"I'm not thinking about anything." Those jaw muscles still worked so hard in his face, practically screaming how worked up he was. "Now, sit back."

"You know," I said, sliding my hand into the shoulder sleeve of my robe and pushing it down, "I'd say you were being especially bossy, but I know better. You're always a big grump."

As the fabric fell down my arm, I lifted my bra strap and put it between my teeth, holding it up away from my skin. Flicking my eyes to Reagan again, I saw that delightful fire burning in his dark irises, the silent question of what the fuck I was doing written all over his face.

Returning my attention to my shoulder, I scratched beneath where the bra strap had been, pretending this had just been the best way to get to it. Letting it drop back in place with a little snap, I leaned back on my hands, gazing up at Reagan with all the attitude I could muster and doing nothing about my robe.

"A big grump who's all talk, too." Reagan glared daggers at me. "You should just be grateful that I haven't said anything about what I saw yesterday in Edward's office."

That should do it.

Quicker than I could comprehend, Reagan snatched me up

by the throat, holding me in front of him as he scowled down at me, his shoulder-length, dark hair falling slightly in front of his face.

"That's some mouth you got on you, Lila? Is that what these fuckers are paying you for?"

"As a matter of fact–"

But the words I uttered through a tight throat were abruptly silenced as my godfather put more pressure on my neck, and I hissed.

"I didn't tell you to respond, princess." The barest hint of a smirk touched the corner of Reagan's mouth, and if he'd have asked me to do anything right then, I would have fucking done it. "But that's so like you, isn't it? Always quick to open up that pretty little mouth of yours."

I whimpered. I couldn't help it. And I was completely frozen in his grip, too, my entire body screaming for more of Reagan, so much more. My thighs pressed together instinctively, and fuck, I was *wet*.

"What? Cat got your tongue?" Reagan chuckled, darkling, but he shook his head, his hold on me changing so that he could drag his thumb across my bottom lip. "This is a dangerous game you're playing, Lila. Use your head. Back. Off."

Absolutely not. I was a damn brat. I'd learned as much about myself, and it was hitting all of Reagan's buttons, the *impressive* evidence of it pressed to my hips right now.

"Or what? Is my big, bad godfather going to punish me?"

He growled again, and I was going to explode. No human should have to contain this much unanswered lust in their body.

"You are such a little brat." Reagan smoothed his thumb back in place around my throat, squeezing lightly. "You'd probably love that, wouldn't you?"

My heart hammered against my ribs, and I made the bold move to lean into Reagan's hold, lean into his erection that I wanted so badly I could taste it.

"Maybe." I stared up into his eyes, the knowledge of how close we were to the line burning in my veins. "And I've never been one to play it safe. You should know that."

That growl again, but Reagan yanked his hand back, nearly causing me to fall. He stood there, still so fucking close to me, and swallowed hard.

"Princess, you–"

The door to the changing room opened, and as quickly as he'd got me to my feet, Reagan backed up, putting several feet between us. When I looked over at the door, totally thrown for a damn loop, Edward stared back at me, his brows furrowing.

"Am I…interrupting something?"

"No," Reagan supplied just a hair too quickly. "What?"

Edward turned to me. "Lila, you have a client waiting in the Red Room. She asked for someone fitting your skill profile. Are you good to go out there?"

I nodded, plastering on my go-to-work smile. "Sure thing, Boss Man."

As I headed to the door, I looked back over my shoulder at Reagan, who glared at me like he was thinking about either fucking me or killing me. Maybe both.

"I'll see you afterward, Mr. Terrasi."

He didn't respond, so I just winked at Edward as I left. He was my other mark, after all, and I was looking forward to that interaction just as much as this last one.

7
The Interlude

Reagan

A fire was working its way through my bloodstream, and I had a feeling that it was going to eat through my veins at this point. I wasn't sure if it was rage or arousal—or both.

Yes, you do. You know exactly what you're feeling, big guy.

I shrugged my shoulders, rolling them backward as the door shut behind Lila. I didn't have time for this. Yeah, I knew what she was doing, but it didn't make her methods any less effective, which was a damn problem.

She was my goddaughter, my charge, and one hundred percent off-limits. That was a non-starter. But the little brat still picked at me. Did she really want something to happen? That was nuts. Lila was just some big fucking tease.

Ugh, I could just—

"You alright there, Reagan?" Edward sauntered up to me, a smirk dressing his face and making me want to smack it right off. "You look a little…flushed."

I glared at him, my blood boiling enough to make my skin hot. Edward could be just as much of a brat as his employee, and I was not in the fucking mood. Still, at least he could take my aggression out on. Edward wasn't off-limits.

Or he was, but I'd stopped caring.

"I can't believe I never noticed it before. Though," Edward closed the distance between us, slipping his arm around my neck as he toyed with the ends of my hair, "I suppose I was trying *not* to notice anything about you."

Shrugging him off, I headed for the door. He could play his little game all he wanted, but I was done with this conversation. Moreover, if Edward was going to keep pushing my buttons like this, I needed us in his office, where we could lock the door.

"I don't know what you're talking about. Can we *please* discuss more important matters? What did you learn from your guy?"

Edward followed me down the hall as I headed toward his office. He didn't say anything, but I could feel him smirking behind my back. His ass was going to fucking get it. Lila was *not* a topic of discussion, and I knew that he wasn't about to let it go. We had our rules, which did include him testing his limits, but this particular limit was a downright no.

I should've put it in the fucking contract.

We'd drafted up a loose one the night before Lila made her impromptu appearance, and I believed it was time to check back in and up that bitch.

When we shuffled into Edward's office, I slammed the door closed behind him, locking the door. Edward smirked over at me, but I wasn't about to throw him up against the wall just yet. This wasn't a planned session, and it was very clear we needed to be more careful with those, particularly on the premises.

"So?" I raised my brows at him, folding my arms over my chest as I looked at Edward expectantly. "What'd you learn?"

"Who me?" He put a hand to his chest, really playing it up, and it took everything not to cross the room and throw Edward down to the floor. "Well, I learned that there are some extracurricular activities that your boss is involved with, details to be revealed, and that, apparently, you have a crush on Lila. How sweet."

My stomach dropped, my jaw clenching, so I had to speak through gritted teeth. "What?"

"I'm sorry. Did I stutter?" Edward cast a glance at me that was so fucking *much*, that latent dom side of him coming to the surface as he bratted enough to make my head spin. "You like Lila, and going off of what I saw before you too pulled apart like the ground was on fire–she likes you, too. How. Fucking. Sweet."

I was at him in a heartbeat, flying across the room and seizing the asshole by the throat. Edward hissed in a breath as I squeezed, and I dragged him from where he stood to the rack of jackets hanging up in the far corner. Shoving them to the side–hard enough that a few fell to the floor–I pinned Edward to the wall right next to the shiny chrome bar that made up the back half of the rack.

"You have two seconds. Two seconds to come up with some fucking excuse for that little speech of yours, or I'm pounding you into the ground so goddamn hard that you're going to avoid sitting for a while."

Edward didn't say anything. He only stared into my eyes with that fucking smirk painted across his face. When his throat worked beneath my hand, his Adam's apple bobbing against my palm, I was sure he'd thought better of his actions and was ready to make it up to me like a good little slave.

"I can hardly blame you, baby. I'm sure it's been a long few years living with Lila and not stuffing that sweet little thing like a stocking." He leaned forward, choking himself further so that he could hover his lips over mine. "Does it kill you seeing your goddaughter go to work when she should be swallowing that thick cock of yours?"

I was wrong.

Gripping him, I slammed Edward back against the wall.

He groaned, the pain no doubt zinging through the back of his head. I was familiar with the sensation. With him planted there, I took his tie in my other hand, yanking the thing free. Glaring, I pushed Edward backward before gradually pulling my hand back.

"Stay, slave."

He smirked, still so fucking proud of himself, but he stayed.

Taking the tie in hand, I looped it around Edward's wrist and then the uppermost bar of his clothing rack. It hoisted my slave's arm over his head, leaving him with just one.

"Color," I demanded, knowing that this session was going to require some frequent check-ins, but he'd certainly asked for it.

"Green, baby."

I slapped him across the face. He'd get this one because I knew not to leave visible marks. But Edward needed his fucking punishment.

"Color."

"Green," he paused, licking his lip as he stared directly into my eyes, "Master."

"That's better." The rage that boiled my blood, the undeniable lust that had been coursing through me when Lila teased me, all funneled into focus, this moment giving me the chance to use it all. "Take off my tie."

Edward reached out with his one free hand, yanking me close by the tie. I grunted, eyeing him as he kept up with that smirk of his. Still, he did as told, working the knot free by using his hand and his teeth, which was quite fun, I had to admit. When the fabric was loose, I stepped back, making it slide free from my shoulders.

"Jacket next."

The suit jacket I wore hit the floor as Edward pulled the second sleeve from my arm. I looked down, scoffing while I kicked him in the shin.

"Rude. Pick it up, slave."

He groaned, eyeing me hard after the bite of pain registered through his leg. Without breaking eye contact with me, he sank down as low as he could, his tied arm preventing him from bending over, and then reached for the jacket. He had to struggle to get enough of the fabric in his fingers to lift it.

"Aww, look how hard you're trying. You know," I said, stepping over the jacket and hovering my lips over Edward's ear, "if you say sorry, I'll help you."

A heavy breath left Edward, and he grunted as he was finally able to get a grip on the jacket and pull it up.

"I'm good, Master." He turned and smirked at me, holding out my jacket. "But thank you."

I just smiled, taking the thing and then tossing it on his desk. Edward sneered a me, his jaw working as he pushed his tongue against the back of his teeth, a habit I'd come to notice. As I walked back over to him, however, Edward's eyes landed on the holster I wore beneath my suit, my gun catching his attention.

"Something you want to ask, slave?" I glanced down at my pistol again, then met his stare, smiling. "You keep looking at it like that, and it might go off from the excitement."

"You're wearing a gun in my club, and while I had a background knowledge of that, it's another thing to see it. It…"

Edward searched for the words, and at that moment, as much as I wanted to make him suffer for how he'd spoken to me, I could see the need for understanding and intrigue in his eyes. So I gave him the space required–for some fucking reason.

"…It reminds me that you are indeed dangerous, that all of this," he gestured around himself, "is dangerous."

"Am I hearing a red?" I cocked my head, keeping my expression neutral because as much of an asshole as I was, I could respect a limit.

"No. In fact," Edward's eyes went to the gun again, "quite the contrary."

Lust surged through me, a tsunami of potent arousal that made my cock kick behind my slacks. I walked up to him, placing the gun against his chest as my other hand went to his belt.

"I see. Well, that can be worked into your punishment for backtalking me." I flicked his belt strap free, getting it out of the way as I unbuttoned his pants and yanked down the zipper. "Since I'm such a *nice* Master."

Edward flicked his eyes to mine, the sarcastic expression on his face too fucking pretty. Now that his pants were undone, I let them fall to the floor, his dick bobbing free and already sticky with precum. As he stood there, one hand tied to the bar over his head, I raked my gaze over him, needing just a bit more.

Leaving him, I walked to the desk, retrieving my tie from the floor as I did. I snagged the phone, the long cord able to reach Edward where he stood.

"We're going to need some time, slave. Call your assistant and have your calls held. You're not to be interrupted."

At this point, Edward could hardly deny that it was necessary, and I was pleasantly surprised when he did so without argument. When he was finished, I returned the phone to the desk and then walked over to him with the tie in hand.

I grabbed Edward's free hand, lifting it up to the other and securing it to the bar with my tie. He grunted when the fabric pinched his skin, and I stepped back, slapping his cock, which elicited a delicious little moan. He really could be such a pain slut.

"Shh, you're fine." Seeing my slave all trussed up for me was such a delightful sight, and I took my gun in hand, ensuring that the safety was on. "Lick the barrel."

Edward's eyes flared. He was clearly on edge about the whole thing, and that was exactly what I wanted. He'd been naughty. If he was going to get a "reward" and shiny new "toy" to play with, he was going to get it on my terms. Plus, as we both knew quite well at this point, I was an asshole.

I liked to scare him.

Tentatively, oh so slowly, Edward stuck out his tongue. He touched the tip to the area below the hammer, which was not pulled back, and dragged it all the way down the shiny barrel, leaving a fiendish trail of saliva in its wake. Edward shivered when he was done, his cock twitching at his hips.

"Reckless little whore, aren't you?" I smack his cock again, making my slave jerk in his ties. "Stick those hips out, pretty boy. My other weapon wants to get nice and warm."

"Goddamn you, Reagan. You're an asshole."

All I did was smirk. "It's that what you want?"

Edward didn't say anything, but he stuck his ass out, giving me the chance to hook my fingers under his hip bones and get him at the right angle to take my cock. He groaned as I manhandled him, using him like the toy he was. I craned my head over his back, making sure the placement was just right before I sucked up my saliva against my tongue and let it fall from my lips.

It hit his crack, sliding between his cheeks. A breathy groan left him, and I squeezed tighter with one hand so that I could use the other to down my zipper and free my aching erection. My dick sprung free, eager to get inside him, and I rocked my hips so that I could drag my shaft through the saliva and lube it up.

"Do you want my cock, slave? Do you want me to fuck you and then leave you to hang like another one of your jackets?"

"Dammit," Edward hissed, his as rubbing against my cock as he sought more sensation. "Yes, asshole. I want you to fuck me already."

I dug my fingers into his hips until it was hard enough to bruise. "Asshole? Is that what you should be calling me?"

"Ugh," he groaned. "God, fucking…Please, *Master*. Please fuck me."

Relaxing my grip some, I reached up to pat him on the head. "There's a good boy. Now, remember…"

Hoisting Edward up a bit, I nestled my dick between his cheeks, pressing in right on target. My bratty slave hissed, sticking his ass out all the more so that my cock nudged at his hole.

"…keep quiet."

I shoved in, my dick bottoming out in Edward's tight ass. He grunted, muttering a low curse under his breath. Starting up a rhythm, I unleashed the pent-up frenzy that had been waiting to be set free. The only sounds around us became heavy breaths, groans of pleasure, and the filthy slaps of our bodies meeting over and over.

Edward wobbled, his balance shit thanks to the way he was tied up, and I did nothing to help him aside from gripping him tight as I brutally fucked his ass. He took it all so wonderfully, gripping the ties that bound him to the bar at face level. After only a few moments, he tightened around me, his head falling back on his shoulders.

"Oh, fuck. Ugh, yessss…"

Pausing, I stopped Edward from coming right then and there. "Oh, no. I don't think so, slave. Don't you dare come. This is your punishment. You won't be getting off."

"Fuck you." He grunted out the words through gritted teeth. "Fuck you so much."

"Yes, slave, you will." I smacked his ass–hard. "Now, ride my cock, pretty boy."

He thrust his hips back, working as best he could at such an awkward angle. Every time he got too close, I made him stop. Edward was furious, but there was also nothing he could do, and he knew this was part of the punishment. We'd agreed that coming on his end would be up to my discretion, and right now, I said no.

"Ugh, goddamn it!" Edward squirmed on my cock as I stopped again, my own orgasm right on the brink. "I need to fucking come, you bastard. I can't stop it!"

Edward wasn't being loud enough that we'd have to worry, but I could hear his fury through the bite of his words, the way his tone dropped so low and deep. God, I loved the sound of it.

"My fuck slave," I slipped free of him, stroking my cock hard and quick, "I can, though. I can stop you from coming so very easily."

Taking one step backward, I admired him. I scanned my eyes over every inch of Edward's body, relishing in the way he was tied up and dying to come. His cock looked so needy and red. I knew exactly how much that ached. It was gorgeous.

"You fucking ass–"

"Shush, slave. Quiet time."

He glared at me, and I ate it up, stroking my shaft from base to tip, where I rolled my hand around the head. I groaned, the release I'd been chasing right at the edge. My balls pulled tight against my body, my dick throbbing as I ate up the tasty sight of Edward, utterly unable to do anything about his own erection.

It was more than enough.

Grabbing his hip and twisting him toward me, I stroked faster and faster until I came all over Edward's dick. My cum painted it in hot ropes of sticky white. They decorated his skin, making his shaft bob as it twitched. Precum oozed from his tip. Edward wanted to come so very badly.

But no. I wasn't going to let him.

"Ugh," I groaned, the last spurts of my spend launching from me and onto Edward's angry shaft, "look how pretty you look wearing my cum, slave. Does it feel all nice and warm on your desperate little dick?"

Edward sneered at me, his muscles working as he repeatedly clenched and unclenched his jaw. He loved it. I could see how badly he wanted to come in his eyes, how he was right on the edge. I let him go, his body swinging back into place as Edward adjusted his stance for better comfort.

He wasn't looking at me or saying anything. I knew he was walking himself back from the edge, trying not to orgasm.

I closed the distance between us, patting him on the cheek right where his very trimmed, very manicured beard stopped.

"Such a good slave. You took your punishment well."

Edward rolled his eyes up toward the ceiling, sucking in a breath through his nose. He was still concentrating so hard. I chuckled, then walked away, tucking myself back in my pants and taking a seat at his desk.

"What are you doing?" He turned my direction, glaring.

"Sitting. That was quite the workout. I need to rest a bit."

When his jaw dropped open slightly, I smirked at him, shrugging gently as I cocked a brow at him. Rolling his lips between his teeth briefly, Edward blinked once and then met my stare again.

"You're not going to untie me?"

"Of course I am." I kicked my feet up on the desk, lounging back with my arms behind my head. "When that hard-on goes away. Can't have you taking care of yourself quick in the bathroom or something."

Edward murdered me with his eyes. If those hazel beauties could have actually done the job, oh, they would have. His longer bangs fell in front of his eyes, the furious scowl I was used to seeing pinned in place.

I closed my eyes, settling into his chair. "Wake me up when it goes down."

8
The Self-Care Routine

Lila

My socks made a shushing sound as they brushed over the carpet. I was dragging my feet a little more than usual today. I had the day off, much to my annoyance, but the Boss Man wasn't about to let me work. He was a firm believer in taking some "self-care" days, which was bullshit when home was the place I was trying to get away from.

Ugh, this is both boring and stressful somehow. Amazing.

But being around my dad right now was like walking on eggshells. I knew any little thing would set him off. He was in one of his "moods." Moods that seemed to be longer and longer stretches of time as of late. Sure, I wasn't at home much, all things considered, but I was here enough to see that the don was in a shitty mood at least ninety percent of the time.

Which is why I have to sneak past his damn office with my snacks.

It was later in the afternoon, and I'd gone as long as I could in my room. I had to get out of there and stretch my legs a bit. Hell, even Ludo had the dog run. I couldn't be expected to stay cooped up in there literally all day. I'd hit the gym downstairs for a bit, took a swim in the Olympic-sized pool, and even wasted a few quarters on the arcade games I'd convinced Dad to install in the billiard room.

Snacks were mandatory if I was going to hang out in my room for the rest of the night.

"...a task of this nature needs to be handled correctly. I'm not watching you fuck up again."

I halted. Dad was brewing up a storm in there, and I should get the hell out of dodge. But I wasn't moving. For whatever reason–and clearly a self-destructive one–I was intrigued by what he was saying. What was my father talking about, and who was he talking to?

Does it have anything to do with the other day? Is he chewing Reagan out for not protecting me more?

"...If I pay for something, I expect results. And don't give me that bullshit about trying. Trying doesn't fucking win first prize, asshole. Winning does. So get off your fucking ass and fucking do something about this, or it's your head on a fucking platter."

My body went rigid, and I felt a zing of unease work its way through my nerves. Everything was tense, the mood affecting me even though I wasn't directly involved, just overhearing. It was like when you stumbled into an argument out in public. Awkward and uncomfortable, sure, but this one in particular was also terrifying.

I didn't see my dad like this. That was by design, of course, given that I avoided everything that had to do with the Family business if I could. I wasn't interested in my father's dealings. Drugs, guns, real estate, they could all fuck off for all I cared. I wasn't meant for the mob life, regardless of the fact that I'd been born into it.

Hopefully, it wouldn't take dying to get out of it.

My dad finished the last bit of his tirade behind the office door, which was cracked slightly, and I peeked inside even though it was risky as hell. He was at his desk, standing up, and when he ended the call, my father threw his phone across the room.

I jumped as the sound of plastic cracking against drywall echoed through the hall. He'd definitely broken it, and now someone would have to go run out and get him a new burner.

"Carmine!" Dad called out, and through the crack in the door, I could see him hurrying toward the hall.

Shit!

Taking off down the hallway, I rushed around the corner so that my father wouldn't see me. I flattened my back against the wall, the chair rail digging into my spine as I watched the don rush past, heading toward the foyer.

Whoever ran into my dad first was going to catch hell for him breaking his own phone. I would not let that be me, so as soon as the coast was clear, I sprinted down the left-side hall to my room.

As I closed the door behind myself, I spun around, putting my back to the wooden panel after switching over the lock.

I hated my father. I hated this life. I didn't want anything to do with it, but I was fucking trapped. The one person I could stand–the one person I liked, if I was honest with myself–Reagan, was getting chewed out because my father's enemies were after me. How fucked up was that?

You need to get out of here.

Walking into my closet, going faster than normal, I went for the shoebox I kept tucked behind my dresses, pulling it out and sitting on the floor with it. I opened the lid, flipping it to reveal the stash of cash and my passport. I had the club pay me direct in Benjis. I wasn't letting my father get a peek at my money–or worse, get hold of it.

The stack, all sorted and rolled up in balls of one thousand dollars, eased some of the panic roiling through my blood. I could almost leave. I wasn't going without ten grand at my disposal, and I was halfway there.

In nearly a month, I'd made most of the cash. The rest was from the "allowances" my mother used to give me. I never spent it. I'd never needed to. And even now, I wasn't sure I'd be able to part with those particular bills, but I knew Mom would understand.

She'd want you to be free of him, too.

Ludo came in, wagging his tail, and was so happy to see me. He stuffed his cold nose into my face, smearing the tears I hadn't realized had slid down my cheeks. I rubbed his head, packing up the money and tucking it back into its hiding place.

"Okay, buddy. I still smell like shit, and I have no snacks." Exiting the closet, I walked over to my bed, dialing for some "room service," with the instruction to leave it by the door. "Alright, now it's shower time."

Following me to the bathroom, Ludo curled up on my bath mat by the sink and kept a watchful eye on me as I stripped and tossed the dirty exercise clothes in the hamper. I smiled at him as I turned on the water, knowing that it'd get warm in a matter of seconds.

My dad's voice echoed in my skull. *Do something about this, or it's your head on a fucking platter.* He'd been so damn furious. I was nervous for Reagan. He'd done everything he could to keep me safe over the past month. The fact that someone got into the club was nuts. It was so secure.

He has a point about that inside job theory. God, Edward must be livid.

My skin hummed at the thought of those two. I'd hardly forgotten about what I saw, dreams of it filling my sleep. And after that altercation yesterday with Reagan...I *needed* something to happen there.

But I wasn't convinced it would. I was good–hell, I was damn good–but Reagan's stone will was a thing of renown.

He had a rep, and so did Edward, and both of them weren't known for flights of fancy or dallying where they shouldn't.

They're fucking, though. I saw it myself. So, something might be possible.

I stepped into the shower, letting the water caress me with its steaming droplets. The rainfall setting rinsed away any trace of my workout in seconds, and I scrubbed over myself with my lavender and rose soap, the loofa exfoliating my skin. God, it felt amazing.

And the images in my head weren't quitting.

If anything, more and more of those juicy details from the day I'd seen them fuck were coming into sharp clarity. Edward's cock had been pinned to the desk, a sticky trail oozing down from the tip.

Lust kicked through me, physically rocking me where I stood beneath the water. My clit tingled, the need to touch it growing.

I grabbed my shampoo, sudsing up my hair as quickly as I could without damaging my curls. The conditioner was next, and I combed through my strands, letting the moisturizing cream sit in my locks while I walked over to the long bench built into the side of my shower.

Whoever designed the thing likely assumed the bench would be used for shaving. And I did use it for that quite a bit. But it was also a great spot to sit down and practice some of that "self-care" Edward was always going on about. He probably didn't mean masturbating, but to each their damn own, right?

Right.

The marble was cold at first, and I squeaked slightly as my ass touched it. But I quickly adjusted as I lay back on the bench, stretching out one leg while I kept the other up, bent at the knee. The surface was plenty wide enough for me to lie comfortably, and I loved taking advantage of it like this.

A chill worked through me as the water started to evaporate

from my skin, and I pushed a button near my head. An overhead light came on in the shower, dousing me in glorious heat. Yup, this puppy had all the bells and whistles.

Getting set up took my mind out of the moment, so I closed my eyes, enjoying the heat and imagining what Reagan would do if he ever accidentally walked in on me in the shower, regardless of how unlikely that was.

I could see his wide-eyed glare in my mind, the erection bulging in his pants.

One of the best things about having that kind of equipment, it was much more difficult to hide an immediate sexual reaction. God, what would he taste like? Did Edward know?

Oh, fuck, he so has to.

Images of Reagan fucking Edward bloomed–vivid and clear–in my mind. My godfather had been giving it to Boss Man like he owed him money, and hell, Edward kind of did, didn't he? But Reagan wouldn't just fuck someone to get a bit of cash from them. He wouldn't have fucked Edward unless…

He desperately wanted to.

"Ugh," I moaned, reaching for my hardening nipples and plucking at them.

I relished the way they pebbled beneath my fingers, and I pulled harder, *squeezed* harder. Pain and I were interesting bedfellows. I feared it as much as a typical person might. I wasn't here to break my leg or anything, but I adored the way it felt to test my limits during spicy, fun times.

Being rough with myself, I could feel myself flood with arousal. I wanted Reagan to snap and finally take out some of that pent-up tension on me. I wanted to feel how it stung when he slapped his hand across my breast, my ass, my pussy. I was desperate to see the marks he left on my skin–little bruises, handprints, bite marks…

"Ugh." The moan melted out of me, and I slid one hand down my stomach, still twisting my nipple with the other.

The water on my skin made me slick, and when I reached the miniscule section of hair between my legs, I wondered how Reagan would have me, how Edward liked it. I'd do whatever either of them wanted, what they *both* wanted.

Taking them both…Ugh, fuck…filled up in every hole with their cocks…

My entire body jerked as I swiped a finger across my seam, my clit aching for more. The shower mist coated me in a fine layer, which was nothing compared to how I fucking dripped at the thought of being fucked by those two gorgeous men.

I imagined what it would be like if they both claimed me, took my virginity, my innocence. I wanted them to corrupt me, getting me down on my knees for them like a good girl.

Dipping a finger inside my folds, I swirled it over my entrance. I didn't go in, just teasing. My thighs clenched reflexively, and I circled over my clit, lightning firing through my veins.

But it wasn't my finger. No, no, no. It was Edward's tongue caressing my pussy. It was Reagan's hand groping my breast. I smacked it, my tit zinging with sensation. I wanted to taste them. I *wanted* to take them down my throat–no payment required.

Releasing my nipple, I dragged my hand up to my neck, squeezing my throat briefly before sticking a finger in my mouth and sucking it like a cock. My finger hurried over my seam, teasing in and out until I couldn't take it.

I pushed my fingers inside, rubbing over my clit with my thumb. I wanted Edward and Reagan to fuck me so hard that I forgot my name. I wanted to worship them like they were the church I prayed to–an unholy sacrament of cum and lust.

"Fuuuuck…" Pumping my fingers in and out of my pussy, I started to flutter around my digits.

The heat was overwhelming, too much, but I didn't turn it off. I wanted that burn. I wanted to be forced to the edge of sensation and shoved past.

"That's some mouth you got on you, Lila? Is that what these fuckers are paying you for?"

Goddamn, being around Reagan like that had been so fucking hot. The way he'd stared at my mouth, the thoughts I could see spinning through his head, even though he didn't vocalize a single one.

He'd called me...princess.

It wasn't the first time, but it was also a move he only pulled when I was really under his skin. When he was skirting the line between us that I wanted to fucking destroy more and more every day.

I slid in and out of my pussy faster, hooking my fingers up into my G-spot hard enough to see spots behind my closed lids. Oh, to be wrecked by him, utterly ruined and cracked open under his ruthless touch.

And Edward.

"You've gotten quite the reputation, Lila. And it's only been a few days. Apparently, that mouth of yours is a thing of wonder. Naughty little thing."

It was just a little shop talk, some harmless teasing, but holy fuck, when Edward had called me naughty, I'd nearly exploded right then and there. I wanted to be on the receiving end of his teasing words. I wanted him to use me up, making me as dirty as he wanted.

As they both wanted.

The need to come was roaring forward. My clit was burning, and I was fucking drooling around my finger like it was one of those impressive men's cocks. I could just picture them doing whatever they wanted to me–coming on me, whipping me, tying me up...

Whatever they want–a sinful little masterpiece of their creation.

"Ugh!"

I flew over the edge, my orgasm cresting over me so hard and fast that I cried out in the shower. The sound echoed through the room, this bright cry of pleasure as I imagined finally getting what I'd always desired.

The sensations eased off, and I breathed in ragged gasps, my eyes flying open as I realized just how *badly* I wanted those men.

"Woof!"

I jumped, my hands flying away from myself. Ludo stood outside the shower. He whined, scratching at the door. He thought I'd hurt myself or something.

"Oh, buddy. I'm fine. I'm okay." I stood up, my legs a little shaky, and peeked out the door at him. "Go lay down, bud. I'll be out in a minute."

My head was fucking spinning as I went under the spray to rinse my hair. I was reeling from my own thoughts, how intense that orgasm had been, and yet, I was still hungry for more.

No, I was hungry for the real thing, and goddamn, I was going to get it–if it was the last thing I did.

9
The Boss's Dilemma

Edward

I t was a bright and shiny new day, and I was still fucking pent-up like a goddamn prisoner because Reagan hadn't let me come at all last night. Even after the club had closed and everyone had gone home, the fucker just got me worked up again, only to leave for his place a few hours before sunrise.

Yes, I could've dealt with it myself, but I'd been fucking exhausted and passed out straight away. I only woke up when my alarm screamed at me for the third time, reminding me that it was morning and I had to get back to work.

Asshole.

I was this close to taking care of things on my own at the club, but then this voice kicked up in my head.

Prove to him you can do it. Prove to him it doesn't even matter.

Indeed, it appeared that even to myself, I could be a bit of a brat. *Ugh.* In any case, it was nearly opening time, and after the day of digging through the notes sent over by Lavar, I was ready to take a break from staring at a fucking computer screen. This was the time when I usually walked the floor and checked on everything – the setups, the subs, the doms, and so on.

So, that was what I did.

"Ms. Evergreen." I nodded at her as I passed by the front desk, where payments and contracts were handled. "How are we looking?"

"Excellent, sir. Thank you for asking. Is there anything that you require assistance with?"

I smiled, shaking my head. "No, thank you. I'm all set. Just making the rounds."

She nodded back at me, going back to whatever she'd been doing on the computer. I went through the hall that led to the main entrance, accessed through a hidden door on the side. The dark atmosphere was right on track, and the podium the hosts used to greet people was stocked with the appropriate clipboard, waivers, and keys for the guest lockers.

The bright red interior of the main bar and performance area was lit with the flaming scarlet lights, and I grinned all the harder. I'd designed this place from top to bottom, and it never failed to put a smile on my face.

"Hey, boss." Juliet, a sub who also took turns working the bar, waved from the drink station to my left. "Doing the rounds?"

"Yes, is everything up to standard at the bar?" I nodded behind her, where the liquor options were presented to clients.

Anyone participating in the events, as opposed to solely watching, was restricted to a maximum of three drinks, and all my bartenders were well-schooled in how to enforce that rule.

"Yup. I did have to crack into a new box of red blend for the stage bar. The last performance attracted quite a crowd."

"Thank you, Juliet. How is Theo at the other bar?"

She pointed over my shoulder to the man in question as he approached. "Hey, boss. Just need a new box of cocktail napkins, and we're out of olives."

"See that Drake or Ramirez handles it." Theo nodded, and I noticed a non-club-issue collar gracing his neck. "What's that?"

He rolled his eyes, making a sound as he failed to hide his bashful grin. "You were…right. Clive and I just needed to talk. He's…he's properly staked his claim. The club notwithstanding, of course."

"Oh, good. I was worried I was about to lose my best combination of a male bartender and puppy sub on the premises. That would be an extremely hard replacement."

Theo chuckled. "Nope, I'm still here. Clive, umm, well, he likes that I'm on display like this."

Cocking a brow at him, I grinned. I knew Clive well, a dom who had enjoyed our services for several years, and I could imagine that he did at that. However, I imagined he was also insisting on "punishing" Theo a little for the fun of being a bad dog.

Ah, relationships. Yeah…

"I bet. Well, thank you for letting me know. If you don't get the stock, be sure to ask Drake directly."

Nodding, Theo turned around on his heel and headed back behind the bar. As the swinging closure came up and tapped him on the ass, he noticeably flinched. *Staked his claim, indeed.*

There was a pinch in my chest I couldn't place, or at least didn't want to, so I shook myself and decided to head back behind the scenes to check on the sub getting ready in the dressing room. There was one in particular who I believed needed a bit of support.

"Lila," I walked up to her, the other subs in the room knowing to give us some privacy based solely on my tone, "I'd like to speak with you."

She turned over her shoulder, her brown curls bouncing, and offered a slight smile.

"Oh, sure. What's up?"

Eyeing her simple outfit–leggings and a t-shirt since she'd just arrived–I sat down next to her on the bench seat installed in the back wall, right where I'd found her "talking" with Reagan. My cock twitched at the thought, and I had to clear my throat to refocus myself.

"I'm fairly certain you know precisely 'what's up.' How are you since the *incident* the other day? You hardly took any time off, and you know how I feel about self–"

"Care. Yeah, I know." Lila smirked, one corner of her mouth lifting, and she shrugged as she rolled her eyes. "I'm fine, Boss Man. Chill. It's not like I wasn't raised around violence, right?"

She had a point there, which I didn't like in the slightest. "True. Well, has your father said anything about the attack? Did he have any thoughts about who it might have been?"

In a rather startling change, Lila visibly stiffened. She didn't usually react that way about her father, always one to brush him off as if he didn't matter. The armor she wore to protect herself from everything related to her father appeared to be cracking.

"Eh, that's a no. He hasn't said dick."

I couldn't stop the closed-mouth laugh that burst from me. "Always such a poet, Lila."

"Yeah, well, excuse me if I'm a little salty, but Dad seems more pissed about a missing shipment than my near-miss with death. Though I think I heard him chewing out Reagan the other day. He seemed really fucking pissed. Has Reagan said anything to you?"

Pulling back, I regarded her. "Why would he say something to me? He's your godfather and bodyguard."

Lila's brows rose to her hairline as she sent an incredulous look right back at me.

"Aaanndd…"

"And what, Lila?"

She rolled her eyes. "And you're the one fucking him, so I thought maybe he'd let some deetz spill when you exchange sweet nothings."

Clenching my jaw, it took everything in my power not to snap at her. But that wouldn't have been smart. For one, Lila likes to get demeaned, so me losing it on her would only make things *more* complicated, not less. For another, this particular room was hardly soundproofed, and I didn't need anyone else to be privy to our conversation.

I kept my voice low and level, adjusting my tie where it pinched my neck, when I finally responded to her. "Lila, I will not be discussing that with you. Except to say–and I can guarantee you of this fact–there is no universe in existence in which Reagan Terassi whispers sweet nothings to anyone, least of all me."

She held up her hands as if she were surrendering to me. "Sorry, sorry. But like…we *have* to talk about that at some point. I'll keep it on the DL. I promise you, but that… happened."

Sighing, I closed my eyes briefly, pinching the bridge of my nose. "Lila, keep your personal and professional lives as separate as you can. I have clearly…struggled there as of late, but I won't be making a habit out of this. Reagan and I…"

My words trailed off, and I didn't really know what I wanted to say. I wasn't sure of the expression on my face either. So I quickly schooled my emotions into line and regarded her once more.

"We won't be discussing this. Understood?"

Scanning her soft, honey-brown eyes over me, Lila paused. I could see the cogs in her mind whirring away, and something told me I would not be appreciative of the outcome.

"Or what? Are you going to fire me? Are you going to send me packing, knowing that my dad's business has become intertwined with your club, with my life, and he's not even concerned? Would you really risk my safety like that? The big bad boss of the Scarlett Oleander, letting one of his subs fall to the wayside."

My skin prickled. I could see precisely what she was doing. Being a brat was something that we apparently both excelled at, and though I had heard as much from doms who'd requested it, I'd never seen it. I had to admit that the idea of putting little Lila in her place was *appealing*.

But I could leave the brat-taming to Reagan. I was more interested in whether Lila could be controlled via *other* means.

You shouldn't be interested in anything. What are you doing? Edward, she's the don's daughter and an employee. Don't. As much as you want to…God, do I want to…

"Try that with Reagan, Lila." I locked my stare on hers as it went wide, and I swear the tiniest little moan left her, going straight to my cock. "I know that he would enjoy taming that rather insubordinate side of you."

I leaned forward, close enough to see that Lila's pupils were dilated. It was such a sight on her pretty face, those pouty lips of hers spread as she stared at me in shock. Goddamn, she truly was gorgeous. I wanted to fist those silky, brown curls. I wanted to strip away everything between Lila and the harsh truth of who she was at her core. I wanted to bare her–body and soul.

Seeing the feisty girl submit to my pleasure, allowing me to crack her open and expose her down to her core, would be better than almost anything. How lovely it would be to make her face the truth of her inherent worth, praising her, pleasuring her until she cried.

Fuck…she'd fit so perfectly between us–Reagan and me… and Lila.

"Your father is a piece of shit, Lila. You know this. Don't take his lack of concern for anything but that. You're worthy of being protected and cared for. If you can't see that…"

I let the words hang there as I crowded her, making Lila hear my words for what they were despite her obvious discomfort. I was leaning over her now, an arm planted on the back of the couch as she sank into the fabric. I grabbed her chin, forcing her to look at me.

"Then perhaps it would be best to tie you down to a chair and force you to listen?" Lila's eyes flared wide, and the arousal simmering in the room between us was palpable. "Maybe you would be more receptive if that pretty little mouth were occupied with other things? If that brain was too fogged out from orgasming several times over, so all you could do was finally fucking listen to me, hmm?"

Lila was speechless, and hot damn, that was a first. It was also wildly inappropriate for me to be saying these things to her. I couldn't keep them in, though. They were truth, they were always on my tongue, and they were haunting me at every turn.

Because I *did* want Lila, I knew I did. I had known. I wanted to see how she'd break so beautifully for both Reagan and me. I wanted to see how exquisitely Reagan would unleash that passion he'd been holding in. Lord knew I'd been on the receiving end of it, and I knew that Lila would be so damned pretty beneath his rough attention as well.

"I…"

"Yes, indeed. I hope you have a successful shift, Lila. I have business that needs attending." *Which is definitely not the straining erection behind my zipper.* "If you hear anything about your father's insights into the attack, be sure to inform Reagan. I'll see you at the end of your shift."

And with that, I left. Because if I stayed in that room a moment longer, I was going to throw Lila against the wall and fuck her until she couldn't walk.

10
The Questions

Lila

I had to go back out on the floor in a minute, and I was fucking reeling. What the the great goddamn had just happened? There were so many thoughts spiraling through my head at lightspeed that I could barely keep up.

Oh my god, he's so hot. Why is he so fucking hot? Can I actually please get a piece of that? Fuck, I'm dripping like a fool. Jesus fuck. I've never been called out like that. He didn't just…fuck, those words coming out of Edward's mouth. Dammit, and the face he made when he thought of Reagan? That asshole actually really likes the guy. Why does that make it hotter?!

But I also realized something else: neither of them saw it. They didn't see the way they were so protective of each other, *fawning* over each other. Edward and Reagan didn't realize they'd fallen for each other.

I did.

Worse, I knew my godfather pretty damn well, and I knew that it would take an act of god to get that man to admit to having feelings of *any* kind. Reagan was as emotive as a rock on most days, and that had been a constant since I was little.

A part of me was quite interested in getting the guy to open up, and not just to me, but to Edward, too. I...wanted to see them happy. Fuck, what a sappy thought. Still, I knew loneliness, and I had to assume they did too. Wouldn't it be better if at least the two of them were okay? Wouldn't it be easier to ask them both for a favor–of a sexual nature–if they were in good moods?

"Ugh, fuck me."

There was also the question of whether I would hurt their dynamic by trying to be a part of it, even if that were for just a moment. Reagan and Edward didn't necessarily strike me as the jealous type, but I also didn't peg either of them as the type to be fucking on the DL, so apparently, my judge of character was not perfect.

It didn't help that they had both *responded* to me during those little encounters of ours. There was wanting on both sides of the table, but I wasn't a bitch. I wouldn't ruin something between them just because I wanted to piss off my dad. There were other people in the Family I could fuck.

You just don't want them.

Shoving the thought away, I left the bench seat and went to my spot in the long row of makeup chairs. Each of us who used makeup and such had one in the dressing room, and my outfit choices were in a bin underneath. I still had work to do, after all.

I dug around in the bin, looking for something else to wear today. I'd come into the club in just a pair of black leggings and a black tee. That wouldn't do for working hours. The subs had a loose dress code, but it wasn't that loose.

First things first, it was always wise to begin an outfit with fishnets. Everyone seemed to love them, including me. They felt good against my skin, and they made an incredible sound when they were ripped, not that I was betting on that. Second was some type of bottom, and today, I opted for a short pencil skirt.

Something was feeling very "doing the secretary" today, so I went with it.

There was a long slit in the back of the skirt, and it would leave very little to the imagination when I bent over. With that skirt, I'd wear the super high, patent leather heels–black, of course. They looked a little too "mature" for my typical tastes, but it worked for this outfit.

Besides, my smattering of tattoos would give the outfit some cred. I didn't have anything coherent, just black and grey "doodles" all over my skin. I'd gotten several during flash sales and several more from guys in the Family who were coming off a tattoo career. *Go free tats.*

With the short skirt, clients would be able to see the little ghosts I had on the back of my thighs and the swirling script across the front of them that read "always" and "ready," respectively.

I had a little red heart between my breasts, and with the "secretary look" rocking, I wanted to show it off a bit. There was a black bustier that, all things considered, actually covered quite a bit, and it gave me fantastic cleavage. I opted for that and grabbed the thin collar provided by the club that indicated we were a submissive.

Running my eyes over my appearance in the mirror, I nodded, satisfied with the look I'd created. I'd swirl up my hair into a loose bun and secure it with some pins as the final touch. It was sure to rev a few engines, alright, and the ink randomly decorating my arms helped to create a delicious contrast with the faux buttoned-up look.

A few swipes of gloss, and I'll be good to go.

I'd done makeup at home today, so the lips were the only thing that needed that extra bit of shine.

If only you were doing this for the guys…

Shaking myself, I sighed. I didn't have time to be thinking

like that. Clients would be piling on soon enough, and I needed a clear head. Sure, that was a fat fucking chance at this point, but it was whatever.

Still, for the first time in a long time, I was starting to wonder about myself. Did I want something more than just revenge from Edward and Reagan? I mean, I knew I was attracted to them. I wasn't that dumb. I guess what I was curious about was whether there was more to it than just simple lust.

Did I want *them*?

I didn't have an answer, at least not one that I'd be satisfied with right now. There was too much going on, and I was really just looking to zone out. I could count on sub-space to take my mind off things for a few minutes anyway. And I really needed that tonight.

As soon as I finished applying the gloss, one of the handlers walked into the dressing room and gestured with his head at me.

"Lila, you got a request. Pair of clients–male and female-presenting. They're looking for someone who matches your talents and looks. You good to go?"

I nodded, standing from the chair and pulling down the edges of my skirt. It didn't do much since it was barely a scrap of fabric, but still.

"Yup. Lead the way, Diego."

He grinned softly, always the serene figure around here. Not for the first time, I wondered what type of guy he was beneath all those perfectly tailored layers. I supposed it didn't matter, really, and Diego led me down to a private room at the end of the long hallway. His warm tan skin was a deep red beneath the colored lights.

Diego stopped at the door and knocked twice. A "come in" came out quickly, and he opened the door for me to enter. I winked up at him, giving a fake little salute.

"See ya in a bit."

Nodding, Diego looked down at his clipboard and then back up at me. "You're supposed to check in with Reagan afterward."

I sighed, a sarcastic chuckle slipping from me. "If he shows his dumb mug, I'll think about it."

Diego rolled his eyes and walked up, leaving me to it. When I turned around, I pushed the door further open, having caught it to keep it from closing. I entered, my eyes roaming the space until I found the couple in question near the back of the room, seated at the desk–or, in the woman's case, *on* the desk.

Huh, look at that. A desk. It's kismet.

"Hello," I said, allowing my voice to dip into that seductive tone, "I'm Lila. How can I be of service today?"

The guy grinned, and damn, I had to admit that he was one of the most attractive men I'd ever seen. I also felt a flicker of recognition. I'd seen him and the woman next to him–an eleven out of ten by all accounts–at the club before. They were regulars, but I'd never had the pleasure of being in the company before.

"Hello, Lila." The man stood from the chair behind the desk, his eyes running up and down my body. "I'm Westley. This is my wife, Andi. We were hoping you'd be up for something a bit special today. It's our anniversary, and my little pet has asked to perform a bit of exhibitionism. Among *other* things."

Yeah, these two could do whatever they wanted to me. They were so fucking gorgeous, and if it weren't for the dedication to giving it up to Reagan or Edward alone, I would be throwing my virginity to the wind.

"I'm at your command."

11
The Lesson

Andi

The young woman was stunning and fairly close to me in age, I assumed. She had a beautiful tumble of curls pinned up high on her head, and as if she had known the room we were in, she was dressed in a secretary-esque outfit, just one not suited for an *actual* workplace.

"Lila, you said?" She nodded, a blush coloring her light tan cheeks. "We've seen you around, I think. He's usually referred to as Mr. R.O.B. here."

I smirked over my shoulder at Westley, who was preening like a very happy dom in a candy shop as Lila stood in front of us. It was a delight to see his eyes widen. The thought of her watching us, doing what I told her for a change, lit me up like a firecracker.

"Oh, shit. I'm sorry. I mean, yes, I'm familiar with the name. You're a very well-known client." Lila's soprano voice was high and sweet, her light brown eyes gleaming in the low, red lighting.

I liked her already.

"May I approach?" I raised my brows, eyeing the lovely girl from head to toe. "I'd like to sit with you to discuss terms."

She nodded again, her voice seeming to be caught in her throat a bit–which was fucking adorable–and then Lila looked behind her and sat down in one of the other two chairs that weren't part of the desk set up. A Saint Andrew's cross was mounted on the wall behind her.

"Of course." Lila waited for me to sit down next to her, watching me hungrily as I did. "Are you going to be acting as domme this evening?"

"In a fashion," I replied, sitting down next to her and gesturing for her hand. She obliged by giving it to me, and I began to trace the lines in her palm with my finger. "I'm typically always the submissive in our arrangement, but Westley has allowed me this opportunity to *ask* for what I want. Is that alright?"

"Of course. What did you have in mind?" Lila grinned, her eyes gleaming with interest, with arousal.

"I would like you to watch as he fucks me on the desk. I imagine in this scenario, you'd be the secretary tasked with taking notes while he dictates. Though I don't expect you to actually write anything down."

A growl reverberated from the back of the room where Westley waited, and I looked over my shoulder at him, smiling as he ate me up with his eyes.

"I can do that." Lila's breath hitched in her chest, making the supple breasts she had squeezed into her bustier press against the fabric. "Anything else?"

There was this flicker of something behind Lila's stare, and I'd been with my Westley for long enough to know that that was a hint of the true emotions resting within. She was conflicted about something, whether it was this situation or something else weighing on her mind. I also knew, after all this time and all my experiences as a sub, even seeing Westley's, that it was best to let those thoughts out and face them.

"What is your safe word or signal? And your preferences." I smiled, gently caressing her hand.

Lila sighed a little as the sensations melted some of her

tension. "I use the stop light signals like the other subs in the club. So red, yellow, and green. I can hold up three fingers if, for some reason, I can't talk. I am good for, I guess, *seeing* in this instance impact play, praise and degradation, breath play, anal, oral, orgasm control, bratting, bondage, and…Shit. I feel like I'm forgetting something."

"That's excellent. We'll take it from there. Also," and this part I'd just thought of now because Lila intrigued me; I saw myself in her, and I wanted to help get her through the mental block if I could, "I want you to tell me what you'd like me to do during the scene. Not an order, but what's piquing your interest? I want you to be honest with yourself."

"I–" But Lila stopped herself, her stare flicking downward as her fingers reflexively clenched.

I knew it.

Lifting her chin so that she'd look at me, very much taking a page from my sweet dom's book, I met Lila's eyes and offered a sympathetic smile.

"I can see something is going on in there. You're damn good at remaining professional, so don't think it's that. I just have experience with this." Westley hummed knowingly behind me. "Why not use this scene as a way to open up with yourself? What you say in this room won't leave it, but it could be good for you to vocalize it. And I'll enjoy seeing that wall come down. I definitely have a vulnerability kink."

Lila studied me, acutely scanning my face for any hint of foul play. I could see the calculation in her eyes, and I was momentarily saddened by the way her life must be. She was a guarded individual; anyone could tell that, but she also looked at me like she was desperate for this to be real, as if she needed this outlet more than she realized.

It honestly felt damn good to be in a position to help her. I knew how powerful scenes could be for releasing trauma, and I was starting to understand why Westley liked to be the one to take someone through all that and then put them back together.

That person being me, of course.

"You don't have to be this nice. You can just tell me what you want, and I'll do it. Why…why do this for me?"

Chuckling, I shrugged. "Well, Westley here has done it for me, and it genuinely changed my life. Why not pay it forward when I have the chance?"

Relief filled Lila's expression, and she nodded, her smile shining brightly despite the low lighting.

"Okay, yes. I will do that. I will tell you what I'm thinking, what I want to happen."

"Perfect." I leaned forward, reaching for Lila's cheek and pulling her toward me. As I hovered my lips over hers, I whispered to her, "And that includes everything you're imagining as well. Whoever might pop up in that pretty head of yours."

Because I read people well, and I knew that there was a crush buried under those curls, and I'd pull it from Lila's full, pouty lips.

She shivered beneath my touch, and I licked my lips. "I'm going to kiss you, Lila, and then I'm going to go over to that desk. Also, just as a reference, we don't engage in age play, hard pet play, or blood play. But everything you said is on the table. Westley will say 'hard line' if you manage to find one, alright?"

Lila nodded, her chest rising and falling quicker now as the heat between us grew. "I will use the stop light signal as well, so that everyone will hear the same verbal cues. Do you have any questions?"

"May…" Lila had to force herself to swallow, blinking before she met my eyes again. "May I…touch myself?"

"Please do," Westley replied, Lila's words loud enough to reach him. "I'm rather looking forward to that part, aren't I, pet?"

Smiling, still facing Lila, I brushed my lips over hers. "Yes, Daddy, you've been talking about how good it will feel to see someone coming to the sight of us."

"Oh, god," Lila shuddered.

"He's about to get quite the show, gorgeous."

Then I kissed her.

Lila's skin was so fucking soft, and she moaned against my lips. I could feel how much she didn't want me to leave when I pulled back, but I crossed the room and took my place on the desk, seated facing Westley on the edge of the wood surface.

"Lila," I turned over my shoulder, loving the absolutely desperate look on her face, "where do we begin?"

Staring up at Westley, I smirked at him, opening my legs a hair so that he could watch my skirt hike up higher on my thighs. His eyes darkened, hungrily eating me up.

"I want…" Lila sounded so breathy and riled up. God, I loved it. "…I want you to eat her out, Mr. R.O.B. I want you to shove her skirt up and pull her panties aside to devour her."

Once Lila had found her voice, it was clear that she had one hell of an imagination. This was going to be so fucking fun.

"'Sir' is fine, gorgeous," Westley replied, his voice gravely and thick with need. "Might I suggest that I'm rather rough about it? Pet loves that."

"Oh, fuck yes."

With that, Westley shoved me backward onto the desk, forcing my legs wide so that my skirt moved out of the way quickly for him. He took care of the rest by pushing the fabric up higher, going for the fishnets I'd worn here and gripping the crotch. He ripped a hole straight through them, reaching inside and pulling my panties away from my pussy, which fucking dripped.

He began to devour me just as instructed, and there was not a universe that existed where Westley's skills could ever be praised highly enough. I would never get sick of this incredible feeling, no matter how many times he did it.

As I dipped my head back, I looked over at Lila, where she sat on the chair across from me. The soft velvet ate up the light, making her skin stand out in the crimson glow. She reached for her breast, slipping the sumptuous flesh out from her bustier. When she pinched her nipple, I bit my lip, Westley's tongue circling my clit at the exact moment.

"That's so fucking pretty, gorgeous." My words were breathy as Westley licked through my folds, twirling his tongue right at my entrance. "Let me see you play with yourself."

Whimpering lightly, Lila released her nipple to reach for her skirt, scooting the thing up over her hips. She was wearing fishnets as well, but Lila had opted to forgo the panties. *Smart woman.*

Westley pulled back from my pussy, glancing up my body and eyeing Lila. He watched with me as she slipped her fingers into the holes of her stockings and found her seam, sliding up and down over the glistening skin.

"Finger her." Lila sucked in a desperate breath, her eyes flicking closed as she teased herself. "Tell her…tell her you shouldn't be doing this, but you don't care."

My interest peaked, and I gasped as Westley drove his finger into my cunt, his knuckles stretching my entrance.

When I looked up at him, he smirked. "I don't give a fuck if I'm not supposed to have you, pet. I'm going to make you squirt all over my hand for me like a good girl."

"Oh, fuck." Lila echoed my words, and I looked back again to see her slender fingers stuffed inside her pretty little pussy.

"Ugh, who are you thinking of, Lila? Who do you want to fuck you when they shouldn't." Westley smirked down at me, working his fingers deep into me so that I was already right on the edge, my clit burning with the need for release.

A pleading whimper left Lila, and I arched enough to eye

her as she fingered herself. "Tell me, gorgeous."

"R-Reagan. Edward. I…I want them both like this."

"Take notes, gorgeous." Westley jerked his fingers forward, adding a third so that I was squealing at the sensations. "Imagine them doing this to you."

Wetness pooled in my cunt as Westley pumped harder and harder. He hooked his fingers into my G-spot, and stars bloomed behind my lids. I was so close, and I wanted to know if Lila was too.

"Is that pussy desperate to come, Lila? Do you want *permission* to come?"

Straining to see her, I could tell that Lila was on the same page as I was, knowing that I needed permission as well, and even now, I was a good little sub. I'd hold off as much as I could.

"Beg him. Beg Sir to let you come for him." Her stare was lidded, the lust pounding through her so damn brightly, and I could see her still, her fingers waiting.

"Please, Sir, *please* let me come."

Westley smirked down at me. "Oh, come now, pet. I've heard you beg harder than that."

Glaring, I bucked as Westley fucked me harder with his fingers, my brain going haywire.

"Fuck! Please! Please, Sir. I…oh god…."

He chuckled, that dark, delicious sound, and I was going to lose it. "That's my good girl. Yes, come for Daddy, pet."

And fuck did I. My screams filled the room as the euphoria washed over me, and I came, gushing over Westley's hand. From behind me, I heard a needy squeak, and then Lila was crying out, "Do it again. Drink her down."

Westley didn't hesitate to obey *that* order. He knew well enough that I was going to be a fucking puddle after this.

"You heard her, pet. Give me my treat." Westley thrust his fingers into me so damn hard and fast, and I came again, squirting cum across his mouth and tongue. "So good, my little slut. So *very* good."

Just as the orgasm was coming down, I heard Lila moan and whine. Turning to her, I watched–filled with fucking glee–as she fingered her pussy so fast, slipping out of her cunt to rub across her clit. Her cum rushed over her fingers, this delectable steady stream of glistening liquid.

She sat forward abruptly, her skin flushed as she struggled for breath. "Oh, shit. I've never done *that* before."

Westley chuckled, his stare moving from Lila to me. "Oh, that's a damn treat. It looks like I can work my magic without even touching her."

I grinned, pulling him to my lips for a quick kiss. "Are you still hungry, dear? Or should Lila have you fill me up with that thick cock?"

We both looked back at Lila, and she chewed on her lip, the naughty thoughts in her head clear in her expression.

"Turn her around and fuck her ass. Choke her with your tie as you spank her."

"I like the way your mind works," Westley smirked, then yanked me off the desk, only to spin me around and force me back down. "Scream for me, pet."

Smearing my cum over my asshole, Westley got me ready for his cock and then thrust home in one hard push. I was so filled up, his impressive cock stretching my ass. I cried out at the incredible intrusion, and as his hips rocked back and forth fucking me, I could hear him reach for his tie.

Before I could moan again, the fabric slid around my throat, and my breathing was restricted. Slaps on my ass blazed through my skin in time with Westley's thrusts. I adored impact play, and Westley didn't hold back, bringing his hand down on my skin so hard that it was sure to leave marks.

"I want to hear how bad you want it." Lila's words were moaned out of her. "Say how much you want him to take your virginity."

Oh, shit. Well, isn't that a treat? And to the man who took mine no less.

Looking out at her, I held Lila's eyes as she continued to finger herself, her hips rocking against her hand. There was this perfect little spot beneath her pussy that revealed how she'd squirted for the first time, and my pussy clenched as I ate up the sight.

It had become something of an obsession for me–Westley being so very good at making me do it–and seeing someone else like that was undeniably hot.

I didn't blink as I repeated the words for the gorgeous submissive. "Take my virginity, Sir. Claim every one of my firsts."

Westley growled, leaning forward so that his lips dusted the skin of my ear, and I erupted in goosebumps.

"Aww, pet, that sounds familiar. Happy anniversary."

With that, my husband stopped holding back, fucking my ass with abandon as he spanked me. As if that weren't enough to get me coming again, Westley reached between my legs, hooking his fingers into my cunt. I was so blissfully filled, and the cries for release started up again, the functioning part of my brain short-circuiting.

"*Please*! Oh fuck, oh fuck, oh fuck…"

I was a delirious mess as Westley thrust his cock into my ass right up to the hilt. But the floor creaked in front of me, and I managed to get an eyelid open to see Lila on the floor. She knelt before the desk, her eyes pinned on Westley and me, captivated by how he fucked me within an inch of my life.

"You're a naughty little thing, aren't you? Getting up from the chair where Pet put you. Tsk, tsk." Westley clucked his tongue. "Why don't you make yourself useful then and give my slut something to do with her mouth?"

Lila's eyes flared wide. We'd switched who was in control

to a degree, but she could see that I was a goner, lost to how roughly and wonderfully my husband was fucking me. She stood precariously, walking up to me until she was standing at the edge of the desk, her pussy level with my mouth.

"Will you–"

"Any fucking day, gorgeous." I cut in as I groaned, Westley tormenting me by holding still until Lila was in place.

"I...I'll admit..." Lila lifted her leg, perching her knee on the desk so that I could get at her wet pussy. "...I've never had a femme client before. I've...I've never done anything with a woman at all."

"Oh, pet," Westley grabbed my hips and thrust forward hard, making me yelp, "you're so lucky."

"I am." My dom started a slow rhythm again, his fingers going back into my cunt. "Oh, fuck, ugh! Come...come here, gorgeous."

Letting go of the desk, I reached for Lila. She took her place, hovering her pussy in front of my mouth, and I went to work, eating her out with every trick I'd ever felt Westley use. She trembled against me, pulsing and rubbing herself against my mouth.

"You look so pretty with your face stuffed in pussy, pet. Make her scream for you, and I'll let you come."

Westley's fingers dug into my hip hard enough to bruise, while his others hooked into my G-spot. They rubbed against his cock on the other side of my walls, and I was dying to come.

Shoving my fingers inside Lila's pussy, I pumped in and out in time with Westley, sucking on her clit as I did. It wasn't long before she was bucking against me, getting wetter and wetter, until I pressed hard into the magic button we both shared, and Lila's screams filled the room.

"Holy...shit! Ahh!" The lovely submissive came around my fingers, and I lapped up the delicious stream of cum that slowly bled from her.

"Good girl. Ugh, pet," Westley spoke through gritted molars, "that's so fucking good. Now, come for me. I want you to make a nice little puddle on the floor."

He turned up the volume, his efforts doubling down, and I shattered, climaxing so hard that my vision went blurry, my body convulsing. Cum gushed out of my pussy as Westley tore his fingers free, only to rub my clit as he continued to pound into my ass.

Just as he demanded, I came and came, undoubtedly making a mess of the floor, going by the sounds. I knew how much he loved it, my sweet, depraved Westley, and I adored pleasing him. When the sensations were almost becoming too much, he rocked his hips in one hard thrust, and warmth pooled inside me.

I felt Westley's cock kick in my ass as he pumped his cum into me, and the animal groans he let out went straight to my core, making flickers of orgasms tumble through me.

"Tell me what it feels like," Lila whispered, and I leaned back, circling her clit with my thumb as I slid my fingers in and out of her.

"Warm and so full, so very fucking full. His cock twitches inside me as he comes."

Lila whimpered, and another quick shock of pleasure zinged through her, her pussy clamping around my fingers as a tiny rivulet of cum trickled out of her.

It was several long moments of us all catching our breath and getting ourselves untangled. But we did, and as we straightened ourselves, Lila looked about as dazed as I felt. I chuckled as we made eye contact, and she just grinned.

"You should talk to those guys you mentioned. The worst that can happen is they say no, right? At least you'll know then."

Eyes widening, Lila's stare went a little distant, and then she blinked, looking over at me again.

"I…I was going to. I, umm, we're not supposed to per se, but…I think I want something like you have with them." Lila looked between Westley and me. "I get it if they aren't looking for a relationship, of course. Hell, I didn't know I *was* until you, umm, yeah. I guess what I'm saying is thanks, and I'll give it a shot. Can't hurt any more than it does now, right?"

Lila was just a bit younger than me, I believed, and I nodded, pulling Westley close and smiling up at him before meeting her cautiously optimistic grin again.

"It's strange the way fate works, but it does. Go for it. You'll regret it if you don't and if it *does* work out…"

Westley's sinister grin beamed from his face, and if I weren't already so spent, I would've come from the sight alone.

"Just think about how wonderful it will feel."

When I finally broke the loving staring contest with my husband and glanced back at Lila, she was watching us with that look I'd seen on people before. A kind of jealousy, but one that wasn't about wanting Westley or me, but what we had together.

"Yeah, that sounds…pretty fucking great."

Stepping forward, Westley took Lila's hand and kissed the back of it. "Thank you for helping to make our anniversary one to remember. Now, if you'll excuse us, there's some aftercare to tend to and then more orgasms."

Lila blushed, smiling as he nodded at us. "I'm glad I could be of service. You guys are…incredibly hot–and so sweet. I'll see you around."

"Go get 'em, Lila." I winked at her, and she left the room.

"Well, darling, shall we?" Westley hugged me to his side, gesturing toward the door.

"Yes. You owe me ice cream and a bubble bath."

"As you wish, pet. As you wish."

12
The Meet-Up

Reagan

E dward was unsurprisingly cooped up in his office when I found him. He'd been a little grumpy after being unable to come. It was fucking delicious. But unfortunately, I wasn't here to engage in another punishment session or even some stress relief.

Even though I was filled to the fucking brim with the stuff.

No, we needed to discuss what he had learned from his guy and determine our next move. I knew it wasn't over with Lila. You don't try that hard to kill someone and give up after only one miss. Whoever was looking to hurt her, they'd be back.

And I needed a way to fucking stop them.

Knocking on his door, I waited for him to answer, annoyed that it took longer than two seconds. I also heard some shuffling on the other side, and the lock clicked into place. I cocked a brow.

Curious.

"Yes, come in."

I pushed the door wide, entering Edward's office. He was behind his desk, and if my eyes didn't fucking deceive me, he was a little sweaty.

"What were you doing?"

He cleared his throat, sitting up straighter in his office chair.

"Nothing. What's up?"

You fucker. I chewed on my tongue for a moment, pushing inside and closing the door behind me. I also promptly locked it again.

Sauntering up to his desk and sitting down on the edge, I glanced down at Edward. I knew exactly how accusatory my expression was, and I didn't let up for a second as he stewed in his juices, forced to endure my gaze and silence.

"Goddamn it, Reagan. I needed to." He sighed, raking a hand through his hair. "We weren't even supposed to see each other again today. You couldn't have expected me to wait until I saw you next. Whenever that was going to be."

I glared. "Oh yes, I could. You've racked up more punishment time. Is that really what you were going for?"

Edward's annoyed stare flicked up and off to the side. "I was going for a quick release so that I could fucking focus."

"How'd that work out for you?" I smirked, and oh damn, I was really starting to love the way Edward looked at me when he wanted to both murder me and fuck me.

"Fuck. Off." He sat back in his chair, his fingers going through his locks again as he sighed. "Now, what do you want?"

Chuckling, I got up off his desk, taking a seat in the chair that sat before it. "We'll talk about that punishment later, slave."

His eyes glowed–a mixture of rage and intrigue–and Edward nodded. "Fine. Anything else?"

"Yes, as a matter of fact, there is. What did you learn about the attack on Lila? I need more to go on."

With the conversation turning hard into serious territory, Edward visibly refocused, his calculating mind coming fully online. *At least one part of him got to, right? Stop complaining.*

"Well, you know that there's an outside business angle at play here. I've been pushing Lavar for more details, but he's still digging for most of it. It looks like your Family, or at least the don, has been using someone of similar talents to hide their business."

I shrugged one shoulder. "Well, sure. That tracks. We have hackers and shit protecting our digital assets everywhere. Hell, some are in fucking Seuol."

"Of course. That part doesn't surprise me. What does is that this cover up is unique from the other scrubs that Lavar was able to find in the Family records. Those he could open. Tracked it to offshore accounts that coincided with specific 'known' drug and arms networks. He could see all that. This? He hasn't cracked yet. That means his heightened security."

My gut tightened, and I considered what Edward was saying. "Which means that Emilio knows it's worse. He's keeping it from the law and, more importantly, the Family. Jesus fuck. What is he up to?"

"An excellent question. Any information you can gather from within the organization might very well be the key to protecting Lila. I'm not sure if she was targeted because she knows his business, though I doubt it based on how he treats her. So, it's far more likely that whoever he's doing business with outside of his usual jobs has targeted her to send a message. A violent one."

My jaw clenched, the tension in me strong enough to make it crack, and I briefly worried for my teeth before I forced myself to relax. Dropping my head, my hair falling around my face to block Edward's office lights, I gripped the bridge of my nose, pinching hard.

"I'll need to talk with him. And...Emilio's been less than forthcoming with me as of late. Past few months, actually. Something is definitely up. Still," I got up, pushing out of the chair; I adjusted my tie, making this more presentable, "he might let something slip. I can work with that. I just need to... push his buttons a little."

"And you can visit Lila. How wonderful. I'm sure she can give you a few notes on how to push someone's buttons."

Edward's stare found the middle distance, focusing on nothing as he remembered something. I could see those dark brows of his pinch together, and amid the renewed fury I felt toward him was curiosity. Had Lila gotten to my slave as well?

"That's another slight to add to your punishment, pretty boy. Keep at it. We can make the next session one for the record books."

Glaring, but unable to hide the smirk that ticked up the corner of his mouth, Edward recentered himself toward his laptop screen, not looking at me.

"See you later, Reagan. If I hear anything, I'll be sure to ring Lila's phone since I'm sure you'll be with her."

Shaking my head, I left him to his club-running bullshit. But I also took note. Edward was up to three naughty acts that I'd be claiming his ass for.

Hope you enjoy orgasm torture, slave. You'll be in for a treat.

13
The Sight

Reagan

Emilio glared at me from behind his desk. He'd let me into the office, and I could see it on his face how much he was already regretting that decision. It gnawed at me. This guy had been my friend for most of my life, and we were now so distant. I didn't know what had happened between us, but I didn't like it.

"I'm still concerned for Lila, as you know." The don shifted in his chair, narrowing his eyes at me. "An attempt on your daughter's life is clearly a move to attack you and your business. Is there *anything* I should know that I don't already?"

I was trying to give the fucker an out, a way to bring me into the conversation so that we could handle this. Emilio sucked in a breath, leaning back in his chair and tenting his fingers in front of his mouth.

"You really think someone is trying to get at me through her? Why not the direct approach? I mean, speaking purely strategically, killing Lila doesn't stop my business from running. It hardly seems wise as the competition."

Hearing Emilio talk about Lila like that made my blood boil. I had to force myself to keep the torrent of words locked behind my lips. But I wasn't one to fly off the handle, particularly with the don. I knew how that shit went over.

Instead, I clenched my jaw, balling my hands into fists at my sides. Stoic was my reliable mask, and I leaned into it as hard as I could, keeping my voice level.

"*Strategically*, sir, I think they're trying to knock you off your game. Losing your daughter would certainly upset you, cause you to make rash decisions, and that *might,* in fact, affect your business."

Something flickered over Emilio's expression, this odd twinge of annoyance or boredom. I knew it couldn't be either of those things logically. We were talking about his daughter's death, for fuck's sake. But the instinctual part of me that didn't give a fuck about the precedent that Emilio and I had created over all these years didn't agree. It *was* annoyance.

What the fuck is that about? How are you not taking this fucking seriously?

I couldn't let my rage show, so I didn't. But there was no denying how furious it made me to see the don be wildly flippant about Lila's safety. She was my fucking goddaughter. I'd been protecting her for twenty-seven years. Twenty-eight this October, actually.

It had been drilled into me since day one that her safety and livelihood were the two most essential things in my life, which was a hell of a balancing act considering I was still to act as Emilio's consigliere. I was to put my life on the line for her from the time she was an infant until the day I finally kicked the damn bucket.

And I'd done it. I'd done it several times, in fact.

Lila mattered more to me than I was totally comfortable admitting. I always remained at a distance, though, staying in the shadows to do my job and never once interfering with her life or choices. That wasn't for me.

Time had fucking flown by, and now she was an adult. We'd gotten to know each other as a result. Now, instead of her basically ignoring my presence, which I'd mimicked as much as I could while protecting her, Lila was interested in pushing my buttons to no end.

I wasn't sure when the dynamic had changed, really, when I'd started to see her beyond the job I had, but I did. And the truth was, the fact that Emilio–her fucking father–was this unmoved by her near-death experience was enough to strain the already fraying strings of our friendship.

If something happened to Lila because he couldn't get his head out of his ass, I'd fucking kill him.

Calm down, Reagan. Come on. Jesus fucking christ.

"Ugh, this is hardly what I need right now. Do your digging or whatever." Emilio reached for his glass of whisky, taking a swig. "If you can find whoever is responsible, see to it that a message of our own is sent. Pictures, or it didn't happen, too."

I nodded. "Fine. It would still help me do my fucking job if I had more to go off of. It seems a bit…odd that you don't have your own thoughts on who it might be."

"Don't fucking 'odd' me, Reagan." Emilio glared, his dark eyes nearly buried beneath the furrowed slash of his brows. "I'm fucking busy, and it's your fucking job to make sure you know what's going on. So be better at it. Don't fucking come in here and beg me for answers because you can find them."

My jaw cracked, the joint popping from the pressure I was putting on it. Emilio chugged down the rest of his drink, his eyes flicking to his monitor. As he jiggled the mouse to wake the computer up, his jaw was set in a hard line, the black hair of his beard only just masking the tension there.

Apparently, we were both sick of each other. *Surprise, surprise.*

"Get out, Reagan. I have been things to do than entertain your fucking attitude. Go get your answers and report back."

I didn't say another word, spinning on my heel and heading directly for the door. I was liable to grab the asshole by his overly expensive suit and throw him down on his desk. Emilio may have been the don, but he wasn't the best fighter in the house. I claimed that title, and my fists were aching to punch that message into his face.

The door slammed closed behind me, and I beelined toward the kitchen. Maybe some of the guys would know something. It had been a minute since I'd checked in with them. Babysitting Lila at the club–and "speaking" with Edward–had eaten up a lot of my time.

This better not be a fucking waste.

"Well, that was a total fucking waste," I grumbled, speeding down the hall toward my bedroom.

This day had gone drastically downhill since I'd arrived home, and I needed a fucking break. Booze and a shower sounded about as good as it was going to get, too. I couldn't go all the way back to the club without sparking suspicion, so pounding Edward was a no-go, which sucked.

I was really starting to enjoy that particular form of stress relief, which was an issue technically, but I didn't give a fuck right now.

"Meets at the docs. Right, so fucking helpful." I complained to myself as I hurried down the long hallway to the other wing of the mansion. "He's got every type of connection meeting him down there, or fucking Renzo most like. That's not fucking helpful."

Pounding behind my eyes stopped my tirade. I was heading straight toward an all-night migraine at this rate, and I couldn't afford another night of practically no sleep. Caffeine could only do so much, and I was forty-seven.

Going on two to three hours of sleep wasn't as easy to shrug off as it had been when I was younger.

Music filtered into the hall as I got to the wing I shared with Emilio and Lila. Our bedrooms were all down on this end, and I knew for a fact that wasn't the don enjoying some tunes. One, he didn't crank it that loud, and two, nineties R&B wasn't his style.

Ugh, Lila, turn it down. You're obsessed with those fucking CDs.

I marched over to her door. It was across the hall from mine, the banister to my right protecting residents from falling onto the first floor beneath us. If I was going to be spending the night without my go-to method of relieving tension–with a fucking migraine to boot–then I wasn't dealing with her fucking music on top of it.

My steps boomed, and I pulled up to a stop in front of Lila's door with my hand raised, knuckles poised to pound on the wood.

But it wasn't closed, not entirely.

That's why the music was just *that much* louder than usual. Lila's stereo was screaming through a cracked door, the sounds of sappy lyrics bleeding out into the hallway. Still, it was what I saw as I peered inside–my stare landing on Lila as she lay back on the bed–that gripped me by the cock and wouldn't let go.

Oh, fuck. She's...masturbating.

14
The Lack of Control

Reagan

Ineeded to leave. I needed to get the fuck out of here and go into my room. The stupid girl had left the door open for anyone to walk by and see her knuckles deep in her pussy, but I could just close it quietly and leave.

So why was I still fucking standing here?

My cock kicked behind my zipper. She was *right there*. I was watching those slender little fingers slide in and out of Lila's pussy. Holy fucking god, I was going to lose my mind. This was so *not* what I was supposed to be doing.

Sure, I was there to protect her, but this? This was *not* that. This was wanting to shove my way into her room and replace her hand with my cock.

Clenching my jaw, I could feel the joint squeeze, and my molars protested against the pressure I was applying. I needed to move. I needed to go back to my room.

"Ugh. " A tiny squeak left Lila's lips, and she bucked her hips against her hand as she circled her clit.

Fuuuck.

I shook my head, trying and failing to refocus. It had been easy to ignore Lila's looks, her endless flirtations, for so long. Well, not easy per se. When she'd gone and grown up–coming back from a year abroad in Italy without me–I couldn't deny that Lila had become fucking stunning.

It had likely always been there, but it was when she got home, her light tan skin all the more bronzed and her entire being seeming to be that much more mature, that I truly saw how gorgeous she was–how goddamn alluring. I'd wanted to go on that Italy trip to protect her as always, but Emilio insisted she'd be fine and that he needed me in town.

Now, with everything going on, I had to wonder if it was that trip that landed her in an enemy Famiglia's sights.

And I could be dwelling on all of that from the comfort of my room, where I could do whatever else I wanted aside from starting at the prettiest fucking pussy I'd ever seen in my life.

Lila wasn't naked either. She was entirely clothed, just her skirt hiked up with her panties–black and lacey–pulled to the side. Hell, her shoes were on, high-heeled Mary Janes, which I knew she wore at the club.

She'd been at work earlier. I had stayed behind to talk to Edward. Was…was Lila masturbating because she didn't get off from her fucking Johns.

Potent fury pulsed through my veins when I pictured Lila fucking some asshole at that goddamn club. She was an adult, and she could do what she wanted, but dammit, the thought of anyone touching her–of some fucker leaving her wanting–made my blood boil.

Goddamn it, Reagan. Go to your room. Leave.

But Lila's fingering picked up speed, her digits slick with her arousal driving in and out before stopping to work her clit. Lila's hips were bucking against her hand, and she reached up with the other to grab her breast over her shirt.

I knew exactly what those breasts looked like, and my cock ached at the memory. It *ached* to see Lila like this, her cunt glistening and needy, her skin flushed, and her curls tousled on the bed.

Without really thinking, my hand drifted down to my

erection, squeezing the base through my slacks. I was so fucking hard, the slippery, cool sensation of precum smearing inside my briefs.

Go into your room and do this. You're in the fucking hall.

There was no one around, though, and there wouldn't be. The Family was all busy with their own tasks, and Emilio didn't come down to this wing until well into the middle of the night. I wouldn't be seen. And something about doing it right here, knowing Lila had been careless with her door on top of it, made it so much hotter.

Quietly, I reached for my zipper, dragging it down so that I could reach inside and free my straining dick. Lila whimpered as her pleasure increased, her fingers dipping into her cunt over and over. Just as I gave myself one firm pump, Lila pulled her panties further out of the way with her free hand, the fingers teasing her clit.

I thrust into my hand, gripping so fucking tight. I wanted the ache, the intensity of handling myself roughly. I could imagine stuffing my cock into Lila's pussy, how she'd clench around me when she came.

"Ugh, oh fuck…" I could barely hear her over the music, but those words found me, and my stare was pinned to her all the more as Lila toyed with that sensitive bud while her other hand smeared her arousal over her asshole.

Oh fuck, indeed. Such a naughty girl.

Fisting my shaft harder, I stroked, fucking into my hand as I pictured thrusting into Lila's tight little hole. Edward had been kind enough to solidify the belief that I was rather large, and the idea of Lila being forced to take me was too fucking good.

I was an asshole, a bit of a monster, and every part of me wanted to see the pretty girl break for me. She'd be so damn beautiful when she cried, stuffed so full in any one of her needy holes.

Lila swirled her finger around the tight ring of muscle

before plunging her finger inside and then another. Her arm was under her, raising Lila's hips, and it angled her cunt right at me. Getting closer, she rubbed briskly across her clit with her other hand, her fingers flying across the skin in a frenzy.

I picked up my pace, thrusting into my fist as I increased the pressure. The tell-tale burn in my shaft trickled through me, my balls pulling up tight. I was going to come right when my naughty little Lila did.

Her breathing was erratic–quick and hungry for oxygen–and just as the stream of precum that leaked from me got more persistent, she tipped over the edge. I watched Lila's body jerk and pulse as she came, a little rivulet of cum running from her.

That did it.

My cock kicked, and I gripped the head with my other hand, emptying into my palm in what felt like an endless orgasm. Seeing Lila's pussy leak all that shiny cum was too damn good. I wanted to see her fucking rain for me. The thought–the sight of her riding out the aftershocks–had me spurting ropes of warm cum into my hand.

I couldn't let it get on the floor or her door. And I was worried it was going to gush through my fingers because I was coming so much, so hard.

Catching my breath, I snapped back to reality. Oh shit. I spun on my heel, quiet as death, as I shoved my dick away and practically ran for my bedroom. I opened things up, locking the door behind me, and it wasn't until I was rinsing my hands in the sink that my heartbeat slowed.

What the fuck did I just do?

But I knew exactly what I'd done, and there was no going back after this. I was fucking attracted to Emilio's daughter. That wasn't about to go over well. My thoughts churned through worst-case scenarios and how to avoid them all.

I wanted to be furious, to blame this on Lila's little stunt in the dressing room. But I knew better than that. I was an excellent liar, but I didn't lie to myself if I could avoid it–you know, as long as it didn't involve sex. But I was waging a losing battle, it seemed.

Edward might have been my first struggle with a particular set of Emilio's rules, but he clearly wasn't the last. I looked up at myself in the mirror, meeting my dark eyes with a tired sigh. Hanging my head, I turned off the water and started for my bedroom.

"You just…Ugh. God fucking damn it."

15
The New Hire

Lila

Being bored at a sex club shouldn't be possible, but when you're not entertaining a client, it really could be. I sat in the dressing room, lounging back on the booth-like bench that ran along the back side of the room. The velvet felt nice under my fingers, but I couldn't help but think about the last time I'd been in here.

Yesterday...right before that session with the couple...

I could remember their names—Westley and Andi, and what she'd said to me had stuck around. So had the flaring desire that hadn't let up for a moment after I'd finished with them. Even masturbating last night hadn't taken the edge off. I still felt tight in my skin, constricted, and not in the fun bondage way.

I was still thinking about Reagan and Edward, and I was still hung up on how badly I wanted to be *involved* with both of them, not just once.

"Ugh, I hate this." Grumbling to myself was hardly going to help, though.

"You alright over there?" I waved off Demi's concern; they were so sweet, but I wasn't in the mood to talk.

"I'm fine. I'm just going to rest before I'm called out on the floor."

Demi chuckled. "Mood, girl. I'm so close to finishing this chapter."

That switch did love their books. I smiled, resting back on the closest thing to a couch the room offered. It was quiet enough inside, and even with Demi reading and making their little excited noises, I would be able to drift off if I put my mind to it.

Closing my eyes, I focused intently on trying to catch a few Zzzs before I was eventually paged for a client. Resting up was wise, after all. I'd stayed up too late watching movies and then woke up early from an intense sex dream that just had me flicking the bean again.

The silence of the dressing room pressed down on me–almost too uncomfortable to rest–but I began to zone it all out as I slowed my breathing, going for at least a meditative state if I couldn't fall asleep.

Creak.

Cracking a lid, I watched the dressing room door open, and a woman walked over to the usually empty spot in front of the long bank of mirrors. I didn't recognize her, but that wasn't a huge surprise. Edward hired new subs all the time. I'd heard that Celeste was quitting, too. So, it tracked that he'd need a new sub to come in and take her place.

Still, I wasn't really interested in conversing with someone right now, so I stayed lying back on the seat and closed my eyes again. If Elle, our resident domme in charge of the subs, had already spoken to her, the new hire would know to give the other employees space.

Plus, Dmie could take that bullet for me. At least they seemed awake.

"Are you Lila?" Clearly, the new sub had other ideas.

I sat up, glancing over at the woman. She eyed me with this

sense of hope, and I wondered if Elle had told her I was the most recent hire before her. The submissive was probably just looking for a bit of advice. I could muster up some empathy and help out.

"Yeah." I smiled with a nod. "I'm guessing this is your first day?"

"It is, yeah. I'm sorry to bug you; I was just a little nervous. Do you have a second to talk?"

Pulling up all the way so that I sat cross-legged on the bench, I nodded again. "As a matter of fact, I do. What's your name?"

"Joelle." The woman stood, holding out her hand to shake mine. "Nice to meet you."

I waited a few seconds for her to cross the room, noting that she was wearing a rather full-body robe that looked especially thick. She'd need to get over that "modesty" if she was going to feel comfortable working at a sex club.

Shaking her hand, I allowed Joelle to join me on the bench. "Are you nervous? If this is your first time working at a club, I can get why you would be."

"Oh, it's not my first job ever, but I'll admit that this particular club setting is new." Joelle glanced at Demi, running her stare over them like Demi was some type of oddity. "I don't usually see such diverse people."

Joelle's voice was low enough that Demi didn't hear, and they were wrapped up in their book enough to tune us out anyway. I didn't love the way she was talking about her, this false feeling of acceptance accompanying Joelle's words. But I also didn't want to jump to conclusions.

"Oh, well, yeah. The Scarlett Oleander employs all sorts of people. Edward's cool like that."

Offering a smile, I waited for Joelle to ask me something or confide in me about her nerves. That was the usual first-day-on-the-job stuff. She was damn quiet though, watching Demi out of the corner of her eye. It wasn't especially noticeable, but I was the type to pick up on that type of thing. I got good at reading a room or a person thanks to my life as a mafia don's daughter.

It was a pretty useful trick both in and out of the bedroom.

Joelle wasn't fidgeting or changing positions too frequently. She didn't have a layer of sweat across her forehead or a tick she was indulging in as an attempt to self-soothe.

She's definitely not nervous. What's her deal?

"Umm, did you have a question for me or something?" I didn't want to pry, but Joelle was the one who'd come over to talk to me.

"Oh, sorry." Joelle shook her head, paying more attention to me. "I was distracted. Yeah, umm, what do you do outside of this? Or is this like your life?"

It was a weird way to put it, but again, I didn't want to judge her. Maybe Joelle had social anxiety or just didn't interact with people the same way.

"I mean, this is my job, but I go home when I'm done. Hang out with my dog and listen to CDs."

Joelle's brows rose, and she nodded at me with the corners of her mouth down. "CDs? I didn't think people used those anymore."

Feeling oddly self-conscious, I nodded, my stare going down to my hands in my lap. I started picking at the dry skin next to my cuticle, knowing I needed to be careful so I didn't tear the skin too far.

"Oh, well, it's kind of my thing. I like CDs. It's fun to have a little collection of them."

"But you can just stream everything, and it doesn't take up room in your house." Joelle sat with her spine straight, not relaxing on the bench in the slightest. "But whatever."

"Yeah," I bobbed my head in this awkward nod-adjacent gesture that was entirely there to help diffuse some of the tension, "well...Umm, I'm not needed for a client right now, so I was going to try to doze. You'll see how much it helps during your own shift. So...umm...yeah."

I began to lean back against the bench seat, hoping that Joelle would take the hint.

"Demi," Dante leaned into the dressing room, "you've got a client. Mr. Z. Your regular."

They looked up from their phone with a sigh, clicking off the screen and standing up.

"It's always at the good part." Demi looked at their watch before taking it off and putting it in a pile with their phone and short, silk robe. "Huh, he's a bit early today. Wonder what's up."

Walking over to their station, Demi stuffed their belongings into the drawer at the bottom and turned the key, locking it up. They took it with them as they headed toward Drake, who was still waiting at the door.

"Hey, Lila." He smiled as we made eye contact. "There's a new guy out front, too. He might be a good fit, but we're doing the background check."

"Oh, okay. Well, just let me know." I smirked back, shooting him some finger guns–because was I really bisexual if I didn't find a way to use them in conversation?

"Alright, Drake, lead the way." Demi waved back at me, a hint of dislike in her eye as she cast a quick glance at the new girl. "See ya in a few, Lila."

The two of them left, leaving me alone in the room with Joelle. *Goody*.

I just went back to that attempt to sleep, though. I'd told Joelle I wanted to rest, and hopefully, she took that to heart and gave me some space. Elle was going to have some "training moments" with that one for sure.

"Finally," Joelle whispered, her register deeper, "I thought I'd never get you alone."

Abruptly sitting up, I raised my brows, holding up my hand

to keep her from advancing on me.

"Whoa, whoa, whoa. You can't just hop on the train like that. There is a ticket buying process, and I'm all full up on passengers at the moment."

Joelle rolled her eyes, laughing before meeting my eyes again. Her gaze was a laser sight, drilling into me so that I felt far too exposed and on the spot.

"God, you really are a fucking moron, aren't you?" She scoffed, her hands going for the tie on her robe. "I really don't know why they're making such a fuss about you, but c'est la vie. Not for much longer in your case."

My pulse leaped into overdrive, and I reeled back on the bench, trying to put distance between Joelle and me.

"What are you fucking talking about?"

But she was standing up and taking off that overly thick robe. Beneath it, Joelle wore street clothes, but they were all black and... tactical. *The hell is up with that?* On her hip was a small loop of what I could only guess was wire.

Alarm bells blared in my head. She shouldn't have that, and it really shouldn't have two wooden handles on either end. Joelle pulled it from her hip, taking both grips, and sneered at me.

"Oh, shit."

I jumped out of the way just as Joelle swung her hands down to lasso me. She stumbled into the bench but only slightly, and I rolled off the bench toward the door. Drake. He'd be right outside. Hell, I just needed anyone to see what Joelle was up to. She'd run off like the last guy had, worried about being spotted.

Reaching the door, I was suddenly shoved forward, colliding with the hard surface. I didn't hit it too hard, but it stopped my progress, and before I could correct myself, Joelle jabbed her fist into my spine.

"Ahh!" I screeched, pinching backward as I reflexively

tried to protect myself.

Standing there was dumb. I needed to put distance between us, so I took off for the mirrors, hoping to find something I could use to even the fight.

I wasn't hopeless in a scuffle. Dad had ensured that when I was younger, but I didn't do wet work for the Family, so it had been a minute since I'd used the skills. I was a much better shot than I was a fighter, too.

"Oh no, bitch. I have a job to do."

Joelle's voice was so devoid of emotion, so menacing, and then I was forced down to the floor much quicker than I'd intended. She jumped onto my back, keeping me there, and I tried to push up, only to see the wire coming down over my face.

Shoving my hands up, I managed to create a barrier between my neck and the wire at the last second. It dug into my fingers and the sides of my throat, the pressure enormous. I couldn't breathe properly, only managing tiny sips of air through my nose and gaping mouth.

No, no, no. This is really fucking bad.

I couldn't call for help like this, and the weapon pressed to my skin was starting to rub it raw from the strain, threatening to tear my flesh.

Every second made it harder to fight back, my brain screaming at me that I was going to die if I didn't breathe soon. My vision went hazy, black dots floating through the air in front of my face. Pushing with my knees wasn't getting me up off the floor, either.

This is not the type of breath play I enjoy. Christ, Lila. You're dying, and that's what you want your last thought to be? Fuck.

Fighting against Joelle's hold took everything I had, and I needed all that to just breathe. She leaned into my spine with her elbow or knee, and the pain made it even harder for me to concentrate on getting enough oxygen.

"Go to sleep, Lila. This'll all be over, and I can get paid."

Something about the fact that this meant nothing to Joelle made it so much worse. She was just doing a job, getting paid to murder me. And I knew it was all about being a Carpinelli. This was my fucking Famiglia's fault, and I hated them. I hated everything about my fucking life so goddamn much.

Not like this. Not on the floor of a dressing room.

But everything was fading, getting darker and darker, and I couldn't hear right. Everything was muffled. As much as I tried to push the wire away from my neck, I couldn't. The strength in my arms was leaving me, and the pressure on my throat only got more and more excruciating.

This was it. I was going to die.

"Lila, have you talked to the new hire?" Edward's voice sounded distantly in the background. "The fuck?!"

16
The Fallout

Lila

Life was an odd series of ups and downs, shouts and loud thuds, and then I could feel someone touching me. I wanted to scream and flail, knocking away whoever was looking to kill me now.

But the world came into better focus, the mess of reds and blacks finally solidifying as oxygen rushed into my lungs. I shot upright, clinging to whoever was in front of me by the lapels of their jacket.

"Ugh!" I gasped, choking and coughing on the air that could at last make its way into me.

"Lila!" Hands gripped my shoulders, and I recognized that voice. "Lila, it's me! It's Edward."

Shapes crystallized into the proper forms, and I saw him. Edward was on the floor with me, his eyes wide with his brows to his hairline. What had just happened? What had I been doing just now? I'd come into the dressing room–confirmed by the fact that I was still there–and wanted to take a nap before I was needed again.

Demi had been in here, reading. I...I...Joelle!

Panicking, I scanned around me for any sign of her. "She

fucking tried to kill me!"

My throat was raw as I spoke, each word coming out raspy and strained. Edward dropped his stare, and I followed it, seeing the heap in the middle of the room. It looked like a person, and the clothes matched what I could remember of Joelle.

"Is she dead?" I winced as I spoke, and Edward glanced back at me, his brows now pinched tightly together.

"No." He didn't sound altogether happy about that. "I knocked her unconscious."

He reached into his pocket, pulling out his cell. "I'm calling the authorities. The ones I know will handle this discreetly."

I watched as he went into his contacts to dial someone, nodding for no particular reason since Edward wasn't looking at me right now. He was still right at my side, however. His free hand was still on my shoulder, squeezing gently. I really didn't want it to ever leave.

"Morris, I need you at the club. We've had another attack. I apprehended this one. She's currently unconscious on the floor."

Whoever Edward was talking to, they responded, and it seemed to just piss Edward off more because he glared at nothing, his jaw clenching.

"I don't fucking care. She tried to kill one of my girls. One who just so happens to be Emilio's daughter, so if I were you, I'd get my ass down here *pronto*."

Hanging up, Edward returned his attention to me, sliding his phone into his pocket.

"Are you okay? Physically? I can call an ambulance." I knew how much he hated to have cops and city officials in the club, considering it wasn't supposed to exist and all, so it was actually really nice of him to offer. "Lila?"

I shook my head. "No, you don't need to call. I'm...I'm fine. I can hit up Dad's in-Family doctor, too."

Edward nodded. "Okay, but you're not going anywhere yet. I've called for Reagan, who's conveniently not here for some goddamn reason. So I want him at the club to take you home."

"Alright."

Arguing might have been my default otherwise, but right now, I truly loved the idea of having someone with me at all times. I didn't want to be alone.

Still, I couldn't find the words to actually say that. Dazed was a mild way to put it, and I realized that I was still nodding my head way after I'd thought I stopped. It was spinning, though. I could feel my pulse beat in my temples, and my throat hurt– not as much as I thought it might, however. Apparently, I'd protected myself a bit with my hands.

"Let's get you some water. Come here."

Standing, Edward offered his hand to help me up. I took it, following him over to the bench seat. I couldn't help but stare down at the unconscious Joelle on the ground, stifling a shiver.

"How did she get in here?" I hated the way my voice sounded–raspy and small.

"That's a good fucking question. Can you wait right here for me?" He met my eyes, Edward's stare penetrating me in a way that made me shift in my seat as if I were in danger of breaking. "I need to assemble the staff."

"Yeah, of course. I told you. I'm fine."

I wasn't about to be treated like a fragile sculpture or a flimsy piece of wet paper. I grew up in the mafia. I was familiar with violence, even if this was only the second time that I'd been directly involved.

"Okay." Hesitating for a moment, Edward finally got up and walked to the door, leaning through it. "Dante! Elle! Get fucking security and get the fuck in here!"

It was a rare occasion that I got to hear Edward use his "Mr. Scarlett" voice. He reserved it for moments where he had to lay down the law regarding the club or dole out some punishment when someone was caught slacking or lying. Seeing it now was something else.

He's royally pissed…for me. Why does that do something to my stomach?

After that, everything happened so quickly. The detective Edward had called, Morris, arrived at the club and was escorted back to arrest Joelle. She roused slightly before he got there, and Dante and security had seen fit to man-handle her into handcuffs. They stood guard over her, making sure she wouldn't get away.

"Do what you need to make sure she stays behind bars." Edward faced off with Morris, his jaw muscles standing out beneath his ultra-trimmed beard.

"I can't just make up charges, Scarlett. Your girl is going to need to provide a statement if we're going to get her on attempted murder."

Morris didn't seem phased by the fact that he was being called down here to deal with an assassin. Jesus, that sounded fucking ridiculous. But that's what she was–a hired gun. One who' been sent to kill *me* in particular. I hoped she go her ass kicked in jail.

"Lila can provide a written statement that I will have delivered to you. Or…" Edward cocked his head, this look of profound confidence on his face–the Boss Man holding all the cards. "…I can ensure that Mr. Carpinelli's men deal with this themselves. I'm sure that'll come with minimal consequences."

"Ugh, fine. I can hold her for falsifying personal identification until the statement is in." The cop rolled his eyes, pinching the bridge of his nose. "And I'll just assume that all the bruises she's sporting were delivered in self-defense."

Edward smirked. "Absolutely."

As Joelle was getting hauled up and directed to the door

behind Morris, my boss looked back at me for a moment. He held my stare, his gaze so intense, and I could feel Edward eyeing my neck. I shifted uncomfortably under his gaze, seeing his concern was…odd.

Security and Morris were out the door for barely a moment when Edward turned to Dante and Elle. He looked as composed as ever, but there was a darkness around him. Flicking his stare from the floor up to them, Edward sucked in a deep breath through his nose. I watched from the sidelines, guessing that there was one hell of a chewing-out about to happen.

"How the *fuck* did she get in?"

Elle and Dante both looked especially uncomfortable, and as much as I understood why Edward would be angry with them, I didn't think it was their fault. If this had to do with the first time–which Joelle had basically said–then the people funding her knew their shit.

"Because of this." Elle stepped forward, handing her phone to Edward, who all but snatched it out of her grip. "That's the most elaborate, well-done forgery I've seen. I studied the applicants extensively, and it wasn't until right there, right at the end, that I noticed it."

I couldn't see what she was talking about, but my attention switched to Drake as he cleared his throat, taking a step closer to Edward as well.

"I reviewed it twice. We don't have any other recorded accounts of similar filings. Elle confirmed that the digital signature was invisible until she ran the new program you had us install, which we only looked at when the seal pinged during a search."

The two of them must have done their research while we were waiting for Morris. Elle crossed her arms, those curves of hers standing out as she cocked a hip. If it weren't for the fact that I was still shaking from…well, everything, I would have been as turned on as I usually was around her.

Thick, competent queen? Yeah, what bi wouldn't want a piece of that?

"I thought it was legit. The underlying work all checked out—the dates and locations, as well as the name. Joelle Miller is a real person. She just happens to be in Ohio, not in Harmstead. The ID fake was so damn good. Even the holographic seal was imprinted correctly. But they just changed it. This morning, in fact. Which means these were made before today, but not longer than a few months ago, because the seal changed then, too. The guy, whoever did it, just got unlucky. We never would have known otherwise."

Edward was silent, but I could see his eyes racing across the screen as he swiped through the information. What really hit me, though, was how he looked off to the side after he was finished, cursing under his breath. It almost sounded like "lever," but I was too far away to hear clearly.

"Scrub everything. Get all the current protocols up to date across all our systems, and ensure that this digital signature is searched for on every incoming document." Edward sighed. "And goddamn it, start asking for socials. And don't start. I fucking know. But we can't take any chances anymore."

"Of course. We'll see to it." Elle nodded, flicking her stare to Dante as she gestured toward the door. "Let's go."

On her way out, Elle cast a glance back at me, and I smiled sympathetically. She was a good Mistress, taking care of the subs here as well as Edward, and I knew that she'd be beating herself up for this.

I mouthed the words "not your fault" to her. Elle just offered a crooked smirk, narrowing her eyes on me before leaving with Dante.

"Lila!"

Jerking, I sat up straight, immediately recognizing the voice. My eyes went to the door, and as Reagan rushed inside, his expression wild and furious, I couldn't stop myself from running to him. I launched myself off the bench seat and into his arms.

I hit his chest hard, but I didn't care. There was a flare of pain in my neck, but I didn't fucking care. All I cared about was getting as close to him as possible. Reagan had been there for me my entire life. I could count on him, and fuck, I *needed* him right now.

His scent filled my nose as I pressed my face into him. I would know this cologne anywhere. I'd even purchased it a few months ago. I sprayed it on my pillow like some love-sick fucking teenager, and it hadn't been the same as the real thing.

Perfumes and shit were like that, though. People's natural scents mixed with the fragrance creating something unique to each person.

"What the fuck happened? Are you okay?"

Reagan's deep voice was still as sharp as a knife, but there was something behind it—more of that concern. Between his and Edward's, it was enough to finally get the tears to fall.

"She tried to kill me. Someone tried to kill me—*again*."

Hearing my voice all choked up and rough made me furious. I didn't want to be upset. I didn't want to feel so weak compared to the woman who'd tried to murder me. Why couldn't I have defended myself? What were those fucking self defense lessons for?

"Where the fuck were you? Your entire fucking purpose is to be here to protect her."

I looked up from Reagan's chest to see him returning a fiery glare to Edward. They were staring each other down, both of them ready to fight the other. That was *not* what I wanted.

"Emilio insisted I meet him at a job. I couldn't avoid it." Reagan gritted the words through clenched teeth.

"A job? Are you fucking kidding me? Isn't Lila your top priority?"

This was way past "Mr. Scarlett voice." Edward was livid. I'd never seen him this mad, and it was reflected in Reagan.

"I would've been 'seen to' if I hadn't responded to Emilio's message. If I were hobbling around on broken fucking legs, I wouldn't be much good to her now, would I?"

"And what? Now is the time you decide to be a good little boy and do as he says? You've been disregarding Emilio's rules for months now."

Reagan surged next to me, moving to shove right past my body and to Edward. I planted my fingers on his chest, pushing him back.

"Knock it the fuck off! Both of you!"

Both pairs of eyes flew to me, Edward and Reagan staring like I'd yelled about a bomb or something. Tension hung in the air for a moment before I sighed and dropped my hands. Standing between the two of them, I traded glances with the men who were the most involved in my life–these men who I'd finally accepted I had feelings for.

"How is you two screaming at each other fucking helping me?"

"Lila, I–"

"Don't." I cut Edward off, raising a hand to stop his words. "I'm speaking."

I wasn't sure how to describe the look I got from both Reagan and Edward, but it wasn't entirely anger, not solely at least. There was a fire building behind both their eyes, and I sort of loved the feeling of being beneath it, the invisible flames licking at my skin.

"Twice. Two fucking times someone has tried to kill me. Here in this club, and *both* times, the people who were supposed to protect me were otherwise engaged. That doesn't say *anything* about either of you, but it tells me a hell of a lot about the person behind this. They're using every advantage they can find. So, don't squabble like some married fucking couple while I still need your help. Help me *fix* this."

Reagan and Edward exchanged looks, and then they were both closing in on me. I expected a chewing out or for them to lecture me about how I didn't understand what was going on, but they didn't. Two hands landed on either of my shoulders, and I was surrounded by focused, empathetic stares.

"Let's get out of this room so we can talk in private." Edward squeezed my shoulder, gesturing with his head toward the door. "My office is protected and soundproofed."

Gripping my other shoulder, Reagan used his free hand to lift my chin up so that I had to meet his eyes directly.

"We'll figure this out, princess. But you're also coming down from shock. You need to let us get you level."

It was the gentlest command Reagan had ever uttered, and I didn't know what to make of that. I didn't hate it, but I was also eager to return things to our usual dynamic–a battle of give and take where I pushed him to the limits, hoping to break him.

Apparently, nearly getting killed wasn't a total buzz kill in the attraction department. Hell, it was quite possibly one of the best aphrodisiacs. But they were both right. We needed to talk about this in a private space where they could both help me come down after the surging adrenaline.

And you know, if something else happened while we were in the soundproofed room, then so be it.

17
The First Time

Reagan

I'd never seen Lila stand up for herself like that. Sure, she didn't just roll over and take a command, but that was more of a playful way—that typical bratty side of her. What I'd just seen wasn't that, not until the end of our little conversation anyway. Lila had been forceful with both her boss and her godfather, something that we'd needed at the time.

Still, I couldn't deny that something else was brewing beneath the surface, for all of us.

"Come on." Edward gestured inside his office, holding the door open for Lila and then me as I slipped inside last. "You can have a seat on the chaise, Lila. I'll get you some water."

Locking the door, Edward crossed the room to his bar, and I made quick eye contact with him as he paused to pour some water into a rocks glass.

"Water's good and all, but I think I need something stronger."

I flicked my attention to her. Lila's throat was red, this line striped across her flesh, and from what Edward had texted, the assassin had used a garrotte. One that had thankfully been constructed with thick wire as opposed to something more problematic, like fishing line.

"You drink a full glass of water, and maybe I'll consider

letting him pour you a whiskey." I glared at her, this incredible woman who was handling a near-murder pretty damn well. "Your throat won't like it anyway."

Lila rolled her eyes, taking off the purse she'd grabbed from the dressing room and reaching out to take the glass from Edward as he approached her. He sat down on the chaise next to her, and surprisingly, I didn't mind their closeness. If anything, I was fucking thrilled to have someone like Edward around to help care for Lila after all this.

I wasn't big on the comforting gestures and about as soothing as a cattle prod.

"It doesn't appreciate much right now, but it's not terrible." Lila sipped at the water, and I was satisfied when she swallowed without wincing. "I think getting my hands in there helped."

"I'm sure it did. A garrotte wire can cut skin. Your fingers are tougher to get through, with all the bone and shit."

Both Lila and Edward stared at me, their mouths both parting slightly as I furrowed my brow at both of them.

"What?"

"There were a million more tactful ways to put that, Reagan. Jesus." Edward rolled his eyes, but then he was standing again, and when he went to the bar this time, he poured three whiskeys, one for each of us. "I think we *all* need this."

"Ugh, yes, please." Lila smiled, and as she sat on the chaise, I ran my stare over her.

She was still dressed in her silk robe, likely wearing something ridiculous beneath it. Still, she wasn't as roughed up looking as I had expected to see upon arriving. Her curls were a bit of a mess, but the unruly tresses actually looked good that way, and aside from the red line across her neck, she wasn't sporting any bruises or lumps. Hell, her cherry red lipstick was hardly smudged.

Thank God. If something had happened to her...when I was out doing a fucking "errand" for her father...

"Here." Blinking, I looked up to see Edward handing me a glass. "Drink up, Master."

He whispered the last word, but it was still enough of a move that my temper flared, the need to punish him for being so forward with our dynamic surging in my veins. Narrowing my eyes, I clenched my jaw, swallowing down the hefty sip of whiskey.

"Watch it."

As Edward smirked, he sauntered back over toward Lila, leaning on his desk so that he could watch her and me simultaneously. The room was thick with tension again, and I couldn't pull my heated glare from him. I had a feeling he knew precisely what he was doing, as if he was getting both Lila *and* me into position.

"Umm…did I miss something?" Lila looked between us, her lips parted slightly. "I can go if–"

"Absolutely not, Lila." Edward cut her off, but his stare was pinned on me. "You stay right where you are."

Dammit, what is this little brat up to?

Taking a few steps closer to them, I faced toward Edward, putting Lila at my back. I wasn't about to look at her right now. Not when I was about to rip Edward a new one. Still, I needed Lila out of the room if I wanted to do that to *my* level of satisfaction.

Or do you?

I shook myself, trying to force away thoughts like that–thoughts that had become much more frequent since my run-in with Lila in the dressing room, since I'd jerked off to watching her masturbate.

"What are you doing?" I held Edward's defiant stare, my hands balling into fists at my sides.

"What needs to be done." He took a step closer to me, running his hand up my chest, and I tensed as he lowered his voice to a whisper. "We've been fighting this, you and I, and after today, after almost *losing* Lila again, I'm not waiting anymore. I'm not denying what's right in fucking front of me. Life's too damn short."

"Edward, you're fucking pushing it." I gripped his hand, squeezing his tendons together. "I'm already breaking enough rules."

"So what's one more?" He cocked a brow, and damn him. Damn Edward for somehow seeing that I'd been so on edge, so desperately fighting to keep Lila at arm's length.

Slipping backward, Edward went back to his desk, leaning against it like some lithe, graceful predator, and picked up his drink. He broke our prolonged stare, turning to Lila. As I followed his eyes, I saw her there, sitting on that stupid, fancy couch and looking too goddamn pretty.

"Lila." Edward waited for her to look up at him, her gaze having switched between the two of us.

"Yes?"

"You've said some things to both of us, to Reagan and me. And now," Edward sipped once, then set his glass down, "I want you to be crystal fucking clear. Something terrible happened today, and we're going to get to the bottom of it, but..."

Tension hung. This was the moment when I was supposed to say something, to speak up and put an end to this. She was off-limits. This entire situation was off-limits on so many different levels, and I needed to put the brakes on.

But I couldn't.

"...I think the three of us are sick of pretending. I know I am. So, be honest with me, with Reagan. What do you want?"

I scanned my eyes across the short distance toward Lila. I was wound as tight as a Swiss watch, and looking at her was already testing everything inside me.

What the fuck is happening? How is this happening?

Lila gulped down a mouthful of whiskey and then set her

glass down on the coffee table a foot away from her. She looked down at her hands, where she held the two halves of her black silk robe, her purse slipping open a bit on the couch to reveal one of her trademark lollipops. I could hear her audibly exhale from where I stood, and then Lila raised her head, trying her best to make eye contact with both Edward and me.

"You know, you kind of have some clients to thank for this. Me having the balls to actually say something that is. And I feel like if I'm going to, I need to start at the beginning. So, bear with me."

Neither Edward nor I spoke, giving Lila the space she needed. From him, it was fine, but from me? Who was I right now?

"It didn't just start because of the first attempt on my life. I...I've been 'interested' in you both for a while. But...I'll admit that the almost dying thing did have a way of speeding things up. At first, like back when I learned this club existed, I thought that working here would ensure that my dad didn't marry me off. The thought of that has plagued my entire fucking life."

The words hit me hard. I knew that Lila wasn't a fan of the idea, but damn. I guess I didn't fully know that she'd been working every angle to ensure she was "not marrying material."

My guts tightened at the thought. Lila was a fucking catch for anyone–curves, gorgeous honey brown eyes, those curls. It would take some horrible truth to make that girl not appealing as hell, like ate a baby level awful.

"Your father is looking to marry you off?" Edward's brows pinched together as he stared at Lila.

"Not actively, I don't think. It's on the back burner. I, umm, I said I'd already popped my cherry, so that kind of put the kabash on things."

Something tickled in my brain. The way Lila had said that was different. I knew her. I knew that girl so fucking well, and that included her little tells when she lied. How had I not noticed it before?

"You didn't, did you?" Lila's eyes flicked to mine, going a bit wide and then dropping away. "Lila? Fucking answer me."

"Reagan, what's–"

"Lila," I barked out, cutting off Edward's concerned tone, and she jumped in her seat.

When she looked back up at me, she shook her head. "No. I…lied."

"You lied about what?" Edward leaned forward, his head cocking as the puzzle pieces fell into place in his brain. He wanted to hear her say it, and you know what? I fucking did, too.

"I…lied about losing my, umm, virginity. I…still haven't."

"What?!" Edward and I spoke in unison, both of us shocked to our cores.

"Well, why do you think I made sure to be so good at blow jobs?" Lila shrugged. "Anyway, it's mostly worked for now, but I got worried that Dad might try something again with attempts and all. You know, some strange way to 'protect me.' So, I figured sleeping with his consigliere and business annoyance would do the trick. I wasn't going to admit that I also just wanted to…to be with you both. But, umm, yeah, those clients. They sort of helped me accept the truth."

"Which is?" Edward was gripping the edge of his desk so hard that his knuckles turned white, and when I looked from him to Lila, she was flushed so damn pink beneath her soft, tan skin.

I wanted to touch it. I wanted to touch *her*. Edward started this freight train running, and there was very fucking little that was going to stop it now.

Lila steadied herself, sucking in a lungful of air as she stood up and took up the spot between Edward and me.

"That I want both of you. That I want to fuck you more than I've wanted to do that with anyone. That I can't stand being around you both all the time, and not being able to do something about this. That of all the people in the world, it's you," she glanced from Edward to me and then down to the floor, "who I want to claim me for the first time."

It was like touching an electric fence. I was rocked from my head to my feet, a massive punch to my entire system. Lila wanted to fuck us, to fuck *me*, and she wanted to give up her first time.

I'd be a goddamn liar if I said I didn't want that with everything I had, that the notion of fucking her virgin pussy didn't go straight to my head, to my cock. My jaw clenched along with my fists, and I could scarcely breathe around the desperate need to throw Lila down to the floor and claim her all for myself.

Fucking hell...

Frozen in place, I hadn't said a word or done anything else for that matter. Edward pushed off the desk, the noise getting my attention, and then he walked over to me. When he was within a few inches, Edward slipped behind me, turning me toward Lila.

Glaring outward at the only person in eyeline, Lila, I barely allowed him to move me, but it did happen. I was facing off with my goddaughter–the forbidden fucking fruit–with Edward at my back, whispering in my ear like Satan himself who was rocking a wicked hard-on.

"Go on, Master. Get your taste. Then," He sucked in a breath, the sensation tickling my skin, "it's my turn."

Shit. I should stop this. I was already risking enough before when it was just Edward, but if I do this...oh goddamn it.

My stare flicked from Lila to the contents of her purse, the lollipop a bright red batch for her lipstick. I'd thought about it before. I'd thought about wearing the crimson rings of her lipstick down the shaft of my cock.

And I was thinking about it now.

"Come here." My voice was harsher than a growl–all animal possessiveness.

Lila approached, her steps cautious and purposeful. When she was right in front of me, I could smell the spicy floral scent of her perfume–the one that I knew she liked in its tiny red bottle with a black cap. I knew that fucking scent so well.

I sucked in a breath, and then my hand shot forward into her hair, gripping the twisting locks at the root and yanking her against my chest.

"You're a little fucking brat, you know that?"

Hissing, Lila whimpered slightly, the corner of her mouth still lifting in a smirk.

"Yes."

The silk of her curls between my fingers did something to me, and I gripped and re-gripped over and over as I used her hair to make Lila's head dance in a circle for me.

"You're going to fucking listen to me this time, aren't you?"

With my hold on her curls, Lila couldn't really nod, but she tried. "Mostly."

That's my little princess.

I growled low in my chest, my cock twitching behind my fly. "Stop light signals. Three fingers in the air if you can't speak."

Lila nodded like a good girl.

"I will fuck that bratty attitude into submission, understood? I'm not going to take it easy on you. If anything I know how much of a little shit you can be, and I'm going to use everything I know about you to drive you right to the fucking edge."

A desperate whimper erupted from her, and from the corner of my eye, I could see just how fucking happy about this

Edward was from his perch on his desk. We'd work up to him being involved simultaneously. I mean, it was Lila's first fucking time for fuck's sake. And maybe I was being just a hair possessive.

"I like making you do things for me. I like *forcing* you to do things for me. Understood?"

"Fuck yes." Lila's eyes were lidded, and I could feel the heat radiating off her skin. "Please, Reagan. Please, let's go already."

Yanking on her locks, I forced Lila's head back. "It's Master, princess."

"Yes…" She trembled in my grip, and goddamn, I just knew that she was dripping. "...*Master*."

Shoving Lila down to her knees, I glared down at her, hungry and sporting an erection that *ached* to be inside her.

"Crawl to the couch and get that fucking lollipop of yours." I gestured at it with my head. "Unwrap it and suck that sweet little ball like your life depends on it."

Her eyes flared wide, Edward chuckling in the background, and then she did as told, taking her sweet time and sure to rock those hips as she did. *Malicious compliance, indeed.*

I watched, my shaft throbbing, as Lila took out the lollipop, uncaring that the rest of her purse spilled onto the couch. She unwrapped the candy and then turned to face me, her stare locking onto mine. As it did, she sucked that treat like the tiniest little cock, giving it the ride of it's life.

Letting her go for a few moments, I made sure I saw strings of saliva before I stepped forward and snatched the sucker from her grip. I put it between my teeth and crunched down. Her eyes widened just that little bit more, and I smirked– sadistic and so ready to play with my new toy.

Toy….oh, ho, ho, now that gives me an idea.

"Take out your lipstick and crawl back to me."

"My lipstick? I don't under–"

"Did I fucking ask you to speak?" My hands went to my belt, and I unbuckled it, beginning to slide it free from my pant loops. "Do it."

Lila glared at me, that delicious sneer lighting up her expression. I loved how it looked on her, loved to see how much of a fighter she was. I would win her submission, but it would be earned–and that was a fucking delight.

It only took a few moments for Lila to grab her lipstick–the bright red color indicated with a little circle at the butt of the tube–and then put it between her teeth so that she could crawl over to me.

The sight was nearly enough to get me coming right then and there. I loved to see this girl on her knees for me so goddamn much. When she reached me, she sat back on her heels, the perfect submissive's pose, and presented the makeup to me in her palms.

Oh, fuck yes.

"Draw the letters T and Y around your mouth. Make those pouty lips the letter O, princess. Let me see how much you want to be my good girl."

Lila put together what I was asking in seconds, and her eyes flared as she looked up at me. She wore that defiant expression, hesitating instead of getting right to work. When she looked down at the tube, I snatched her hair again, purposefully messing it up.

"Put your money where your mouth is, little slut. Best blow jobs around? Prove it."

Gulping, Lila took off the cap and narrowed her eyes at me. I allowed her to get ready, leaning over to grab the little mirror that fell from her purse and handing it to her. Then, I removed my belt completely, draping it across the coffee table.

Our little game of chicken persisted just a hair longer, and I cocked a brow at her, dragging the zipper of my pants down.

I was going to hell and back for this.

178

But I really didn't give a fuck. Emilio's daughter was still safe per his regulations, and the naughty fucking girl had this coming.

Those lovely brown curls of hers were a mess, tugged and twisted as she knelt before me. Those sinful lips of hers, painted that bright red today, were glistening with saliva, thanks to that fucking lollipop.

Lila's large doe eyes looked up at me, and I threaded my fingers into the back of her hair, squeezing. The soft hazel of her eyes was glassy, and those charming freckles across her nose and cheeks added to her innocent allure.

"I don't have all fucking day, princess. Do it."

Lila trembled, but she wasn't retreating. No, she stared up at me like she was ready to worship her new god as instructed. Her hand trembled only slightly as she reached up with the lipstick and wrote the letters.

I watched, my cock aching, as my sweet little girl obeyed me. *Fucking hell, that enthralled expression is going to be the death of me.*

When she finished, Lila set the lipstick aside on the coffee table behind her, and I inspected her work as she stared in the pocket mirror. Scrawled across her face in fire-engine red was the word "TOY," those full lips the tempting O in the center.

"Perfect."

She grinned, but it quickly vanished as I fisted her curls, pulling her toward my straing cock as I freed it from my pants. Her stare widened as she stared down at me, and now it was me who was grinning from car to fucking car.

Yeah, we're not rookie league in this house.

"Re–Master, I don't know if I can–"

Twisting my grip, I silenced her. "Better take a deep breath, princess. Because I'm not stopping until I've filled that throat with my cum."

"He'll hardly stop there. Our insatiable Master has quite a

way with coming *several* times."

I tossed a glare at Edward for interrupting, but silently appreciated the compliment. Lila would be finding out soon enough, anyway. As she gaped up at me, her stare still so adorably wide, I pulled her head closer to my hips. A desperate tear of pre-cum leaked from my tip, and Lila swallowed hard.

"Suck, princess. I want to see you choking on my cock."

She trembled in my grip, but Lila scooted closer, opening her mouth. Her lips were still a shiny, sticky sight, the effects of the lollipop quite useful. Then, she hovered her lips over the head of my erection, her tongue extending delicately.

A moan slipped from her as she tasted me, her eyes rolling closed, and when she opened wider–her confidence a bit stronger–I yanked her forward, spearing my shaft into her mouth and down her throat.

Lila reeled, her eyes flared wide, and she glared up at me as she fought to breathe. A sadistic smirk was all I offered in return, starting up a rhythm as I pumped in and out of her mouth. She had to fight to keep up, to find a way to manage the pace, but she did, her throat relaxing and letting me slide as far back as I could.

No gag reflex. Oh, that will *be fun.*

Thrusting hard, Lila took my cock so well, like the pro she so claimed to be, and I pictured my cock and cum branding into her hotter and better than any of those pathetic Johns of hers. She was all fucking mine now, and I'd seer any memory of anyone else from her mind.

"Damn, princess," Edward whispered, his fist squeezing his cock through his pants, "you're taking him so well."

Fisting her hair all the harder, I rocked my hips foward then pinned Lila to my hips, making her struggle as my dick bottomed out down her throat.

"That's because our bratty little slut is so fucking desperate to swallow my cock. A dirty slut. My filthy little *toy*."

Snatching up the fabric of my slacks, Lila dug her nails into my thighs as she fought for air, glaring up at me as her eyes streamed with tears. Her pretty mascara ran down her cheeks, and I growled, loving the sight so goddamn much.

A strangled whine left her, and she pulled against my hold. I didn't let up, rocking my hips back and forth so that I could fuck her mouth as deep as I wanted.

"Breathe through your fucking nose, whore." I grinned, utterly lost to this experience. "You want it? You think it's cute to fight me, to tease me? Take your punishment like a good girl."

Her eyes rolled closed for a moment, and then Lila sucked in through her nose, her head bobbing faster as her hand moved to my balls, cupping them and smoothing her thumb against the sack. I groaned, the sensations so damn perfect. Lila was comfortable now, was fighting back like the little brat she was, and I was already so close to coming.

Thank god that I can indeed come more than once.

The rhythm was spectacular, and I was rushing closer and closer to the edge. The sound of a belt and zipper got my attention, and I opened my eyes to glare at Edward.

"Don't you fucking dare, slave. If you need something to do with those hands," I swiveled my focus down to Lila, who I at last allowed to pull back and gasp for air, "you can get that fucking robe off her and tongue her fucking ass."

Lila's eyes went wide, yet again, and it was still such a treat to see her be surprised by me. Edward clenched his jaw, visibly forcing himself to let go of his cock, and pushed off the desk to walk over to us.

"Crawl. Crawl with that dick hanging out of your pants because you couldn't wait." I growled as Lila dragged her tongue up the underside of my shaft, fisting her hair to hold her back. "And you can suck my fucking balls while you stroke me. In fact…"

181

Abruptly, roughly moving us, I got Lila to the side of the coffee table as I let my pants fall and stepped out of them. Planting my foot on the table, I forced Lila's face to my sack.

"...I don't want you to neglect any fucking part of me. Understood?"

She started to speak, the "yes" poised on her lips, but I smacked the side of her face–just a short little jolt to get Lila focusing.

"Nod. Nod and say," Lila looked up at me from on her knees, still one of the best fucking sights in the world, "yes… *Daddy*."

And there it was, the look on her face that was just one step above the previous. Lila fucking beemed, she flared and gasped and reeled, and it all swirled together into this perfect expression of rapt adoration and carnal lust.

She nodded, swallowing before saying, "Yes, Daddy."

I lit up from the inside, happier and more fucking horny than I could fully admit.

"That's right, princess. You want to be Daddy's good little girl, don't you?"

Another sweet nod. "*Yes*, Daddy. I–Oh!"

Lila's words were cut short as Edward yanked her robe open and forced her legs apart. I'd been keeping a keen eye on him, and it was a delight to see Lila caught off guard while I knew what was coming.

"There's a good slave. Don't stray, fuck puppet. I want you on her ass and that's it."

"Works for me," Edward smirked, taking Lila's panties– black lace and hardly an excuse for underwear–and tore them from her body, "Master."

From my angle, it was difficult to see my girl's pretty cunt, but I relished in the fact that her thighs were slick enough to gleam in the low lighting. Edward lifted Lila's leg, tossing it over his forearm as he maneuvered himself between her legs.

He'd be the first to see her, but I'd be the first to touch that fucking pussy.

I could tell that Edward was doing his thing when Lila's eyes rolled back into her head and the tense grip on my pants relaxed.

"You're not finished, princess." I hauled her to my balls. "I believe I told you to suck, to leave nothing untouched with that tongue, and to stroke my fucking cock. Didn't I?"

A whine bled from her, and Lila nodded frantically as Edward toyed with her. "Y-Yes, Daddy."

Lucky for her, Lila didn't hesitate this time, getting straight to work by sucking one of my balls into her mouth. I groaned, the suction almost too much. But I was no stranger to pain either, and as she glided her small hand up and down my shaft, I fucked her little fist, pressing her face to my undercarriage.

She roamed her tongue everywhere, just as told, and Lila was generous with her saliva and quick circles. Finding my ass, she tongued me as she worked my cock, and I couldn't stop the low growl from rumbling from me as the pleasure kicked up even higher.

Edward's actions had Lila whimpering and squeaking at random intervals. It was a damn, depraved delight, and I could hear how close Lila was to climaxing as well.

I had to admit, my sweet, innocent goddaughter did give one hell of a fucking blow job.

Losing myself to the feeling of Lila worshipping my ass and cock with her tongue, my focused faded. It was all about what was going on with that impressive, naughty mouth of hers, and Lila did not disappoint at any time. She took my shaft all the way down her throat over and over, switching to licks and pats of my dick on her face when she needed air.

When I bottomed out once more, giving Lila several good whacks on the back of her head like I enjoyed doing to Edward, I was ready to fill up her pretty throat with my cum.

"Open your fucking mouth." I pulled Lila back, and she did as told, holding her tongue out for me.

Only two more strokes, and I was coming. I painted Lila's pink tongue in my spend, ropes of white filling up her mouth until it began to drip down her throat and past the corners of her lips.

"Ugh," I spurted another thick stream across her face, "that's my good girl. Now swallow every last drop."

Closing her eyes, Lila tipped her head back and swallowed, then lifted her finger to swipe the cum from her face into her mouth. She truly cleaned her fucking plate, and my cock was already hardening again at the sight of it.

Her breathing ticked up, a squeak leaving her as Edward continued to toy with her. I smirked down, loving the sight of both of them all tangled up.

But it was time. It was time to claim that virgin pussy as mine.

All fucking mine.

18
The Cherry Pop

Lila

I was going to come. It was *right there*. But…some part of me knew that Reagan would have "words" about that. I didn't really care, being the brat that I was, but god, with his taste lingering on my tongue and Edward's shoved up my ass, I was about ready to do whatever Reagan wanted if I could just climax.

"Stop, slave." I looked up at Reagan, whimpering out a needy whine as Edward pulled away from me. "Get our pretty Lila up on the coffee table. I want to see her hips raised in the air for me."

Turning over my shoulder, I looked at Edward. It was the first time we'd really made direct eye contact since we began, and my skin was on fire thanks to the expression painted over his handsome face.

He stared at me, his lids low over his hazel eyes. My thighs clenched as I saw the saliva smeared over his mouth, my skin still burning where his ultra-short beard rasped against me.

"Show off those curves, princess." Edward stood up, holding out his hand to me. "Let Reagan see what I've been enjoying."

My cheeks burned, embarrassment warring with arousal, or

maybe feeding it. I took Edward's hand, crawling on top of the coffee table. My knees immediately protested the surface, but I knew Reagan was going for that. Hell, the couch was right there, but no. He wanted me to suffer for him.

Delicious, sadistic asshole.

In a harsh, quick movement, Reagan shoved my shoulders down to the table, forcing my hips up and back. I was so fucking exposed like this, the air tingling on my sensitive, wet skin. A hard crack came down on my ass cheek, and I yelped, jumping in place as I hissed.

"It is *quite* the sight, isn't it?" Reagan's voice was so damn deep, a growl more than anything else, and I looked over my shoulder, my pussy clenching. "Such a needy, drippy little cunt. It's just begging for Daddy's cock."

One of his fingers smoothed down my seam, and I damn near exploded. My nerves were set to overdrive, and it wouldn't take much to have me falling apart. Arching, I moaned, balling my hands into fists. Edward was in front of the coffee table, his scent so strong in my nose, and I felt his hand come down on my head, stroking my hair.

But then it stopped, the crack of another slap sounding. My ass didn't sting, however.

I looked up, seeing that Reagan had a hold of Edward's throat, my boss's cheek flaring red. He'd slapped him. *Oh, fuck.*

"You're a naughty slave. It's Master right now, and you fucking know that," Reagan challenged, and I would've maybe been worried if it weren't for the mezmorizing look of defiance in Edward's eyes. "You're not going to touch her until I'm finished. You watch, slave. You *watch her* as she falls apart on my cock. While she coats me in her innocence."

Edward's cock twitched right in front of my face. He was clearly into this, and fuck, I was too. Watching Reagan absolutely ruin Edward, tease him and degrade him, was a damn treat I wasn't going to tire of any time soon.

And even more, the words Reagan had uttered, declaring his intent to take my virginity right the fuck now, were enough to have fresh slick dripping down the inside of my thighs.

Reagan shoved Edward back, and he knelt in front of the coffee table, his stare glued to me. We were so close, the temptation to touch him so *very* strong, and I slid my hand forward to where he planted his on the table.

Crack!

A smack landed on my ass, making me jump and whince, hissing in a sharp breath after my yelp rang out in the room.

"No touching, princess. You're going to be my good little fuck table and not move a goddamn inch while I use you."

Humiliating, degrading, challenging, Reagan was doing it all, and damn me to hell and back, but my cunt fucking *throbbed* from it. I could only just make him out behind me–with my head lying on the table as it was–but I pulled my hand back and nodded.

"Yes, Daddy." I could feel my pulse in my pussy lips. "But please. I need you to fuck me. *Please.*"

A mean chuckle left him. "Aww, is my dumb fuck table needy? You're lucky I'm feeling generous. But…"

I sensed him step back. I had no idea what Reagan was up to, and I glanced at Eddward, who only wore a hungry smirk, his cock straining behind his zipper.

"You're doing so well, princess," he crooned, and I fucking melted. "You're going to take Master's cock, and then I'm going to feel you clench around mine. You're going to be dripping with our cum."

Yes, sir.

Shuffling against the carpet brought my attention back to Reagan as he approached. I could hear clinking, and I had to guess that he'd grabbed a bottle from Edward's bar. My suspicions were confirmed when cool liquid rained gently down on my lower back.

It stung horribly as it dripped down my crack to my pussy, and I flinched, groaning loudly. Another smack came down on my right cheek, and then the left. My stick was flaming where Reagan's palm had undoubtedly left a mark. I watched through bleary eyes as a little puddle of liquid appeared in front of my face on the coffee table.

"Drink it up, slut. Daddy wants to hear you fucking slurp up every drop."

Fisting my hair, Reagan shoved my face into the wooden surface, and I scrambled to reach my mouth forward and suck up the alcohol.

"Is she pretty like this, slave? Do you like seeing her work so hard for me?"

Edward sucked in a breath, his body still so close to mine that I could feel the heat radiating off him.

"Yes, Master. I fucking love it."

"Hmm," Reagan hummed, and his arm appeared above me, "open your mouth, slave."

I did my best to move imperceptibly, needing to see what Reagan was doing to Edward. Just managing to crane up enough, I watched as our intense dom poured whiskey into Edward's open mouth. It dribbled down his chin, and Reagan didn't stop as Edward forced himself to swallow repeatedly.

Fuuuck.

When he finally stopped, Reagan took a swig of the bottle himself. He flicked his attention to me, our eyes meeting. My blood went cold, the tilt of his brow telling me that Reagan was going to punish me for moving. Shit, it was too damn sexy to see him like this. My pussy tingled all the more, but I couldn't squeeze my thighs together.

"Hold your hands up by your head."

My joints were already screaming at me, my knees and elbows pushing into the coffee table. I flicked a wicked glance up at Reagan, frowning.

"Seriously? I'm already a fucking pretzel on this desk."

I was getting punished. That much was clear before, so what was the harm in really earning it right? *This brat be bratting.*

Smack! Smack!

Two consequetive blows landed on each ass cheek, and I nearly jumped off the damn table. My skin *hurt*, not needles in my flesh. I whimpered, trying to suck in air as I reeled from the impact.

"How your hands up by your fucking head, slut." Reagan stood as a menacing shadow above me, and I glared–my eyes tearing up–as I did as told.

He placed the whiskey bottle in my palms, and I had to rest my wrists against my head to keep them up.

"You're going to hold that like a good fuck table. Don't you dare spill a single drop." A slap came down on my pussy, making me jerk, and I had to grip the bottle so damn hard to keep from dropping it. "Just like that. Though I do believe you've earned yourself another challenge."

My mind was spinning. I was dropping further into sub space as my pussy throbbed and the need to come built from just the torture Reagan inflicted. The sound of his jacket shuffling was as loud as a cannon behind me, and all the more so when I heard a tell-tale click.

He unholstered his gun.

I knew it was in his jacket. All the men in the Family wore one like that. I'd seen Reagan take the holster on and off a million times over the years, so that noise was one that wouldn't go missed on me.

My mind blanked. Before I knew it the cool weight of something settled on my lower back, perched precariously near my ass. It had to be the gun, and I shuddered.

"The fuck? Did you seriously just–"

Another smack on my pussy, and I nearly dropped the bottle

191

in my hands. The pain flared through me, and I had to squeeze my eyes shut.

"Did I ask you for questions? For your opinion?" Reagan's lips found my ear, whispering the following words. "No. I didn't, princess. You need to trust me. Color?"

Steadying myself, I nodded ever so slightly. Yeah, how was I doing? "Umm…yellow."

"Good girl," Reagan said so damn softly, and then nothing mattered. I was on cloud fucking nine, and I was going to be his little fuck table for as long as he wanted.

Dragging his nails over my heated skin, Reagan teased the places he'd smacked me. I was so damn sensitive, and I hissed as I held the whiskey tighter, pressing the bottle against my head.

"You're doing well, princess. You look so pretty laid out for Master like this."

I'd nearly forgotten Edward was there, my focusing entirely settling on Reagan's torment. His words were a balm, though, and I beamed, so thrilled to be making them both happy.

I really am a fucking sub slut. How is it this hot to be degraded? To be humiliated as I play table for Reagan? Ugh, fuck me.

"Now," Reagan was behind me again, and the head of his cock brushed against my seam, forcing a moan from me, "scream for me, princess."

So much pressure, so much fullness, and my mind whited out, all thought disappearing as Reagan thrust his erection into my wet pussy. Pain flared through my walls, the stretch of accommodating my godfather's thick, long cock profound enough to reach to my very soul.

I was screaming before I could comprehend what I was doing. Everything was instinct, Reagan bottoming out in my cunt. He reached so damn far, hitting my cervix, which ached and ignited my nerves in equal measure.

My throat finally gave out, my howl dying out, and just as it did, Reagan started up a rhythm, fucking me hard and slow. Numerous cries tumbled from my lips as his girth stretched my once-virgin walls. He's obliterated it, popping my fucking cherry like he was actually looking to break me.

Christ, maybe he was. I didn't care. In fact, I welcomed my ruination.

Holding onto the whiskey for dear life, I moaned and hissed and mumbled incoherent words as Reagan's dick slid in and out of me. The pain was quieting down, giving way to unbelievable pleasure.

I wouldn't drop the alcohol. I wouldn't slip or let his pistol fall. This was the best fucking thing I'd felt in my life, and I would do anything Reagan demanded if it meant I could have more of it.

In one long pull backward, Reagan came all the way out of me, and I whined, aching from the loss.

"Needy little slut. My little goddaughter is a whore for Daddy's cock." He swirled the tip across my clit, and I clenched, about to come before he stopped. "And you've painted my cock so pretty, princess. Would you like to see?"

Without thinking, I nodded, suddenly desperate to witness the destruction of my virginity on his dick.

"Yes, Daddy, *please.*"

I wasn't sure how long it took him to reach me, hours or seconds, but Reagan pinched my chin and tipped my face toward him. I forced open my eyes, which had been squeezed shut so damn tightly, and looked at the erection that had just driven into my cunt.

Blood coated Reagan's skin, these delicate whisps of red that smeared all over his shaft along with my slick.

"Holy fuck," I whispered, and then Reagan was gripping my hair craning my neck panifully.

"I assure you, princess, there is nothing *holy* about it."

Pushing his thumbs into the hollow of my cheeks, Reagan got me to open my mouth for him, shoving his cock between my lips. "You're a filthy little sinner. Corrupted *so easily* by the promise of my cock. Fucking your godfather, your boss about to follow, and you're going to suck all that virgin blood off my dick."

And I fucking did. I sucked Reagan off, tasting the copper and salt of the fluids mixing, until he yanked himself away, leaving me gasping. Reagan let my head go, moving back behind me again and licking up my seam before poising his cock at my entrance again.

"You're close, aren't you, princess?" He kept teasing my clit.

My nerves screamed out, begging for release. "Yes! Yes, Daddy!"

"You're not going to come until I tell you to." He smacked my ass again–hard. "You'll hold it back because if you don't, it'll be the last time you come for a week."

I trembled, goddamn shaking beneath Reagan's presence, his touch, his massive cock. Nodding, I whimpered, renewed tears prickling at the corners of my eyes. Suddenly, something cold was sliding through my folds, and the rigid, uneven surface told me it was Reagan's gun.

Oh shit, oh shit, oh shit.

"That's it, princess. I want my gun wearing your cum and ruined innocence so I can think about you every time I fire it."

It dipped into me, the shape odd and wrong, but I all I could do was take it, squirming just slightly as the edges bumped my clit and brought me closer to the edge. As quickly as it was there, though, the weapon was gone, and I was left inches from the edge of that looming cliff.

"Beg me. Beg me to fuck you."

Not being able to see Reagan was infuriating, and I glanced up at Edward, looking for something to anchor myself to. He

194

smirked gently, looking so pleased with how distraught I was. But there was also such adoration in his stare that I melted all the more.

"*Please*, Daddy. Please use me like your fuck table. *Please* let me feel you fill me up."

A satisfied growl rumbled out from behind me, and I locked eyes with Edward as Reagan rammed his cock inside me again, right up to the hilt. The scream was unstoppable, and I was going to come. Reagan was pistoning into me without mercy, and I was going to *fucking* come.

"Ugh!" I gripped the bottle as my palms went sweaty, the glass sliding down just a hair as the gun bounced on my lower back again. "Please! Oh, fuck I'm so close! *Please*!"

"Why?" Reagan gripped my hips hard enough to leave bruises in the shape of his fingertips, not slowing down in the slightest. "Why should I let you come?"

"Please," I whimpered, tears streaming down my face now, "I can't take it. It's so fucking much. Please, Daddy. You control my body, and I *need* to come. I…I'm yours. I promise I'll always be yours, Daddy."

It was strange, but I think we both needed to hear the words. Sure, we both knew that Edward was a part of this. He was the necessary third leg of our unique little unit, but Reagan had known me for so long. After everything, after all that we had denied for so long, we both needed to hear how we had accepted it.

I was his–irrevocably.

"Come on my cock, little girl. Come for Daddy."

I lost any sense of control or resolve I'd mustered. My body exploded, the orgasm taking over, and so intense my vision went black and spotty. I clamped down on Reagan's cock, gripping him and pulling him deeper as he thrust. Warmth gushed from me as he sank all the way into my cunt, stimulating that spot I'd found during my session with the

R.O.B. couple.

Squirting cum over Reagan's dick, I lost track of the world around me, pulsing and shuddering as the most powerful orgasm of my life took over for several long moments.

Reagan grunted behind me, the noise filthy and wonderful, and I felt his cock thicken, getting even harder before it twitched and he pumped his cum into my cunt. It seemed endless, the sensation of my godfather utterly filling me up persisting until I felt our combined fluids dripping down my thighs.

When I thought we'd finished, Reagan, likely about to step away, went and shocked me again. Sliding back, he brought his erection nearly all the way out of me, but then clucked his tongue.

"Tsk, tsk. No, no. Every drop is staying inside my slutty princess. You're going to feel my cum filling you as Edward adds his."

Oh my fucking god.

He stuffed the cum back in my pussy with the head of his cock, and another burst of wetness oozed from me as a tiny orgasm went off.

How I was going to make it through Edward was a fucking mystery.

18
The Blindfold & Bondage

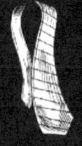

Edward

Lila was a damned dream, a godsend sent from on high. But that wasn't quite right, was it? No, this little minx was far more like a sinful, curvaceous demon sent by the devil to drag Reagan and me down to the depths of hell.

I'd go happily if it meant more of this. And it was my fucking turn with her.

"Good girl," I praised, taking the bottle of whiskey from Lila's hold. "You didn't let anything fall."

Her eyes still closed, she let out a little whimper as the weight left her, and I removed the gun from her back, allowing Lila to slip down onto her side.

Reagan groaned, satiated and so very pleased with himself, with the scene he'd created with Lila. I smirked over to him. He'd said that I was supposed to fill our girl–*ugh*, the way it felt to use those words–with my cum, but he was a bastard at the best of times, so I needed better confirmation.

"Do I have free rein, Master?" Reagan cocked a brow at me, narrowing his eyes like he wanted to say no, but then nodded ever so slightly. "Thank you."

I was high, damn euphoric after everything I'd seen, and so many of the thoughts I'd had when I first saw Lila bloomed through my mind. *You can't want her. You do want her. She's your employee. She's fucking stunning. She's the damn don's daughter who has your club in a fucking chokehold. She's a reason to break all those fucking rules.*

Between Reagan and Lila, I was so fucking done for. I should have realized it sooner, but apparently I have as much of a blind spot regarding my lovelife and desires as the next asshole.

Lila was still lying on the coffee table, lightly dozing as she caught her breath from all the previous excitement. I'd give her the chance to regain some energy, but it would be filled with *my* tastes in foreplay.

Stroking the side of her face, which adorably made Lila turn into the warmth of my hand and nuzzle it, I roused her some.

"You're not done, princess. But I'll be kind and give you a better spot to lie while I get you ready for me."

She hummed, her eyes flickering open. As she looked up at me, realization spread across her features, a deep pink coloring her cheeks. It was so damn pretty, the warm tan of her skin creating this unique shade as the arousal and worry flared in her expression.

"Seriously? You still want to…have sex? After all that?"

I chuckled. "I didn't get that pleasure yet, little one. But I'm about to."

The wide flare of her eyes was perfection, and I scooped her up into my arms, carrying her to my desk. Resting her ass on the edge, it was easy to sweep my papers out of the way and create a spot for her. I could feel Reagan's eyes on us from behind me, his stare burning where it touched me.

He liked this.

"Stay." Pointing my finger at Lila's chest, I focused on her hard, and she nodded.

I needed to gather a few things and make sure that the lock on the door was still firmly in place. Checking it first, I returned to where Reagan now sat on the couch, eye fucking

Lila as she perched on my desk. I stood in front of him, taking off my tie and then holding a hand out.

"May I borrow your tie, Master?"

He cocked a brow, that gorgeous look of intrigue on his stern face, and as he narrowed his eyes, he regarded me.

"What do you have up your sleeve, slave?"

"Blindfolds and bondage, of course." I smirked, hearing a tiny gasp from Lila.

Reagan's face lit up, and he went for his tie, loosening the knot and then pulling it all the way through to free the fabric from his neck. As he handed it to me, Reagan pulled me down by my shirt, crashing his lips against mine.

When he finished ravishing my mouth, he whispered in my ear. "You are the only other person on the planet I want touching her. Make her stupid from coming so much."

Smiling so damn big, I reached for his cock, already–*miraculously*–swelling to half-mast. "That's the plan, Master."

I released him, eliciting a delicious moan from both him and Lila, and then stalked back to her, two ties in hand. As I reached her, I began to wind one of them around her eyes.

"Do you like seeing Reagan and me together?" I watched as Lila stiffened slightly as the blindfold settled into place, her nerves peaking. "Do you want both of us to fuck you next time?"

Lila shuddered, a low groan melting from her as she squeezed her thighs together. She couldn't see it, but I fucking beamed. *That's my girl.*

Fisting the front of her bra, still somehow on, I tore the stupid thing from her chest. Lila yelped, jumping slightly in place.

"Yes, oh god, yes." She nodded eagerly, and without another word, I snagged her wrists, winding the other tie around them and leaving plenty to secure to the desk. "Oh, fuck…I should probably mention that I *really* like being tied up."

"Oh, I know, princess. It's in your file."

Reeling, Lila chewed on her lip before whispering, "This is really happening, then. Jesus, first Reagan and now you? How'd I get this lucky?"

That made me smile, because hell, I felt damn lucky myself. "Fate's weird like that. You think I saw Reagan in my future?"

She chuckled, and I could hear said mafioso groan in the background. "Ha, no, probably not."

Making sure the tie was good and snug, I leaned Lila back across my desk, holding onto the tie and walking around to where I sat to tie it to the underside. I'd installed a hook there a while back, hoping to take advantage of it with Reagan.

This was certainly just as good.

"And what's that, slave?" Reagan demanded from the couch, his hand idly stroking his dick.

"Little surprise I was going to show you." I nodded at the other corner of the desk and the ceiling by the suit rack. "I installed a few hooks last week."

"I like them," he drawled, and damn, I did love a lazy, satisfied Reagan almost as much as I enjoyed the raw, unhinged side of him.

"I'm tied to your desk?" Lila asked, and I looked down at her with a grin, adoring that she couldn't see me. "Aren't you afraid of…getting it messy?"

Laughing easily, darkly, I leaned down, hovering my lips right next to Lila's ear. "Oh, princess, I sincerely hope we do. I want to see your glistening cum paint my desktop so I can think of Reagan *and* you whenever I sit down to work."

She blushed all the harder, her skin flaming from within, from her face all the way down her naked chest to her taut nipples, which were straining and hard, desperate to be touched.

"Oh my god." Lila shook her head. "This is so wild."

"Oh, Lila, sweet, naughty Lila," I brushed my lips across

hers, "you haven't seen anything yet."

Before she could respond, I planted my lips on her, searing our skin in what was the first of many kisses we'd exchanged. I'd crossed this line, after all. I'd done it with Reagan, and I'd done it with her. Now that Lila was ours–*mine*–I was going to enjoy every fucking minute, every goddamn inch of her.

And oh, the taste of her. Lila swirled her tongue across mine, both of us wasting no time in getting to the heart of our kiss. I could taste Reagan on her tongue, and it was sinful, pure wicked delight. No doubt, she could taste herself on me, because that pussy had dripped all the way to my mouth when she was taking Reagan's cock.

It was a moment before I pulled back, but I did. I could kiss her for years, but I had *other* things I was dying to get to.

"You're going to do everything I ask you, princess. You're going to take everything I give you. Because I want you to fall apart as many times as I can force you to. I like to pleasure, and I love it when your body breaks because of it. Understood?"

"Y-Yes." Lila's voice trembled, her skin heated beneath my fingertips as I roamed them freely over her naked breasts. "What…What do I call you?"

I looked over at Reagan, knowing without asking that I wasn't about to have her call me Master or Daddy. Those were his. He cocked his head, his stare going up as he thought it over, still slowly toying with his dick.

When he returned his gaze to me, Reagan smirked. "She already calls you 'Boss.'"

Lila chuckled lightly. "Boss Man, to be specific. But I think I like Boss. Edward?"

Plucking at her nipples, loving that she couldn't get away from me, I grinned hungrily down at her.

"Very well. Be a good girl for me, princess, and do everything your Boss tells you."

She pressed her thighs together, the flesh this shiny and

appetitzing as the cum mixture smeared over her skin. Circling to the other side of my desk, I grabbed her knees, forcing them apart and baring that pussy to me.

"Starting with keeping your legs spread wide for me." I knelt down on one knee, blowing across her seam. "And you're going to tell me how good everything feels, whenever it's too much. I want to hear everything. Understood?"

Thighs trembling, Lila moaned. "Yes, Boss. Please, please. I need you to touch me."

Smirking, I slid my hand up the inside of her thigh, the other gripping my erection and stroking in slow, rough pulls.

"Remember you said that when you're coming down from your fourth orgasm."

"Fuuuck, do you really expect me to–" But her words died as I swiped over her folds and then leaned forward, sucking her wet clit into my mouth. "Ugh!"

Working her, lavishing her cunt with pliant, hungry strokes and flicks, I edged myself, getting so close to that edge and then stopping and shoving her legs up and out so I could get at every inch of her. I'd already tasted her, but I'd eat Lila's pussy, her ass, all damn day.

"Yes." I sucked hard on her clit, letting it pop out of my mouth as I sat back. "Yes, I do."

Lila reeled, her pussy fluttering against my mouth and fingers as I rushed her toward a release. I pressed my tongue into her, fucking her entrance with it, and when I firmly circled her clit with my thumb, she exploded.

Cum–hers and Reagan's–swirled around my tongue, but I didn't stop sinking my tongue inside her, creating a barrier that kept his spend inside her for the most part aside from a few glorious dribbles that leaked down my chin.

Bucking against my hold, Lila fought to push her legs together, the action involuntary, but I didn't allow it, eating her out until the aftershock of her orgasm receded. She still twitched and sporadically pulsed as I slipped my tongue free.

"That's my good girl. And Master will be happy to hear his cum is still so warm all stuffed up in your tight pussy."

An appreciative moan left Reagan, and I looked over my shoulder with an evil grin. He glared–hungry and deadly– and I licked my lips for him. Regan remained sitting, giving me this, but his lazy strokes quickened, his grip on his cock tighter.

"Oh god, I...I don't know if..." Lila breathed hard, her words sloppy through rough sucks of air, and I stood, slowly swirling my fingers across her clit, soaking them in her juices. "Ugh, dammit...I'm so sensitive!"

"You *will* take it, princess." I reached up her body with my other hand, pinching her nipple. "Tell me what you're feeling."

"Oh shit, umm, fuck...it's...it's so much! It's...ahh!" She cried out as I squeezed down on her nipple and clit simultaneously. "Dammit! Yellow! So fucking much, Boss! It's...oh god, why is it too much and not enough?"

That was exactly where I wanted her, and I privately beamed down at Lila as she reeled for me, her hips bucking against my desk, a slippery, gleaming stain of her cum smearing underher ass.

"That's so good, princess. You're going to give me two more before I fuck you. Two more and then I'm going stuff my cock into that tight little pussy and add my cum to Reagan's."

Lila whimpered, and damn, it was the most beautiful sound. "I...I...I'm not sure..."

"You're doing so well, princess. Do let your Boss, or your Daddy, down now." I drove my fingers inside her cunt, pumping in and out as I thumbed her clit and plucked at her nipples with my free hand. "Come on my fingers, Lila."

"Oh god, oh god, oh god..." She tightened around me, but there was this delicious roll to her lips. She bit the bottom one enough to turn the skin white, the determination to please and the need to come taking over. "Boss…oh shit. It's…it's right there. Oh fuck, it's so much!"

Tears streamed down her face, adding fresh tracks to the ones that already streaked her cheeks. She writhed beneath my touch, clenching down on my fingers so damn hard. I groaned, my cock twitching and leaking an endless stream of clear precum.

This was by far one of the most gorgeous sights I'd ever had the privilege of laying my eyes on.

"That's it, baby. My sweet girl," I soothed, fucking her with my fingers quicker, harder. "You look so damn pretty crying for me. Come, princess. Come for your Boss."

"Fuck!"

Lila's tight cunt clutched at me, pulling me deeper as she fell apart. Her slick juices leaked all over my hand, and I pressed in, hooking my fingers up into her G-spot. I knew if I didn't let up, she'd crash over that edge immediately after this orgasm.

And that's exactly what I did, fucking her hard with my hand and getting another climax out of her that left my girl sobbing and twitching.

When she calmed some, thanks only to me slowing down, I gently slid my fingers free, careful to keep Reagan's cum inside her.

"That was so good, princess. You did spectacularly. How are you feeling?"

It took Lila a good ten seconds to respond, her chest heaving as she fought for air.

"I…I'm…umm…still yellow but…maybe orange?"

I couldn't help but chuckle. That wasn't on the list of colors, but I knew what she was getting at. Stroking gently up and down her thighs, I smiled down at her, watching the tension in her body fade some.

"Orange isn't strictly on the list. But," I leaned over her, kissing along her sternum and breasts; damn, those pert tits were a fucking dream, "it's also not a red. So, you're going to take my cock now, baby, and I'm going to fill you up so damn full."

Lila whimpered. She didn't offer anything else, but she didn't use "red" either.

"Good girl."

Gripping my cock, I lined the head up with her entrance, sinking in a few inches. Lila tensed, hissing as I demanded more from her abused, swollen cunt. It was so fucking gorgeous.

She fought against the binds, pulling down to no avail, and I pressed in a bit farther, now half-way inside her tight pussy. Lifting from the desk, Lila arched, her knees digging into my side as she whined.

"Oh god…too much," Lila mewled, shaking her head and hyperventilating, "Boss, it's too much. I can't."

"You can, baby." Angling over the top of her, easily able to reach her hard nipple with my superior height, I sucked it into my mouth, suckling on her and imaginging this needy, sinful little thing taking Reagan's cock as well. "I'm going to fuck this tight cunt and feel it grip my cock as you come once more for me."

Crying out, Lila began to babble incoherently. She writhed on the desk, and I pushed further in, bottoming out inside her pussy. The warmth, the clutch of her walls on my shaft, the liquid feeling of Reagan's cum coating my cock along with her slick, it was all perfection.

And more than enough to start a chain reaction.

I fucked her. I fucked my beautiful employee, this incredible woman I just couldn't stay away from, and I gave it everything I had. Lila's curses and whimpers were endless, and in between them, I could pick out the sounds of Reagan grunting and groaning.

Just as I looked over my shoulder, he was standing up, hurrying toward the desk as he stroked himself.

"Oh, it looks like your Daddy can't stay away from you." I pistoned my hips, pushing Lila's legs up and back to get as deep as possible. "You're just too fucking pretty, aren't you?"

"Boss! Oh god, it's…I need to…fuck, fuck, fuck…"

Reagan stood near Lila's face, angling his dick so that he could come all over her chest, and I knew he was close. And fuck, so was I.

"Take his cock, little slut. Take your boss's fucking cock and come. I want to see you rithing so I can paint those tits with my cum."

"Shit! I…It's right there! I…"

All of us were on the edge, and I fucked mercilessly, loving how Lila's cunt gripped me, fluttered around me. She needed something, though. Lila needed one more spark to get her flying over the cliff that was so hard to reach now that she'd come so much.

Dragging my hand over her chest, sure to pinch her nipple quickly before moving on, I found Lila's throat and squeezed–hard.

She reeled, her body spasming and careening toward release as I cut off her air.

"That's it, princess. You're going to fall apart on my dick while I choke you." I grunted, my cock thickening all the more as my orgasm rushed closer. "You're going to come for me because you want pleasure more than you want air. You want it–*So. Fucking. Bad.*"

That did it.

Lila screamed, this surpressed, strangled cry as I clamped down on her throat and barreled into her cunt until we both saw stars. I felt her come undone, surging about my shaft, and I climaxed hard. Jets and jets of cum spurted into her, filling Lila up all the more and mixing with Reagan's. She took it all, getting dressed with Reagan's fresh spend across her tits, and her sweet pussy pulsed around me until I was sure that Lila had actually passed out.

It may not have been illegal to have that much fun, but it had been real fucking risky.

I didn't care. I didn't fucking care. They were both mine now–Lila and Reagan–and I wasn't letting either of them go.

20
The Come Down

Lila

"We'll get you home, Lila." Edward stood in front of his desk again, and I wasn't sure when, after all *that*, but somehow we were all dressed again. "Did you have anything else you wanted to bring with you?"

My brain was still a little foggy, so I looked down at myself. I had my purse, which was packed again, and I was wearing the clothes I had worn to the club: my black sweats, a black tank, and a grey zip-up hoodie. Thanks to the soft hands of both Reagan and Edward, I was cleaned up. The makeup smeared on my face washed away with swipes of a warm washcloth.

They were both so nice to me after…cleaning me up and helping me redress…Why had they been so nice? …Oh, shit… is that after-care?

As a sex worker, you don't really ask for that when you've finished servicing someone. At least, I didn't. I was usually fine, too. But after this–after finally losing my virginity in a two-fer that I couldn't possibly have been prepared for–I did feel a little adrift. My body had been put through so much.

It felt like a combination of post-workout exhaustion and trying to piece yourself back together after something huge happened.

You know, like my mother dying or the fact that I was nearly killed. Jesus, I almost forgot. What the fuck is my life?

"I think I'm okay. I didn't bring anything else here. I don't need–" My eyes went to the trash can that I knew was full of shredded undergarments. "Those are done for, so, yeah."

Edward nodded, offering a small smile, and the tension in my shoulders eased some. We'd been coming down from the sex for at least an hour now. The club had long since closed up and emptied out, particularly since Edward had demanded everyone go home after my run-in with *Joelle*. Reagan was still sitting next to me, his hand gripping my knee protectively.

Turning to him, I met his eyes as my throat tightened. "Umm, are you...Did you want me to...My dad–"

Sitting forward, my godfather took my chin in his firm grip, effectively silencing me.

"I just want to get you home, princess. You need your rest. I'll be there when you wake up, right across the hall. And I won't let anything get into your room while you sleep. Nothing touches you that you don't want."

Relief coated me, making me sag into the couch. I leaned into Reagan's hand, a little–no, a lot–embarrassed that I was feeling this vulnerable and shaky. I wasn't like that. I was *not* a wilting flower, but...Hell, I could admit that today was a hell of a day, and I was allowed to fall apart a bit.

Weirdly, the sex had actually really helped with that. As up for grabs and submissive as I'd felt with Edward and Reagan, it was so freeing, so distracting from the reality going on outside of me.

"Okay," I said quietly, nodding. "Edward, will you–"

"I'll ride back with you if you want. I can be back at the house in the morning, too. Just call if you want me to come over, and I'll be to you in less than thirty minutes. You're also taking the day off tomorrow. You need a break."

I wanted to protest. I hated my life being controlled since that was the norm with my father, but I knew Edward was right. And at least he was coming from a place of concern, not overbearing domination, at least not *outside* of the bedroom.

My cheeks heated at the thought, and a gentle wave of relaxation eased over me. I would be looked after. Both these powerful men had my back. That was…nice.

"Okay. I will. How will you get home tonight, though?"

Edward walked over, smoothing his hand down my cheek as Reagan pressed in closer on the other side.

"I have drivers, princess. They've come and gotten me from the Carpinelli estate before."

"You're going to lie down in the back of my car and sleep on the way home. Then I'll tuck you into bed with that dog of yours. At least I can trust him to look after you."

That made me smile. "Ludo is only slightly less protective than you are, *Daddy*."

Groaning, Reagan's eyes rolled back as he sucked in a breath. "You're going to be the death of me." He looked up at Edward and then back at me. "Both of you."

"Never," I whispered, snuggling into him and breathing in Reagan's scent. "You're probably bulletproof. And we *both* need you around. Who would be our grumpy, possessive dom?"

Reagan chuckled, stroking my other cheek before he and Edward helped me up to standing.

"Absolutely fucking no one, princess. That's *my* job. Now," he laid a brief kiss on my lips, "let's get you home."

***

The next morning was a slow one. Reagan had been forced to sleep in his own room for fear of us being caught together, and Edward had to go back to his penthouse. I hated that they were so far away, but this was all so new to me. Maybe it was good that I had this time alone to myself…to gather my thoughts or whatever.

My thoughts were centralized. They revolved around Reagan and Edward, focused on how everything with them had felt and how much I wasn't feeling them now.

How am I this hooked already? It's like being a damn drug addict. I am hopelessly addicted to both of them.

I stretched out in my bed, my feet bumping into Ludo, who groaned and let out one of these squeaky dog yawns that were so adorable. Ruffling his ears, I soothed him back to sleep, but there was none of that for me at this point. Nope, I was too fucking awake.

Feeling too restless to lie there, I got out of bed, making sure to leave the covers as undisturbed as possible so my Doberman could snooze away. A shower seemed as good a plan as any. Lord knew I needed one after last night's *exercise*.

"Okay, shower, food, then…something. I don't know," I mumbled to myself, stripping off the sweatpants and tank I wore to sleep.

My skin prickled. Dad insisted on keeping the house at arctic temperatures, and the chilly air immediately hardened my nipples. As I dropped the dirty clothes in the hamper, I noticed the soreness, mild aches, and pains that accompanied me whenever I moved. My body had certainly been through a lot.

You're not a virgin, Lila. You've officially been fucked–twice.

A pleasant hum filtered through my body at that thought. I enjoyed not being so "pristine" anymore; the lie I told was finally true. I hated that it had been necessary to keep my father's attempts to marry me off at bay, but I had to admit that now I'd actually gone and done it, I was so fucking thrilled it had been with Reagan and Edward.

It couldn't have been anyone else. They were meant to be my first experiences, and I was meant to be their naughty little princess.

Yeah, I knew that was some grade-A instalust, even more instalove if I was brave enough to admit it. But I'd known both of them for so long, especially Reagan. And hell, sometimes you just knew. You knew who you were meant to be with.

I was more sure about my men than I was about anything else in my life.

The echoey bathroom was cold as I stepped inside, and when I reached into my shower to turn on the water, I cranked that sucker to roasting. I also made sure to detangle my curls and put in a deep conditioner before I got to scrubbing.

As the cream sat in my curls, I took the loofa attachment to my shower massage off the rack and secured it to the thick handle. It spun in circles as I switched the device on, and I used my favorite shower gel to clean up. My muscles protested the stretches I demanded of them, but I needed to. They'd just get tense and stiff if I babied them.

Still, when I reached my inner thighs–switching to my hands because I wasn't that big of a masochist–I flinched slightly at the burning soreness and sensitivity that zinged through my pussy. Looking down as I stepped out of the spray, I noticed just the faintest hint of red still clinging to my skin right at my folds.

Fuuuck.

My heart thumped against my chest. Reagan had shown me the results of his efforts. I'd...sucked them off his cock. My pussy fluttered at the thought, making me whine as even that stung.

But I wanted more. I wanted more of Reagan and Edward and everything they did to my body. I wanted *them*–so fucking much.

I was gentle as I rinsed away the last remnants of my

obliterated virginity, and then finished up in the shower, exiting the steamy chamber with my gel-set curls hanging in my face and a towel wrapped around my body.

I'd diffuse them, get dressed, and then get some breakfast. I wasn't about to make any more decisions on an empty stomach. Still, I had a feeling that angling for more information about what was going on with my multiple run-ins with mercenaries was going to be at the top of the list.

Reagan had already left by the time I got out of the bedroom, dressed in ass-hugging leggings and a sports bra beneath a slim zip-up, and I was royally pissed about it. Hell, I'd gone through all that work to make myself look casually sexy so that I could get my boys' soldiers standing at attention. But nope.

Ugh, and I'm not going to bother Edward. Everyone's out. I don't need him to swing by like I'm some baby.

The only good thing about Reagan being gone was that my father and his new bitch boy–aka Renzo–were with him, meaning the house was basically empty for all intents and purposes.

The low-ranking Family members who watched the house and crowded the downstairs wouldn't bother coming up here to check on me. Hell, they probably thought I was at work since I should have been. And all that meant that I could do a little snooping in my dad's office.

It was always off-limits if my father was out, and while I'd risked it a few times before, it had been just to say that I did. I didn't have a goal at the time. I did now.

"Alright, Lila. Find something you can use."

I crept into the silent room, closing the heavy wooden door behind me. The place was so fucking big, the size of a typical family's entire upstairs or apartment livingroom. It dripped with pretentious bullshit that my father just couldn't do without, and I went straight to his fucking wetbar for a shot of whiskey to settle my nerves.

Knocking it back, I enjoyed the burn and then turned to face his desk. His computer and books sat on the surface, and I hurried over to his chair, sitting in his chair. It felt wrong on so many levels, and not only because I was breaking more rules. The chair was basically his throne, and I wanted no part of running this Family.

Sure, this was my life, and if I wound up the heir, I'd figure it out, but it had always been a not-so-secret hope of mine that he'd pass me up and just give it to Reagan. He'd make a much better don than I would, and a much better one than my father currently was.

But there were rules. Dad had to attempt to give leadership to me. He could pair me off with some guy, essentially giving *him* the seat, but I'd gone and made that difficult by not being a virgin. I had to admit that I'd kind of fucked my dad's plans up by doing that, but fuck him. I'd made it clear what I wanted, and the only person stopping him from "breaking with tradition" was himself.

If he really wanted someone else to lead, Dad could just pick one. I wasn't about to challenge it. Didn't he know that?

I shook my head, lifting the lid of his laptop. I was letting myself get distracted. I was here for a reason, and I needed to focus up.

"Okay, asshole, what are you up to?" Dad's password was easy enough to guess, taking me only three attempts to land on the initials of his favorite pistol of choice. "Now, if I were secret shit, where would I hide it?"

Dad wasn't especially tech-savvy but he wasn't a moron either. I went through the drives of his computer, ensuring I "unhid" any folders that had been made invisible.

Turns out he had a whole separate partition of the drive relegated for shit that couldn't get found by the feds if they ever got ahold of his computer. It took longer to crack the password to the protected drive, but I had a leg up, having known the guy my entire life.

"Mom's maiden name...no. My full name...no. Shit, it's not going to be something sentimental. Umm..." I scanned the office, my stare landing on the oversized portrait of the late Salvatore Carpinelli, my great-grandfather, who'd passed before I was born. "What did they call him? ...Family savior? No, no, no. It was..."

My words drifted off as I typed in "tiranno della famiglia." The Family's Tyrant, not its savior. How very fucking fitting.

The file unlocked, and I was treated to a host of folders and encrypted documents that didn't make a lick of sense to me. Still, I selected them all and had everything sent to the printer behind me in the bookcase. The device whirred to life and started to spit out paper after paper of documents written in cold or cryptic language. With the folders I still couldn't open, I copied them and uploaded them to my own private drive on the cloud. I kept a brief rundown of my financials and any important information there, and Dad still had no idea it existed.

The loud ass printer was a fucking problem though. I didn't want anyone to find me in here, and it was taking too goddamn long. I looked up at the door, willing anyone still in the house to stay the hell away.

As I waited for the pages to finish, along with the upload, I scanned through some of the documents saved most recently. Most of them were receipts, transcripts of conversations, and there were emails too. I was a little overloaded from the options, so I clicked on the one from only a few days ago and began to read, the printer cycling through its jobs over and over behind me.

"Come on," I whispered, reading through the opening of the email. "Tell me something about how these guys are getting to me. Did Dad spill information about the club by accident? Is it one of the guys we'd just brought in?"

The email was too vague to gather anything from, though, so I jumped to the next. Hovering my mouse over the print queue, I noted that there were only three items left. *Thank god.*

Clicking open the next email, I started reading. It only took a few lines for the words to make my stomach drop into my feet, and I stared at the computer in shock as a tiny gasp escaped. Did I really just read that? Did he–

"What the fuck?"

The room went silent now, my documents weighing down the tray of the printer as they sat waiting for me. I snatched them up and tore from the office, sprinting to my bedroom. My heart pounded too loudly in my ears, too hard against my ribs, and nausea crawled up from the depths, choking me.

He couldn't...he just...couldn't. ...Right?

21
The Confrontation

Edward

Lavar had to be associated with the latest attempt. The thought had been burning in my mind since I'd seen the digging that Elle and Drake had done. That work was too similar to his, and I knew that fucker's digital signature because I'd seen it on my own shit. He needed to be dealt with–now.

Sure, he was a glorified tech bro. Someone who took any job that was offered to him, concerned with money not morals, but that was the fucking problem. Because of his laissez-faire attitude, Lavar had nearly gotten my girl killed.

My fucking girl.

A rumble oozed out of my chest as I sat behind the wheel of my car, stationary thanks to the red light that kept me from speeding down the road again toward Lavar's little abode. I was going to fucking kill him. Fury and disgust roiled through my guts as I considered the fact that Lavar had just taken the job without a second thought.

Loyalty meant everything to me, and it meant a hell of a lot to the fucking mob as well. How he thought he was going to get away with working both sides was beyond me.

One thing was clear to me, however, and as I got moving again, the light turning green above me, he wasn't going to get away with it any longer. His actioned had risked Lila, and that…Would. Not. Do.

It's been less than twenty-four hours, and you're wrapped around that girl's finger.

Yeah, that was certainly something. But there was a part of me that knew it was going to happen. That's why I'd kept Lila at arm's length. She was perfection, and as much as I had not let myself admit that, it had always been true. I secretly knew that once I let her in, there was no getting her out.

And her fucking godfather was no different. They were mine, and they were both getting screwed over by someone. I wasn't about to stand for that.

Possessive had been a word I'd tossed around in the past, connected to the few attempts at relationships I'd made before the club opened. Apparently, it was truer now than it had ever been. If anyone so much as touched a hair on either of their heads, they'd find those fingers on the floor next to their feet.

I couldn't help the sarcastic chuckle that bled from me. Reagan would be so proud of my unrestrained bloodlust. Hell, if he'd known about Lavar, that glorious bastard would be on his way to the guy's office just like I was.

"Fucking move, you fucks!" I honked the horn, trying to will the cars in front of me to move faster, steering to the side in some vain attempt to cut around them.

I was so fucking over this. Everyone was driving too slowly, and no one knew what they were doing. Zero signals, grandmas in the middle lane going twenty, goddamn morons trying to cross the street in the middle instead of using the fucking crosswalk.

I was going to murder everyone.

My watch chirped at me, and I glanced down, skimming the text. It was a warning that my heart rate and blood pressure were spiking. Yeah, I was a bit…pissed off.

Okay, I was a lot pissed off, and I was ready to burn the

damn world down. I was a regular Reagan at this point. But that wasn't going to change until I got some answers out of Lavar.

Lila...some fucking bitch and some asshole before that tried to kill her...Absolutely not. No one is taking her from me now that I've officially staked my claim. No one.

By the time I'd reached Lavar's "office," I'd managed to wrangle my rage into a low simmer. It was his penthouse, of course, the place he shared with his partner, whom I knew little about–other than that they were both very "loud" when they were together. *Annoying.*

They were well-off, judging by the size and location of the place, which was secured uptown instead of downtown, unlike my own. Lavar had been an established hacker by the time I needed one for the club, and he was a few years younger than I was, which had suggested he was good at his job.

That was true to this day. I just didn't like that he was so flippant about who he let purchase those skills.

Pulling into the underground parking structure, I received a ticket from the guard and pulled into a spot on the second level. I knew that Lavar was on the top floor. I'd been here before, and a small part of me wondered at just how he and his boyfriend had secured the place.

It had to have cost a pretty penny, and moreover, they were in an uppity part of town. Not many in this area had property that wasn't a family heirloom. Did Lavar come from some secret family money he didn't want to admit?

Ha, that'd be so on the nose—the blueblood hacker with a client roster full of anti-establishment mafiosos and sex club owners.

Riding the elevator up to the top floor, my blood hummed as the doors slid open to reveal a short hallway with a single door. It was surprising they bothered with the hall at all, but at least I didn't have to say who I was visiting to the guard. My trip here was still traceable, of course, but this bought me a few minutes of discretion.

I approached Lavar's door and gave a thorough pounding on it, ensuring that no matter what the asshole was doing he'd hear me. It didn't take him long to open things up, and as soon as the door was cracked, I shoved inside and thrust Lavar up against the wall.

"Jesus, Edward! What the fuck?!"

Pinning him back with my forearm pressing against his throat, I pushed harder, cutting off his air.

"You serviced someone who needed a personalized identity under the name Joelle Miller. Who was it?"

His eyes flared, and I offered a knowledgeable smirk. When he didn't respond right away, I pulled him off the wall only to ram him back down against it.

"Who?!"

Lavar hissed as his spine hit the wall, the shaggy sections of his blonde hair fluttering past his bright blue eyes. The asshole looked like he was better off surfing as opposed to sitting behing a computer screen and assisting with who knew how many illegal activities. As he blinked up at me, the hard set of his jaw accompanied a narrowing of his eyes.

"Be pissed all you want, fucker. You're giving me what I want."

"You know," he adjusted, pushing himself to stand taller, which put him just a hair above where I stood, "we've always had such a great working experience. What crawled up your ass and changed that?"

"Not your business, Lavar." I glared, gripping the unbuttoned lapel of his white shirt, which hung open over a faded black tee. "Who?"

"Funny, that's none of *your* business. It's *my* client. If I gave away everyone who worked with me just because someone roughed me up a bit, I'd lose all credibility."

He was such a shit, a tall, handsome shit who put Ken's looks to shame, and I wanted to punch that smirk right off his face. I'd settle for another hard shove, this one that included far more pressure on his windpipe.

"You're going to tell me, and I won't let it get out how I learned the information. Besides, whoever hired you is as good as dead when I find them. I'm really not looking to add another name to my list, but by all means…" I leaned forward, making sure Lavar's eyes bulged slightly. "…Test me."

The pretty boy glared until he nodded–just once. I let up, and Lavar sucked in a deep breath through his nose before clearing his throat.

"Your rates just went up, asshole." He gestured toward the desk that was set up in the south corner of the massive open-concept room. "It'll take me two minutes."

Following Lavar to the computer, I loomed just over his shoulder as his fingers whizzed across the keyboard. I was getting more impatient by the second, and if this went on for even a second longer than those "two minutes," I was going to punch him.

Silence stretched uncomfortably, and given the opportunity now, I couldn't help but look around at the penthouse. Everything was so stark and clean, so meticulously organized, a fact I could tell because each item or group of items was set perfectly in its place or housed within clear plastic containers.

"Hurry up, Lavar." I flicked my attention to him, but he didn't seem to pay me any mind, his fingers too busy clacking away through his own set of firewalls and protection.

Swiping my finger across his clear glass desk, I found not even a speck of dust. When I glanced through it, I saw that the wires from his monitor and devices were all perfectly tidy. Each was wearing a colored strip that I had to guess allowed Lavar to tell them apart at a glance.

I cocked a brow, my curisotiy undeniably piqued. A pen and

paper were on the desk in front of me, lined up precisely next to Lavar. I pushed the pen with my pinky, making it look like I had bumped it while standing up.

Without even stopping what he was doing, Lavar straightened it and got back to clacking.

Huh. Okay, then.

Glancing at my watch, I cleared my throat. "You've got ten seconds. Nine, eight, seven, six–"

"One R. Venuti. No first name given. Paid in a wire transfer that originated from a private account in Morocco. Information delivered via an encrypted drive that he was taught how to access."

Lavar looked up at me, sitting back in his chair. He flicked an appraising stare at the rest of his desk, likely ensuring it was still as tidy as everything else. But he took the pen and tapped it three times on his notepad–the one that was blank and didn't even show the torn paper from the previously front piece–before setting it back down in its rightful spot again.

"And with four seconds to spare. I guess I work just a hair faster under the threat of death. I'll factor that in for the future."

"Print it. I want to see this on paper." Lavar rolled his eyes but did as told. "I catch you working for someone who's trying to kill my employees again, and it's your balls."

That actually stopped him, Lavar's fingers freezing as he reached for the printout that would come from the machine under his desk.

"The information was used to kill someone?" His voice was level enough, but the slight narrowing of his brow gave him away.

"Thankfully, no. The target is alive and well." Lavar seemed to relax, but I stared at him hard, leaning over as he sat in his desk chair. "I can assure you that if they weren't, I'd be in a much worse mood. Consider yourself lucky."

I'll hand it to him, he didn't balk or start blabbering. Lavar simply nodded once and swallowed that information down.

"You can imagine why I don't ask what it's being used for, but I'll add this client to a tally that I keep of blacklisted individuals. I'm not looking to aid murders when I can help it."

"Do better at your own background checks, then." I sneered, snatching the paper from him. "And while you're at it, add the woman whose picture was swapped on the ID. She took the liberty of volunteering as muscle for this little attempted assassination."

"Of course." Lavar nodded, his eyes dark with contained anger. "If there's nothing else I can do for you…"

He let the words hang, standing up from his chair and sweeping a hand toward the door. I didn't bother responding, allowing him to walk me to the exit and open it wide. Just as he did, that partner of his appeared on the other side.

The same age as Lavar, Kendrix–a man I only knew the name of because I'd had the displeasure of hearing it called out while we were on the phone–was the exact opposite of his lover.

Where Lavar was light and sunny, Kendrix was dark and shadowy angles. He had shaggy black hair that resembled mine if I went too long between cuts, long bangs that hung almost to his lips, and a tidy goatee that framed his mouth. Dark slashed brows over brown eyes and deep olive skin that bordered on tan. He had gauges in his ears, a pierced brow, and the inklings of several tattoos poking out from his collar and sleeves.

"Problems?" He eyed me, a familiar protective gleam in his eyes.

"I'm just leaving. Thank you for the information, Lavar. We'll be in touch." I nodded at him, and it took a second for him to do so back, likely hedging his bets.

"Indeed. Now," he stepped further back into his penthouse, allowing Kendrix to slide in and stand protectively near him, "if you'll excuse me."

"Have fun, Lavar." I smirked, eyeing his boyfriend, who had taken a step in front of the hacker. "Kendrix."

With that, I left. I had shit to do now that I had a name, and I had a feeling that Reagan would want to hear it as soon as possible.

I'd ditched Emilio not long after he'd forced me to accompany him, a task I knew he was using to get me out of the house and away from Lila. I just couldn't quite piece together why. I knew the don was pissed with me for letting another attempt slip past me, but why would he want me away from her? I was supposed to be her bodyguard, for fuck's sake.

He's off. He's just…goddamn it. What am I missing?

At least he'd let me leave. Sure, I'd faked this call, but Emilio couldn't play it off like he wasn't interested in what the Vitales were up to. They'd been a thorn in our side for a while now, never securing enough ground to be a true "Famiglia," but still disrupting our business.

That, of course, was not who I'd gone to keep an eye on.

"We got another shipment coming in soon. You're gonna have to be patient."

The voice came through my headset, picked up from the conversation being conducted across the parking structure from me. I'd found a reference in the data Edward's contact pulled to one "Alexei Tsyrinsky." He was a big time player for the local bratva, and the Famiglia mostly stayed away from his territory–too evenly matched to do anything more than just piss each other off—mutually assured destruction and all that.

But I also knew that fucker was into just about anything that stood the chance to make him money.

"How soon is soon, Tsyrinsky? I have my own clients looking for new furnishings." I glared through the binoculars that I was using, the old flame of dislike surging at the sound of Dan fucking Brown's voice. "And keeping them waiting affects prices, which'll bounce right back on you. 'Cause I ain't paying for late deliveries."

Dan was low on the organized crime ranking, but he was a little shit who stuck his nose in everything. He knew too much about what was going on with every major player, and even the Carpinellis were forced to do business with him fairly regularly.

He'd eye-fucked Lila during a meeting with Emilio once, and that sealed my death warrant for his dumb ass immediately.

Why is Emilio talking with Tsyrinsky? What is this shit about shipments? If he's fucking working a deal, why the fuck don't I know about it? I don't like–

But my thoughts were interrupted as my phone went off, buzzing in the cupholder. I set the binoculars down, grumbling to myself as I picked up the cell to see that it was Edward. He must have found something.

"Yeah?" I kept my voice low like those asshats would actually hear me. "D'you get something out of your contact?"

There was a light chuckle, and then Edward sighed. "In addition to the annoying headache, yeah. It turns out that Lavar didn't know who he was working for. He didn't ask for details beyond the job, some bullshit about protecting his business."

Rolling my eyes, I adjusted in the driver's seat, my ass aching after hours of watching this spot before Dan finally arrived for the meetup—tardy bastard.

"Whoopie. Did you learn anything useful?"

"Unbunch your briefs, Reagan." I could hear the clink of a glass against Edward's mouth, assuming he'd poured himself a scotch. "Client paid through an offshore account centered in Morocco and had the assassin's information ready to go for a rush job. I've got the print-out of the account details."

Irritation flared. That was nice and all, but I wasn't his tech buddy. I needed a name to go off of so that I could track them down and put a bullet between their eyes, after hours of torture, of course. You didn't put a hit on Lila and get away with a quick death.

"Edward, unless you've got a name for me, I don't know why you had to interrupt me. I'm watching fucking Tsyrinsky. The asshole we swore to never to business with that magically appeared in the last chunk of bullshit you got from your guy."

"As a matter of fact," I could hear the smirk in Edward's voice, "I did get a name."

"And you didn't open with that because..." I squeezed my cell, glaring at nothing as I focused through the windshield.

"Dramatic flare, baby." Another drink of that damned scotch. "R. Venuti."

My stomach clenched as my heart all but stopped. Like some goddamn movie, the world tilted and sucked in on itself as if I was traveling down a never-ending hallway.

"What. Did. You. Say." It wasn't a question but a demand.

The temperature of the cab seemed to drop several degrees, and even Edward's attitude through the line switch gears abruptly, his rough intake of air audible even as my blood screamed in my ears.

"R. Venuti. Do you know him?"

"Know him?" I was going to crack my damn phone in half, having nowhere to go to relieve the need to fucking destroy something stuc in the car like I was. "He's Emilio's new fucking pet project. The asshole is with the don right now. I left them to snoop on fucking Tsyrinsky."

"He's with the Family? Are you fucking kidding me?" The hurried sounds of a glass being set down and several doors opening and closing filtered through the line. "Does–Jesus, I can't believe I'm fucking asking this, but...do you think Emilio knows?"

I didn't want to consider that. I didn't want to believe that my friend since childhood could be responsible for the hits on Lila, his own fucking daughter. But he's been so flippant about the attacks, so unnecessarily upset with her.

"I...I can't prove that right now. I need to confront them both, see how it goes. But if he *is*...Get to the house. I'm not waiting another fucking second on this. Lila is there and–"

"You can't tell her yet. If we're wrong, she's going to get upset for nothing. We need to be sure." Edward's voice was low, dripping with restrained fury and an abundance of concern. "Lila needs us to be one-hundred percent certain about this."

Clenching my jaw, I gripped the steering wheel until my knuckles hollered in protest. Only then did I start the car and slowly back up to get out of there. I needed to get back to the fucking house as quickly as I could, hopefully before Emilio got home so I could check on Lila. She was alone back there, and if Renzo knew that...He could be taking matters into his own hands as we speak.

"Fine. I won't say anything, but we both need to get there right the fuck now. Renzo has access to the house. Lila is there alone–"

"I'm already in the car. I'll meet you there."

Sucking in a deep breath, I waited to be far enough from Tsyrinsky and Brown so that I could flip the car around and hit the freeway with the gas pressed to the damn floor.

"If he hurts her, if that fucker touches her, and I'm not there to keep Lila safe, I'll never fucking forgive myself."

Edward was still on the line with me, and for whatever reason, I was glad, not wanting to hang up until we were both at the house.

"He won't. I can get there in fifteen if I push it. And she's not stupid. Lila keeps her door locked, she's a hell of a shot according to her, and Ludo is there."

That fucking dog. "If he manages to keep her safe, I'll buy the damned mutt a fucking stake."

"We'll get there, Reagan. It's going to be fine."

I sucked in a deep breath, absolutely tearing down the highway like a bat out of hell. My girl, our girl, was in danger. She needed us, and I was off on some pointless recon because I hadn't pegged Renzo's betrayal sooner.

"It fucking better be."

Lila

The email that I'd read happened to be one that I'd printed out as well, and I sat on my bed clutching at the paper until it crumpled beneath my fingers. My eyes burned as I ran over the words, again and again and again. I had to be misunderstanding this. I had to be.

I didn't recognize the name listed, which I supposed was telling in and of itself. I knew most people my dad worked with. Tsyrinsky wasn't a name that lit up any sparks in my mind. The unlisted address–that only certain individuals who'd passed background checks should have access to–did, however.

The club. The address to the fucking club in some email chain between my dad and whoever the fuck this is.

My fingers trembled as I held the page, just staring down at it like magically the names and odd phrases and bullshit would suddenly make sense. Amid all the things that I couldn't understand, though, there was one other thing that made the hairs on my neck stand up, my skin rippling with goosebumps as Ludo settled next to me on the bed.

"You can tell I'm upset, huh?" I stroked over his head once, unable to bring myself to give him more, even though he definitely deserved it. "Yeah. Pretty damn upset."

Ludo's fur was soft under my fingers, and the room smelled like the vacuum powder the maid used. Any other day, the smells and sights and sounds–right now being Ludo's little whine–would be so comforting. But I didn't know what to do with any of them. Nothing felt right.

"What the fuck does 'seasoning up the fresh meat before running the circuit' mean?"

All I got was a whine from my Doberman, but it was more uneasy, reflecting my own mood, I was sure. Still, it didn't sit right, like Ludo knew something was up, just like I did. I had to stifle a shiver, that prickling feeling of something being right on the edge of my brain nagging at me. It was *right there*, just out of reach.

What was I missing?

Standing, I brought the printed email with me as I walked toward my closet. I couldn't be in these clothes anymore. I'd put something on that might attract Edward or Reagan's attention, but now it felt wrong. Weird somehow. I needed sweats and a tee.

Comfort clothes for the win.

I wasn't willing to be too far from my evidence, though. I needed to be sure it was still in eyeshot, so I stared at the print-out as I pulled off my leggings and zip-up exercise jacket. I threw a t-shirt on over my sports bra, deciding that it was as good an option for the girls as any. But I couldn't find my favorite sweats in the drawer.

Groaning, I left the closet, hurrying to the door, which spooked Ludo. "Sorry, buddy. I need to check in the laundry room for my sweats. I'll be–"

But my words were cut off as I opened my door and crashed into a body. Reagan had a habit of being right outside my door, and my heart leaped at the thought of him finally being home.

Righting myself after nearly falling on my ass, I shoved the hair out of my face. "Reagan, I'm so glad you're…"

It wasn't Reagan.

"Oh, hi, Dad." I was still clutching the printed email, and I tried to slip my hand behind my back casually. But where the fuck was i supposed to put it? I wasn't wearing any pants.

"Lila, you're still home. I thought you worked today." The man looked as relaxed as a rectum getting to know a proctologist.

"Oh, right. Edward. He insisted I take the day off. What with all the attempted murder and stuff." My spine tingled as I stared up into the wildly unimpressed expression on my father's face. "You're back sooner than I thought you'd be."

The mood felt wrong, the air between my dad and me too tense and on edge. It was right about then that I put together the fact that he'd been right outside my door, thinking I wasn't home.

"Were you looking for me? Or, umm, something else?"

I hated how insecure I sounded, but I wasn't looking to rile the man. I had no intention on pissing him off right now. I was a damn good shot, I was decently fast, and I had absolutely zero way to use either of those skills if my dad was feeling fiesty. Not that I really expected him to do much more than verbally berate me. The guy had never raised a hand to me once.

"As a matter of fact," my father pushed forward, gesturing toward the bed for me to take a seat, "I was."

With little choice, I backed up until my knees hit the mattress and then plopped down. My father wasn't a small man. He still hit the gym in the basement on the regular, and I felt dwarfed by him. It wasn't nearly as comfortable as when it was Reagan or Edward, and I swallowed hard.

"What?" I looked up at him, channeling the years I'd spent

lying to the man's face about the dumbest things.

"My office door was open." Shit, I'd left it open? Fuck, I was in such a hurry, I didn't notice. "You weren't in there, were you?"

What was the play here? My dad already knew it was me. He'd probably checked the security footage. He wouldn't have thought to look if I'd remember the door, but there was no use in being upset about it now. Did I fess up? Come clean about snooping? Or did I say it was for something else?

I'd at least remembered to log out of everything and close out the windows. I could go with the using your laptop for porn, checking your calendar for a surprise…but none of that felt right.

I knew something was up, and I was tired of being on the outside looking in. This was my life, and if he was messing with it somehow, I wanted to know.

Flicking my stare down and then back up, I met *Emilio's* eyes, holding out the paper I'd been hiding behind my back.

"I was. I'm sure you knew that already. I was curious. There have been so many meets and new contracts over the past few years that I wondered if you accidentally let it drop that I was working at the club. I found this. Listing the address doesn't seem super accidental, Dad. What's that about?"

His eyes flared wide, and I could see the cogs in his brain spinning at double time. He didn't think I'd gotten into the files. That was clear. But he wasn't as quick to defend himself as an innocent person or someone with a lot of guilt might be.

In fact, he broke eye contact to shake his head, pinching his brow between his thumb and forefinger. A long exhale left my father then, and something about it–the resignation to the situation–was more telling than anything else.

He knew about this. He'd *given* whoever that person was my work address. And that had been just *before* the first attack.

My heart dropped, my stomach sinking like ooze into my

feet as I stared up at the man who helped to raise me, my father, and was forced to face the fact that not only did my dad not seem as concerned about my attempted murder as he should...

He was responsible for it.

Emilio sighed, snatching the paper away. It crumpled in his tight grip, and then the don tossed it to the ground, where it landed silently at my feet.

"You know," I backed up, trying to put as much ground between my father and me as possible, "I've always said that if you can't get something done right..."

I stumbled when I hit my nightstand, but thankfully, it made Ludo perk up. I snapped my fingers and pointed at my father, at Emilio Carpinelli, and my rained attack dog got to work. He leaped over the bed, knocking my dad to the ground.

Turning, I fled toward the door, but my exit was blocked as Renzo stood before me, his smile sadistic and cruel. I couldn't get by, and it was a split-second move to rush past my father and take off toward the doggie door that led to the run I'd had installed. The gate there opened so that it could be cleaned; I just needed to make it to the gate.

But Emilio grabbed my leg, sending me to the floor just in time to see Renzo grabbing Ludo, who bit into his arm viciously, and throwing him against the wall. Ludo his hard, whimpering, and when he tried to stand, his front leg buckled.

"No!"

I reached out, trying to get to him, but my hand was kicked away, and Emilio fisted my hair, craning my head back so I was forced to look up at him. Cursing and fighting, I panicked as my stare darted between Renzo and my father. Renzon was grabbing a gun, and I screamed, yanking hair from my head as I struggled to get to Ludo.

"No guns. I want a *relatively* quiet exit. Get the car ready to go."

Renzo hesitated to listen, but my father glared, putting his mutt in its place. I was only briefly relieved before Emilio turned back to me with a cruel mask over his features. He wasn't the man I knew. He wasn't the man who'd fallen in love and created a child with a woman who was honey and silk.

He was a monster, plain and simple.

Dragging me up by the hair, Emilio pulled me to the door. I did everything I could to fight, but I was no match for the man who'd spent his life as a wrecking ball.

"As I said, if you want something done right," Emilio snarled as I fought, getting annoyed and smashing my head into the door, "do it yourself."

The world went fuzzy, pain flaring through my skull, and as hard as I fought, as desperate as I was to stay awake, everything melted into a staticky TV on the blink before fading into utter blackness that dragged me down into the depths.

24
The Empty Room

Reagan

Driving across town to the house had been the longest fifteen minutes of my life, during a trip that should have taken at least twenty-five. I'd sped down the interstate so damned fast, I actually worried about being stopped. Most cops knew a Faily car when it was in their face, but I didn't have to get pulled over and intimidate them.

Thankfully, I'd gotten to the Family mansion without issue.

"Lila!" I called out, not giving a single goddamn fuck about who else might here me calling for her as I threw open my door and headed for the house. "Lila!"

As I sprinted up the steps and inside, there were a few of the low-ranking members milling about in the living room and kitchen. They stopped what they were doing, casting glances my way. One in particular, a newer recruit whom I'd actually brought in a few months back, named Valter, stood from his seat on the couch and approached me, his brows drawn together.

"Reagan, everything alright? You seem–"

"Where the fuck is Lila?" I glared, unable to keep the seething fury at bay.

"In her room far as I know." Val pulled back slightly, his stare scanning me as he assessed my threat level. "She hasn't come out since you left this morning with Emilio."

Tension ratcheted up my spine, and it was all I could do to clench my jaw, my eyes darting around the house as I half-listened to Val. She'd been here all day. I wasn't sure if Emilio had come back to the house. *I never should have split from him.*

"And have you seen him?" I flicked a glare back at Val, his usual 'fuck-boy' vibe so much more annoying right now.

"Him? The boss? Yeah, he was in with Renzo about—"

Grabbing Val by the lapels of his motorcycle jacket, I yanked him toward me just a hair. The guy was about as tall as I was, but he was in his early thirties, no silver streaks, no years in the business. He'd come from a local MC who'd been all but obliterated last year by the Feds.

"Did you see them leave with Lila?"

Val looked up at me like I'd lost my damned mind. He wasn't wrong, not really. With Lila under threat—again—I had lost it. And it wasn't going to get even a fraction better until I found her.

"No, Reagan. I didn't see them leave at all, actually. They both went upstairs." Slowly but purposefully, Val pulled my hand away from his jacket, forcing me to release the leather. "You need to explain what crawled up your ass, yeah?"

"No time. I need to get to her." Practically launching myself at the stairs, I took off at a dead sprint. "Edward Scarlett is right behind me. Let him in when he arrives. My orders."

There was a pause, but then Val called out, "Alright, Terrasi. You owe me, though."

I didn't bother responding; instead, beat-feeting it toward Lila's room. The halls were quiet, which was a fucking signal in and of itself. Lila had those damned CDs, and if she wasn't blasting them or watching some fucking movie in her room, it didn't bode well.

Please. Please let her be in there. Please let Lila be in that room just fucking napping or something.

Reaching her door, I stopped dead in my tracks. It was open. Lila never kept her door open because of Ludo. My brain emptied as I rushed forward into the bedroom. The place was a fucking disaster. The bedding was all messed up, there was a crumpled paper on the floor, and there was no sign of that damned dog.

Scratch, scratch.

Something sounded from the closet, and I rushed over, flinging the door wide to find Ludo pawing at the baseboard. He was lying down, and even as he perked up—the light from the room spilling into the pitch black space—he didn't move to get up. That dog was tackle central.

"Shit."

I hurried over, noting that he was whimpering quietly and his leg was swollen.

"Dammit. He fucking came in here, didn't he?" Ludo looked up at me like he was trying to confirm my suspicion, and his little eyes were scanning the bedroom for any sign of Lila, which of course he wouldn't find. "She's not there."

A whine echoed from him, and I stood up, taking a step back as I gripped the bridge of my nose. The tension flared, this nauseating light behind my veins that threatened to end me as sure as any form of radiation.

Lila wasn't here. Emilio and his little rat had fucking taken her.

"Fuck!" I kicked out, smashing my foot into her dresser. "No, no, no. This can't be fucking happening. Not after... Dammit!"

Ludo was still whining, about as upset as I was, and I just stared at the damn floor. I didn't know where Emilio would take her. Clearly the asshole had a whole separate life I wasn't aware of. He'd been planning this. He arranged the fucking hits on his own goddamn daughter.

Emilio was a monster, and I was going to watch the life leave his eyes for touching what was mine.

"He got her."

Spinning around, I found Edward just outside the closet, his breath coming in harsh bursts like he'd sprinted up here from the foyer. All I could do was nod.

"Dammit." Edward's brow pinched together, and he scanned over Lila's room, probably searching for a clue or something, before they landed on Ludo, who looked up at him with so much worry in his dark eyes. "And he hurt her dog? Your boss is a real prick."

"*Ex*-boss." I shoved out of the closet, going for the paper I'd seen earlier.

"You quitting?" Edward asked, following me toward the exit where I stood with what was apparently a print-out of an email.

"No." I flicked my stare up from the piece of paper. "I'm gutting that bastard and Renzo, too."

A slow smirk spread over Edward's face, and he offered me a single nod. "I support you fully." And then he gestured down at the paper with his head, his arms folded over his chest. "What is that?"

"Some email. It looks like Lila printed it?" I stared back down at the message, skimming over the words. "It must've been interesting for her to actually want a copy of it, so—"

I stopped short, the truth of content crystallizing as I read over it. In all my years, I'd assumed that Emilio and I would never disagree about one critical limit we put on our business. A hard line that separated us from the handful of people who were actually *worse* than the Family.

I'd been wrong.

"What is it?" I could hear the worry in Edward's voice.

"He's…" I almost couldn't bring myself to say the words, and in the moments between, Val came rushing up to the room, looking between Edward and I. "…Emilio is selling Lila to fucking traffickers."

"The fuck?!"

The chorus of two perfectly timed outbursts sounded around me, and I crushed the paper in my fist, imagining Emilio's head in place of the print-out. The thing was, traffickers moved fast, driven by sheer necessity. We didn't have long if we wanted to get Lila back.

And then another puzzle piece fell into place. The name I'd only briefly glanced at in the signature line had been Tsyrinsky.

"That's why he was meeting with that fucker. Ugh!" I balled my hands into fists, needing to pace the room to keep myself from tearing into anyone who happened to be close. "He's working with fucking Tsyrinsky. That asshole will sell Lila like a piece of fucking property to the worst of the worst. She'll be a fucking sex slave."

"No," Edward walked up to me, gripping me by the shoulders, "she won't. We're going to get to her."

"We don't know where he took her." I shook my head, clenching my jaw so tightly I was sure to crack a tooth.

"Lavar sent a lot of fucking shit. Give me two minutes."

Glaring at him, I didn't bother nodding. He could have the time, but I was moving the moment it was up, even if I didn't know where to go.

"Did I catch that right?" Val spoke up, stealing my attention momentarily. "The Don is going to sell his daughter to sex traffickers? That's typical around these parts?"

I shook my head, nausea crawling up the back of my throat. *Lila. My fucking Lila. This couldn't be happening.*

"No. In fact," I cocked my head, regarding Val for any tells I needed to be aware of, "it was the one line he swore he'd never cross. Apparently, Emilio changed his fucking mind."

Val was quiet for a moment, which allowed him to hear the whining coming from the closet. He glanced past me and gestured at Ludo with his head.

"Lila's dog?"

"Yeah, and he's got a broken leg from what I can tell. Get him to the vet."

"Excuse me?" Brows shooting to his hairline, Val eyed me. "Do what now?"

"Get the dog to the fucking doctor. When Lila gets back, she'll lose her shit if something has happened to him." I met Val's stare hard, looking for that spark of understanding I saw in him when we'd first met. "Consider it a test of commitment."

Which hell, any task assigned to you by the mob was, but his was about him obeying me, effectively choosing a side. Mine, not Emilio's.

"Done." He nodded, then proceeded to the closet and scooped up that Doberman like he was cradling a baby.

As Val walked past to leave, I landed a hand on his shoulder. "Get everyone loyal to me on board for the fallout. Either we fail, and you're Lila's last chance, or we succeed and I want every fucker who thinks this shit is okay strung up by their cocks. Understood?"

Nodding, Val didn't even so much as blink at the order. I had to hand it to him and myself. He was a decent guy, and I'd been smart to bring him into the fold.

"Go."

With that Val was off, and I was left standing in Lila's empty fucking room with nothing to go after. I turned to Edward, the fury in my blood boiling hotter with every second.

"Tell me you fucking found something."

"I'm working on it. There's a lot to go through." Edward was scrolling through his damn phone, his eyes scanning the screen in a quick flurry of activity.

"Edward, I'm not fucking standing here while Emilio *sells* Lila. Get me something or—"

"Here!" Edward paused, looking up at me and then back at

the phone so that he could highlight a row of text and shove it in my face. "A warehouse. Recent purchase. Abandoned and on the waterfront. It's a solid place to store the girls and do the transactions."

I glared at him, narrowing my eyes to silently remind him this was Lila we were talking about. She wasn't just some girl, and this wasn't just some *transaction*.

"Their language. Not mine. But it's solid, Reagan. We need to move." His brows dipped lower, the usual air of smugness that he wore at all times cracking just a hair. "I've brought girls into the club who were once trafficked. We…we need to get to her now."

My stomach pinched. Edward had heard stories then.

"Then we fucking go. We get weapons and we go get our fucking girl."

Edward held my stare, both of us locked in an unspoken agreement that nothing would make it out of that warehouse alive that touched her. We were killing everyone in that fucking hole, even if it meant dying in the process.

God, I fucking lo—

Shaking myself, I refocused. There was no fucking time for that.

Edward turned on his heel, running out of the room. "My car. It's faster."

"Faster?" I hurried after him, gesturing toward the back stairwell that would get us to the armory quicker. "It's a car. They'll all go to fucking ninety if I shove the damn pedal down."

"Yes, but I parked you in."

25
The Warehouse

Lila

Ringing in my ears got my attention first, which was quickly backed by the sensation of immense pain that built behind my eyes. My head swam, feeling too heavy and too tight. Blinking my eyes was a nearly insurmountable task, and I immediately regretted it. Everything outside my head was too bright.

"Lila?"

A familiar voice. I tried to concentrate on it, finding that it was very much like I was drunk on too much tequila. I'd managed to fuck myself up good with that one, and I swore off the stuff ever since. Did I break my rule? Where even was I?

I tried to reach up for my head, to pinch the bridge of my nose in some vain attempt to make the throbbing headache stop. I knew that wouldn't work, but sometimes you just did shit because…that's what you did.

"Lila?"

Ugh, yes. I'm here. Shhh. You're being too loud.

I wasn't sure who exactly I was talking to, but I recognized the voice. It was one I knew well, right? Yeah, I knew him. He was…

Pain speared through my head as I tried to focus, and I suddenly realized that even though I'd been reaching for my head, I never made it there. My hand was stuck. Why was my hand stuck?

A spinning nausea took over as I forced myself to open my eyes. That voice continued to call out, and after what felt like about a decade or so, I processed what I was looking at. The floor. I was staring down at the floor, and it wasn't my floor. It didn't belong to any of the house or even the club, for that matter. This was…concrete?

"There she is. Finally coming around. Took you long enough."

Wait. That was my dad. Why was I looking at concrete with my dad yapping somewhere in front of me? And I was in…a chair. I scooted around, regretting the way it made my head throb, but I was able to get my bearings more. I was seated in a wooden chair, and I couldn't reach up for my head because my arms were bound—by ropes.

Fuck.

Like a fuzzy image coming into focus on a staticky TV screen, I forced my head up higher and there in front of me, folding his arms over his chest like he was so fond of, was my father. And we definitely weren't at home.

What happened, Lila? Think. Come on. Think!

Racking my brain was a physical challenge, but it started to filter in. I'd found that odd email on his computer. That's right, I'd been snooping around. But then I'd gone to my room. Why were we here?

"You look a little off there, sweetie. Having trouble concentrating?" Even if I was unsure about the details right now, I still glared at the man. I knew I had every reason to be pissed at him—especially considering, you know, the fucking ropes tying me to a goddamn chair—and I snarled at him, giving the don my best Ludo.

He snickered at me, had the gall to just stand there and laugh.

"Well then. Maybe you don't need the refresher. Still…" My father turned toward his left, and I followed him, trying to peer into the shadows next to him. "I imagine you'll have a few questions."

Out of the darkness stepped a figure. It took a moment for me to recognize, likely concussed as I was, but after the guy was fully situated in the overhead light of what I was now realizing was a warehouse, it hit me.

"Renzo?"

"Hey, bitch."

The sneer on Renzo's face was all cocky bravado and unearned confidence. He had always thought he was a the real top shit, and whatever was going on between him and my father was giving that inflated ego something to draw off of.

Disregarding Renzo, I turned my attention back to Father Dearest. "Why am I fucking tied up in a goddamn warehouse?"

"Because you wouldn't die when told, so I had to resort to more creative tactics."

My stomach plummeted.

Sure, I'd had an idea that my father wasn't the man I'd thought he was, that he was up to something foul, but the fact that he'd confirmed that he was trying to kill me—that he had been responsible for the two attempted assassinations—was something I didn't think I would ever process easily.

More of the past few hours crystallized in my mind. He'd come to find me in my room. Renzo had been there then, too. I'd had that email…the one with the club's address listed. Shit, what had happened after?

The thoughts spun, the sound of Renzo's amused laugh the soundtrack to my mental anguish. My dad had said…Oh, shit. That was right. He'd said that "if you want something done right, do it yourself." And he hit me, smashed my head into the door.

Well, that explains the horrendous headache. What little remained of my faith in my father crumbled. *I…I can't believe it. He really…he really wants me dead.*

My eyes burned, threatening to spill over with tears, but I held them back. I wouldn't shed a single drop for this fucker. As far as I was concerned, the man I was looking at now might have been the don of the Carpinelli Family, but he *wasn't* my fucking father.

We met stares again, and my—Emilio seemed to recognize the conclusion I'd come to.

"So, she's understanding at last. Again, it took you long enough."

"Why?" My voice betrayed the emotions surging through me, and I swallowed hard, trying to rid myself of that sound. "Why did you try to kill me? I'm pretty sure I stayed out of your business, so enlighten me."

Emilio sucked a deep breath in through his nose. I watched him as he tilted his head to the side, considering. A familiar pace set up in his walk, and he ambled back and forth in front of me, clearly weighing his options, deciding what to say— and what to keep locked away.

"Because you aren't fit to be the heir of the Family. Not the Family as I would like to see it run. You don't have the stomach for it."

He wasn't entirely wrong there, but I'd always assumed marrying me off was the next logical step. Would my not being a virgin actually divert those attempts? If I were honest, which it was becoming ever easier to be, I had never really thought sleeping my way through the Family was going to work.

I'd just hoped that it would provide me with a bit of fun before my time was up.

"So why not marry me off like you always said? I can't imagine you *actually* care that I'm not a virgin."

Scoffing, Emilio turned to face me, the backlighting of the warehouse bulbs creating stark shadows across his face.

"I didn't really. Sure, there were several Familias who were pissed about it. It did cause me a number of problems there, but there were a handful who didn't give a fuck. They could have been options."

"So? Why not just—"

"Because I will not see the Carpinelli Family in the hands of *anyone* who might ruin its reputation."

I couldn't say why exactly, but Emilio's hang-up on the Carpinelli reputation infuriated me. All this, my fucking life, was worth less than what some assholes said about us on the street? Seriously?

"I can see you disagree, Lila. You never did have much of a poker face." Emilio's stupid waltz about the room started up again, and I fought against the ropes on my wrists, looking for some weakness there. "And that's precisely the problem. You don't have a fucking clue about how this world works, how to put it beneath your shoe and claim dominion over it."

"And you do?" I bit out, glaring. "The Familias all do the same fucking bullshit. What makes you think that we're any better than them, huh? What puts them so low in your books that you'd kill your daughter instead of selling me to one of them?"

"Oh, Lila," Renzo stepped forward, getting way too close as his eyes roamed over my body, "it's also a lot more profitable this way. And that's what you don't get. We are better than those fucks, and it all comes down to the fact that they aren't willing to do what it takes to ensure the best profits. *We*," he gestured at Emilio with his thumb, "are."

"I don't—" But I stopped myself. This had something to do with that email, with the name I saw signed at the bottom. *Tsyrinsky.* Why had we cut ourselves off from him? What was it about *him* that was so important in all this? "Tsyrinsky.

You're working with him."

Emilio paused, glancing at me. I did my best to actually use my poker face, allowing just my rage to billow out through my expression.

"Huh, I honestly didn't think you remembered who he was. I'll hand it to you, Lila. You might be a fraction less stupid than I believed."

"Your beloved godfather kept us from an excellent profit margin," Renzo added. "Emilio and I have been really fucking busy repairing those business contacts to get back in Tsyrinsky's good graces. But hell, it'll be so worth it when the new operation gets up at running. Starting, of course, with you."

With me? Why with me? What did that mean?

Everything was coming and going too quickly, and my head still ached with each bump of my pulse inside my skull. I remembered Reagan being upset that Emilio wanted to work with Tsyrinsky. I could see that conversation playing out in vague shapes if I focused on it. I'd been in the room. I couldn't remember why, but Emilio...he'd looked so annoyed. It was the first time I wondered about the longevity of their friendship.

Come on, Lila. Think.

I dropped my head, feigning exhaustion, which, of course, wasn't hard at all. Focusing on a speck of black burned into the concrete, I let the memory play out in my head.

They had been in Emilio's office. Reagan had objected to working with Tsyrinsky. Emilio had been silently furious. He'd clearly wanted what that guy offered. But Reagan...he had been so shocked by the suggestion. The look on his face was...disgusted. Why had Reagan been so put off? He'd said something like, "I won't be a party to it. I have to draw the line somewhere..." and something about, "they're not guns or drugs, Emilio. They're—"

People.

Reagan had been disgusted because they were people.

I slowly lifted my head, and the pieces fell into place as my stare landed on my father once more. He was through "chatting" with me, his attention on Renzo now as they spoke too low for me to hear.

Emilio Carpinelli was broadening his financial investments. And hell, I knew the guy. It made sense. The man who'd raised me had always been very concerned about how far he could take the Family, how much he could grow our "market share" if you will.

So, he'd diversified, or he was in the process of it. And the latest venture he was adding to the portfolio was human fucking trafficking.

Fuck.

"So," I announced, breaking up the conversation being had a few feet from me, "are you selling me directly to Tsyrinsky or does he have a different buyer lined up? If I'm going to be sold like all the other girls you've likely trafficked, I'd like to have a vague idea of what's in store."

Slowly, Emilio traced his stare toward me. When it hit, I stifled a shiver, the cold dread surging through my veins as I was met with the cruelest sneer I'd ever witnessed. There was nothing good in the man before me. And it couldn't even be said that he got some kind of sick joy out of this. No, Emilio looked impassive and collected.

This was just business to him.

"If you insist, though, you might change your mind about knowing your fate after this." Emilio sauntered closer until he was just a foot from me, leaning over so that he could stare directly into my eyes. "Tsyrinsky does have a special interest in you. I imagine that he'll keep you 'nearby' instead of shipping you out with the rest of them. So, good news, Lila. You'll be staying right here in Harmstead. Hell, you might even see that

Reagan of yours if Tsyrinsky parades you around one of his parties. Then again, perhaps not. Considering."

Nausea was everywhere, bile crawling up my throat in a terrible burn. I was inches from tossing up whatever I had in me right at Emilio's feet. The man was perfectly okay with me being used as a goddamn sex slave. How…how had I never seen who he truly was?

Wait, what did he say about Reagan?

A renewed sense of dread washed over me as my mind hovered around that word, "considering."

"What do you mean? What does Reagan have to do with this?"

Emilio actually laughed at that, tossing his head back as he stood up. "Don't act so coy. I could see something happening between the two of you for years now. I had to admit that I never did think that asshole would actually act on it, but what do you know?"

"There's no way you could possibly know that. Reagan and I have done nothing."

I wasn't letting him get roped into this. If he could get out of the Family quickly enough, Reagan might stand a chance. And there was no way that Emilio could go after Edward, not yet, not with everything Edward knew.

"You utter fucking moron. Do you think all assassins can do is kill people? They're pretty damn good at watching, too. And I've had several *fascinating* reports given to me since that first attempt."

Dammit. Fucking Joelle and whoever the fuck had sold me out. It made sense, of course, but how was I supposed to protect Reagan now?

Panic and indecision and the desperate urge to move battled for dominance within me. I needed to get out of here. I needed to find Reagan and Edward, and we *all* needed to get the fuck out of dodge. Emilio was going to sell me, I was going to be raped by some Russian mobster, and both Emilio and Renzo were going to take over the Family and ensure shit like that happened all the time.

I couldn't let it happen. I had to do something. But one more question nagged at me, and I risked asking it, hoping to at the very least buy myself some time.

"Why not kill me? Why bring me here if I'm such a nuisance? Surely Tsyrinsky would understand."

"I'm sure he would, but," Emilio pulled on the lapels of his suit jacket, straightened the fabric as he wandered back over toward where Renzo waited for him, "that wouldn't be taking advantage of some truly fantastic leverage I now have against Reagan."

I didn't respond, chewing on my lip so hard that I tasted copper. I couldn't break. There was no time, and I needed to do what I could to protect Reagan.

"Trust me, Lila. It doesn't matter what you do. That dog will come running for his little bitch, and when he does, I'll put him down. Tsyrinsky will come and collect you, and I'll head back home, rid of two very annoying problems."

"He's not that dumb. He won't just come running in here to get me. He doesn't like me that much."

My eyes were glassy and my throat tight as Emilio cocked his head. Deciding to approach me again for one last jab, he leaned forward again. The gesture made me feel tiny, and then Emilio's fingers were gripping the roots of my hair and craning my head back.

Genuine hatred radiated from him at that moment, and an expression of condescending irritation.

"You really don't get it, do you?" Emilio's hand shook with barely restrained rage. "That man has gone against direct orders in favor of keeping you...happy."

Disgust filled Emilio's voice on the last word, and the pain flared through my scalp, forcing out a tear even as I furiously fought against them.

"Reagan cares about very few people in this world, Lila. We've had that conditioned into us from the beginning. But I've never seen that asshole look at anyone the way he looks at you."

My head was shoved down, driving needles of pain through my neck and shoulders, which amplified the throbbing inside my skull.

"Don't bother with your pathetic attempts to keep him safe. He'll die, Tsyrinsky will take you, and I get my Family just how I like it—forever. Thanks to old Renzo here."

There was nothing left to say at this point. I knew Emilio. I knew when he'd made up his mind about something. The only solace I had was knowing that he hadn't seen Reagan and Edward together except for one time. Their connection was unknown to Emilio.

Blinking through tears, I was just able to look up as Emilio patted Renzo on the shoulder, and the guy walked toward me. Something dark and sadistic loomed in his eyes, and it wasn't the kind I enjoyed or consented to.

"What are you doing?" The question was reflexive, my voice so goddamn small as it left me.

"Having my fun. A bonus your father agreed to since I've been helping him with all this." Renzo took off his suit jacket, rolling up his sleeves, and panic exploded through my veins all over again. I fought against the ropes, thrashing wildly, and I kicked out at him. "What are you so worked up over, bitch. This is your fucking job, ain't it? No do as your fucking told and let me see if those rumors about you are true."

"Get away from me!" I screamed, glancing past Renzo to see my father walking off to the far end of the warehouse, not a single glance back at me. "Fuck off!"

Renzo's hand went to the small of his back, freeing a pistol from his waistband. He pressed the gun to my temple, and I seized up, the fear choking me.

"Hold still, cunt. You may be promised to Tsyrinsky, but he ain't gonna mind a few extra holes."

No, no, no. This isn't happening. Oh god...Don't come, Reagan. Just...run.

26
The Confession

Edward

I'd cut off the engine at the top of the gravel drive that led down to the warehouse. It was near the waterfront, and the smell of salt water and stale fish was way too fucking strong. Coasting in neutral along the decline, I maneuvered the car into the shadows, still a distance from the stout concrete building.

It was nondescript, made from stacks of oversized bricks in that drab gray color, and there were large windows at the top of the walls that were coated with grime and age. Any light inside the place would be dull and barely functional.

"Not a lot of options for a sneaky entrance. From what I can see," I pulled out my phone, using the camera as a pair of makeshift binoculars, "there are only the two ways in: back and front."

Reagan had been oddly quiet through the drive here, and I could guess why. Hell, I was on edge. Lila was in that fucking building with her shithole father and he'd planned on selling her. But my way of getting the tension out involved meticulously planning how we'd get in.

Unfortunately, all of the plans I'd come up with on the drive were shit now thanks to the limited access and inability to reach the windows.

"Any thoughts?"

I waited a full five seconds for Reagan to say anything.

"Alright, that's enough." Pushing back my seat so that I could properly lean over toward him in the passenger seat, I grabbed Reagan's chin, forcing him to look at me. "You're not going to protect her like this. We need to think of a way inside. Okay?"

It was soft dom as far as aggression went, but it was enough to get Reagan shaking his head, trying to right himself. He cleared his throat, yanking his chin away before glaring over at me and then the building.

"Fine. Two entrances. Emilio'll be at one. Renzo at the other. Renzo isn't as much of a threat. You could handle him."

"To what end, Reagan? You're holding out on me. Come on. Out with it."

His icy stare shifted down, becoming focused on the recently detailed carpet of my Taycan. Scientists had long determined that air did have mass, and right now, Reagan looked weighed down by it so much that he might actually crumble.

Risking another glare, I pulled Reagan's chin up again. "I can see something cooking in that head of yours. I'm not a child, Reagan. Just talk to me."

He scoffed, rolling his eyes at me as he pushed away my hand with his. His fingers lingered on mine for longer than usual, and I couldn't deny the pinch in my chest. Something was off, something was up, and I had a feeling I wasn't going to like it.

"They took Lila, and according to the tracker in Emilio's car, which I have to assume he knew I'd used, they're in there. They're still in there and they're waiting."

"For what?" I hated to ask.

"For me."

A chill worked down my spine, and I sat up straight in my seat. It took me only a moment to realize what Reagan was implying, and look at that. I'd been right. I *didn't* like this.

"No. That's a terrible idea."

Chuckling, Reagan glanced over with a smirk, his brow cocked. "What is? I haven't even told you yet."

"I know how your head works, asshole. You're going to go in the front to 'distract' them while I try to sneak in through the back. I don't like it. And we aren't doing it."

He scoffed, meeting my gaze again with an intensity now that felt wrong and…terrifying.

"Got any better ideas? Because I'm thinking you don't." Reagan reached into his jacket—to the holster I knew was strapped onto his back. He pulled his gun out, checking the ammo he'd fed into it less than thirty minutes ago. "He wants me. Emilio…he's been looking for a way to get rid of me. I knew it all this time, and now…he's figured out that I've slept with Lila. But he hasn't figured out how you're involved. You're the linchpin to this plan."

"It's a shit plan, and I don't want to do it." I sighed, pinching the bridge of my nose as a migraine built behind my eyes. "There has to be another way for us to get in there. Why can't we both sneak around back?"

The gun was back in his jacket, and Reagan turned toward me, putting his fist on the dash as he leaned forward, really looking to make his point.

"Lila. She's too vulnerable in that situation, and if we're both on one side with them near her, they can hurt her too quickly. I'm a damn good shot, but it'll be easier for them to get the drop on *us*. We can't have that."

The logic was sound, and, again, I hated it. I didn't want to move forward with this plan. There was a damn good chance that Reagan could get shot or even…

"And what if they shoot at you while I'm dealing with Lila? You got a bulletproof vest on under there that you didn't tell me about?"

"No. Look, Edward," Reagan eyed me, determination and something unreadable shining in his eyes, "I probably will get shot at. I expect to. But getting Lila to safety is more important. Besides, Emilio hasn't done wet work in some time. I'm banking on the fact that he's rusty."

"Rusty?! Are you serious? You could—"

But I stopped, the words stuck in my throat. Because I was about to say, you'll be killed. And something about that possibility cut through me like a blade. That couldn't happen. Reagan wasn't allowed to go and get himself killed.

And what exactly was with me that I felt that so strongly?

Dammit. I…Shit. This wasn't supposed to go this way. It's been a few months. There's no way. We've just been fucking. That's all…

I wasn't convincing myself. There was a way. It was possible. I did. I fucking cared for that bastard more than I'd cared for…anyone. And then there was Lila, pulling those same strings in my fucking heart.

The fear of losing either of them was enough to make me nauseous, the need to force out the nothing occupying my stomach really fucking strong.

"I know." I nodded, and Reagan mirrored the gesture, his posture relaxing. "I know we can't let anything happen to Lila. She's ours, and we protect what's ours. But you need to know that I can't watch you get killed, Reagan. It'll…it'll destroy me. You're *both* mine. I won't sacrifice one of you for the other. I need you both."

Reagan Terrasi, consiegliere for the mob, had a damn good poker face. He was excellent at remaining a stoic fuck. In fact, I didn't think I'd ever seen him truly rattled like he was today.

But nothing compared to the look on his face now.

"I will do this, but that means you have to do everything in your goddamn power to stay alive. You aren't leaving Lila behind, and you aren't leaving me. Understood?"

He was still frozen, his lips parted slightly as his brow remained raised at his hairline.

"Edward, I—"

"Don't. Don't you dare. We're all coming out of this together, and when it's all said and done, you're going to admit to Lila that you've been in love with her for years, and you're going to admit to me that this isn't just fucking."

There was a gun stuffed in the center console, and I took it out, ensuring it was loaded, and opened my door. As I got out, I turned around and peered into the car at Reagan, who was still frozen in place.

"We both love you, fucker." I cocked my head briefly, releasing a shakey exhale. "Now, let's go get our girl."

27
The Showdown

Reagan

I'd had no chance to say anything before Edward sprinted off to the back of the building, and our plan was in motion. With no other choice, I hurried toward the front. My gun thudded against my ribs as I jogged for the warehouse's main entrance.

At least, I assumed it was my gun. It very well could have been my heart beating against my ribs.

Probably both.

He fucking said—No, you don't have time for this.

I waited a good minute before I stepped out of the shadows and approached the front door, pounding on the steel entrance to let Emilio know I was here. It didn't take long before the door flew open.

The barrel of a gun was leveled at my chest as I locked eyes with my old boss, and I held up my hands.

"Hey there, friend." I cocked a brow, unable to keep the hatred from my voice. "You know, there were better ways to ask me to meet you."

Emilio only sneered back at me. I didn't know how I missed it. That evil glint in his eyes had been there since I'd first met him. I guess I just never thought he'd loose his venom on his own kid.

He asked me to protect her.

"And miss the show? No, no. I think I quite like how this turned out."

I stepped further inside, sneaking a glance over Emilio's shoulder. The back of the warehouse was so much darker than where we stood, the single working bulb overhead providing a dull yellow glow.

She was back there. Lila was back in that darkness somewhere, and I didn't have any eyes on Renzo. *Dammit.*

"She's your daughter." I flicked my eyes back to Emilio's face. "How could you do this to your own fucking daughter."

Scoffing, Emilio rolled his eyes. "I think you took that protector thing a bit too seriously. She was an asset. One that proved less than useful, and I'm here on the earth to make money, to ensure the Carpinelli Family reigns for decades and decades."

Nausea pulled at the edge, and I clenched my jaw, my fists balling up tight at my sides. I was going to put a fucking bullet in this asshole's head.

"So that's all it is? Money?" I jutted out my chin for a moment, keeping my senses on alert to make out any sounds of impending danger. "Seems like a waste. Why'd you even bother to have me protect her?"

"A marriage was a possibility—once. Lila saw fit to ensure that wasn't an option with her work at the club. Not everyone needs a virgin but none of the Families in this town want to be shackled to a slut they didn't make themselves."

The sound of grit moving beneath my feet boomed. It took everything I had to not rush the fucker. But I needed to know if Lila was safe. I wouldn't risk her.

"So, I'm afraid this is goodbye, old friend." Emilio grinned at me, gesturing with his gun toward the wall to my left. "Be a dear and stand over there so the clean up is easier."

Come on, Edward. Give me some kind of fucking sign.

I walked over to the side, turning so that I faced left. I was careful to be silent as I clicked open the snap on my holster. And soon as I had something to go on, I'd—

"Ahhh!"

The scream that pierced the ominous silence went straight through my spine. It forced my attention to the back of the warehouse again, and before my brain could catch up with my movements, I was pressing in that direction.

"Lila!"

A shot whizzed by, the bullet landing in the wall as it passed just a few inches in front of me. I was damn lucky. But then Emilio was sprinting toward me, his shoulders low to take me down into a tackle.

"Just kill her, Renzo!"

My stomach dropped, and I jerked my head toward the rear of the room again. I needed to get past Emilio first, however.

Just as he charged at me, I side-stepped and rolled forward. Emilio crashed to the ground without his target to absorb the impact. He was down but not out. Still, it was enough to start running for my girl.

I took off, and as I flew into the shadows, my eyes adjusted to the lack of light. There. Lila was just there. Tied to a chair. Renzo was over her, his hands on her.

His fucking hands were *on* her.

My vision tunneled and went red. I put everything I had into gunning it for him, and in moments, I was there, tackling Renzo to the ground. We hit with a heavy thud, the pain ricocheting up my shoulder. But the asshole was pinned beneath me, and I drove my fist into his face over and over until I was bucked off.

Blood streamed down Renzo's face as he glared at me. "You fucking cock-sucking prick! I'll fucking kill you."

"I would very much like to see you try."

Renzo rushed me, swinging wild and only just able to

connect with my jaw as I leaned backward. The blow was nothing, and I just smiled at the fuck, eager to tear his hands from his body.

Clang!

The sound of the back door opening forced my attention away from Renzo. Edward was there, and he rushed forward into the building toward Lila. If he'd only now gotten in, something had been wrong with that entrance. I didn't peg Emilio as smart enough to check it, and it wasn't like there were keys lying around.

It was fucking jammed? Amazing. Just our fucking luck.

A fist collided with my face, Renzo using my distraction to land a solid punch. I reeled back, shaking myself into focus before the next blow hit. I caught his hand this time and cranked it backward before shoving the little shit to the ground.

Copper flooded my mouth, and I spat on the floor, a blob of red splattering across the concrete.

"You hit like an elderly fucking woman."

Renzo glared, but it was fine. I needed his attention on me. I needed the fucker focused right here so that Edward could get Lila free.

I'd barely had a chance to look at her after tackling Renzo, and as I took this brief opportunity to do so, my heart felt like it was being ripped out through my chest.

She was disheveled, her hair and clothes a mess of frizzed-out locks and rumpled fabric. Her eyes met mine, and I held them. I held them with everything in me as I offered the barest hint of a nod.

It's going to be okay. Go with Edward.

Unless Lila possessed mind-reading abilities I wasn't aware of, she couldn't hear me. But she read the subtle change in my eyes, and the slick sheen coating hers doubled down.

"You're fucking dead!"

Launching at me again, Renzo charged, sloppy and inaccurate. I leaned back on my right foot, cocking my fist and waiting until just the right moment. When he was in range, I swung forward, smashing my fist into his nose with the force of a jackhammer.

Renzo went down, collapsing to the floor. He mumbled explitives, but his nostrils were red fucking waterfalls, and he couldn't stand up.

"You know," I stood above him, pulling out my gun from my holster, "I really hate long goodbyes."

Aiming the gun at his head, Renzo's eyes went wide. A stream of pleas for his life tumbled from his blood-stained lips, and I heard none of them. There was no mercy to be delivered today.

"No one touches what's mine."

The crack of the gun going off echoed through the warehouse just as Edward got Lila free from the chair. Renzo's body jerked as the bullet passed through him, and it was done.

"Good fucking riddance."

I lowered my arm, and then from the side, a small body hurtled into mine. My arm was around Lila in a blink, and I hauled her against my chest, breathing her in. It felt damn good to have her in my arms.

"He...Thank you." Lila sounded exhausted as she spoke, and I craned back to look down at her. "Oh my god, if you hadn't come, I—"

"None of that. We're here." I lowered my face into the crook of her neck, surrounded by all those curls. "*I'm here.*"

After a few seconds, Lila stood up. She wiped her fingers under her eyes, cleaning up the mess of her running mascara, and smiled.

"Let's get the fuck out of here."

I smiled, taking her hand and leading us toward the front door. "Sure thing, princess."

Edward stepped in line beside me, leaning on my shoulder. "I swear to god that door was a thing of evil. I had to throw my entire body at it. At least Lila's ropes were child's play. Renzo clearly didn't know anything about shibari."

Crack!

Another boom echoed through the warehouse, and I looked down at my gun. I hadn't fired it. What had—

"Reagan!"

Lila's high-pitched wail knifed through my spine just as the pain flared through my upper left shoulder. I pitched into her, the burning agony making it difficult to stand. Immediately, sweat poured from me, my vision going a little hazy. But there, up ahead, just coming into view from his position hiding in a shadow, was Emilio.

I've known that prick since we were kids, and he shot me. That friendship—

"Aww, fuck." I dipped, my left leg going out as warmth oozed from my chest.

The ground was coming up to meet me fast, and I wasn't processing right. Emilio had hit something juicy, and I was leaking like a damn sieve. Blurry images in front of me showed Lila doing her best to keep me from hitting the floor, her tiny frame trapped under my arm. Edward was rushing forward, and the loud "oof" that echoed confirmed I was actually seeing him tackle Emilio.

The gun went clattering off to the side, and Edward's shoe kicked it even further away.

"No, no, no." Lila's frantic words pulled my attention back down to her. "Reagan, come on. Please. You can't."

I groaned, reaching for the floor so I could just sit and not worry about my legs giving out beneath me. Small hands pressed into my shoulder roughly, and the pain jolted me back into the moment, at least for the time being.

"Fuck!" I shook my head, trying to focus on Lila's face.

"I'm alright. Just my shoulder. Make sure Edward is alright."

Holding my arm up was a no-go, so I took my gun from my own hand with the other and pressed it to Lila's chest.

"Shoot that fucker for me, will ya?"

"Reagan, I—"

"Go," I growled, using what energy I had to give urgency to the word. "Don't let Emilio out of here alive."

Lila's eyes were wide, saucers in her face, and they leaked streams of clear liquid that looked like they might never stop. But she nodded, her hand wrapping around the gun.

The world got blurry on me again, but Lila was pressing her lips to mine, and damn, the feel of that girl. God, I loved it. It was everything. *She* was everything—my little spitfire.

Then, she was gone, rushing forward with the gun raised toward her father and Edward.

Crack! Crack!

Two shots rang out, and the commotion that was constant from Edward and my ex-boss died abruptly. I was slumping further down, crumpling to the floor as I watched Edward pull away from Emilio, his clothes mussed and his lip bleeding.

To my lover's credit, Edward had left several large red spots on Emilio's face. I cackled to myself. *Serves you right, you traitorous douche.*

"Check on him." Lila's voice was loud, echoing through the room, and then Edward was rushing toward me.

Even half-passed out, I could feel the tension and fury rage higher like a towering flame as Lila approached her father, gun raised and pointed directly at his head. Her arm didn't even shake.

Lila was in her bare feet, only wearing a t-shirt. It hardly covered her, and the filth and blood that smeared across the hem of her tee coated her skin. The messy bun she'd stuffed those curls into at some point was lopsided now, hanging more to the right side.

And she was as beautiful as ever. I memorized the way she looked…in case I wouldn't be seeing her again.

"Reagan, stay with me." Edward was close, his voice right above me, and I blinked up at him. "You're not fucking dying on me, asshole. Stay here."

He sounded so furious, so over my shit, and I could hardly blame him. Edward's bangs were hanging limply across his forehead. He was sweaty too. But those hazel eyes. Damn, they were so fucking pretty, these swirls of green and brown and blue against his warm tan skin.

I patted his cheek. "Eh, you'll be fine."

"I absolutely will not."

Crack!

Another shot rang out, and we both turned to see Emilio crumple to his ass, his left leg giving out and dripping the red stuff just like I was.

"You fucking piece of shit." Lila walked closer to her father, her eyes blazing as she let the anger take over. "You were going to kill me, to sell me, and now you've shot the man who stood by your side as your friend for decades. The man who stood by *my* side my entire life!"

Another squeeze of that trigger and a new hole was punched through Emilio's other leg. Lila didn't let up, closing on Emilio until she was standing right in front of him as he lay useless on the cement floor.

Red puddles swelled beneath my former friend's body, and even if she didn't put a bullet in his brain, Emilio was done for.

"I am not a commodity. No human is. I was your fucking daughter. And I won't let you take another goddamn thing from me."

A shaky, blood-covered hand reached up for her. "Please, Lila. Please, I promise I won't—"

"Won't what? Let someone try to rape me again? Kill one of

the two most important people in my life? Kill both of them?"

Lila shook her head, her arm dropping only slightly. "I was never good enough for you. I was never going to be enough because all you care about is money and power. I don't know how Mom even married you, let alone let you get her pregnant. But it doesn't fucking matter—"

"Lila, don't do this!"

"   because you're done, old man. Me, this family, Reagan. We don't belong to you anymore. You lost."

With her eyes back on Emilio, Lila leveled the gun perfectly for the crease between his brows, smirking.

"So go fuck yourself, you sick bastard."

"Li—"

Crack!

The final shot rang out through the warehouse, and Emilio was dead.

Silence and the smell of gunpowder lingered in the air, and then Lila collapsed to her knees, the sobs she'd been holding in breaking through. It only took a moment for her to realize Edward and I were still behind her. She ran over, and suddenly that gorgeous face was clear in my vision.

"Reagan! Oh fuck. We need to get him somewhere." Lila turned to Edward. "A car. You have a car, right?"

"We do. I'll get it. Call the house doctor. I'm sure the number is on your phone." Lila nodded, and Edward took off, calling over his shoulder. "Use my jacket! Pressure on the wound!"

Reality wavered at that point, and I just looked up into Lila's face as she tried to wrap the sleeves of Edward's suit coat around my shoulder. It burned, but my head was lolling, too hard to keep upright.

"Reagan, don't you fucking dare. I didn't just kill my father to see you die."

A muted, dull chuckle left me as my eyes began to close. "That was a hell of a sight, princess. Almost perfect as far as last ones go."

"Reagan." Lila's voice was a warning, and then she was holding my face, forcing hers into my view.

"Ah, there it is. Perfection."

My entire body was racked with the shakes, but I brushed my fingers along her jaw, trailing red over her pristine skin before the darkness melted in.

"Reagan? Reagan!"

Lila

"**B**eep, fucking beep." I rolled my eyes. "I can't believe we even have that."

My voice was shaky, this rattle to it that suggested I might start to cry at any moment. I hated it, but it was incredibly accurate. I was about to cry–again. Apparently, there was no end to the number of tears I could shed.

"You have your Family to thank for that." Sloane, our Familia doctor, eyed me, his mismatched gaze too bright in my face. "And I'm fucking grateful for it so I know what's going on. Now, shush."

He was working, doing fuck if I knew, to assess Reagan's current status. We'd gotten him back to the house faster than I thought possible, but everything had slowed down so much once the resident doc had gotten a hold on the crisis. Val had let us in, his eyes the picture of shock.

"Holy fucking shit. You did it. Christ!" He'd seen Reagan at that point. *"Sloane!"*

That had been, what…an hour ago? Less? It was so damn hard to tell.

Sloane's equipment was reading Reagan's vitals, and

his heart was beating. Slowly, but it was. There were other lines on the screen, too. But I didn't know what they meant. I was pretty sure Sloane had tried to tell me, but I couldn't remember. I could hardly think.

"He's going to be fine, Lila."

I jumped as Edward's hand found mine. He was standing behind me as I sat in a chair, pulled up to the side of Reagan's bed. I'd forgotten he was there. *Ugh, that's such a shit move, Lila. Christ.*

"I'm sorry." I looked up at Edward, and dammit, my eyes glossed over just looking at him. "Your face. Are you sure you're okay?"

Edward held my hand as I reached up to his cheek, smirking. "You think this is my first fight? I'll be fine. And so will Reagan. He has too much to say to me, to both of us, for him to get out of it."

I chuckled, absorbing the warmth of Edward's presence. "I'm really fucking glad you're okay. I...I really care about you, Boss Man. I'd be even more of a wreck if you weren't here."

Narrowing his eyes and looking right into my stare, Edward hit me with a look that was so damned intense that I shifted in my seat.

"I love you, too, princess."

If that monitor had been hooked up to me, I was pretty sure it would have shown my heart stopping for a good ten seconds. All the air left my lungs, and I coughed when I tried to breathe in, choking on my own spit.

"Oh, don't look so surprised. I already told Reagan. I would have told you earlier, but there was a shoot-out in progress. Priorities."

Flying up out of my chair, I planted a hard kiss on Edward's lips. "I love you. I... holy fuck. This is...my head is fucking spinning."

"That's very adorable, would you please take your conversation somewhere else?" Sloane glared at us. "It's impossible to hear thoracic sounds with you yapping."

The doc had alwasy been a bit of a dick. Honestly, I'd always assumed it was why he had such an antagonistic relationship with Reagan. They were both stubborn assholes, and neither one of them was going to budge.

Edward looked over at Slonae, sending one of his classic "boss" looks his way.

"Could we have a few minutes with Reagan?" His tone might have been level, but the slight squint to his eyes and the aura of darkness Edward radiated were anything but. "I'm fairly certain he's stable right now, and we will scream if something happens."

"Who the fuck do you think—"

"We need a few moments with the new don. Get. The. Fuck. Out."

Sloane jerked backward, scanning Edward with a silent, "who the fuck is this guy?" But there was intrigue laced behind the man's blue and green eyes, an expression of reluctant respect.

"I'll hear that monitor. A beep goes awry, and I'm inside in two seconds." Sloane headed for the door, grabbing Val, who stood watchfully in the corner, and hauling him out along with him. "You have five minutes, fuckers."

"Why am I leaving?" Val raised a hand, gesturing at me with his eyebrows up. "I did fuck all. In fact, I got her damn dog to the fucking vet."

"And I'm really super grateful for that, Val!" I called out as he was dragged away. "And for this!"

When the room was empty and quiet, aside from that fucking beeping, Edward shoved me back down into the chair and angled me toward Reagan.

"He's right there, baby. I think you need to talk to him when you know he won't interrupt you."

"I..."

But my objection faded away as I looked from Edward to Reagan. He looked so vulnerable lying in his bed, all hooked up with those numerous wires. My eyes burned as I stared at him, and every time I blinked, I saw the bullet slicing through his shoulder, the blood that leaked from him, and dripped down his shirt.

"This is really fucking hard." I sucked in, my entire body shaking, and Edward put a hand on my shoulder, offering his silent support. "You really weren't supposed to come, Reagan. I begged in my head for you *not* to come because I knew my dad was going to try to kill you."

The image of blowing my father's brains out replaced that of Reagan lying on the concrete, bleeding out.

"I hated him for so long. I hated you a bit, too. You were his second, his consiegliere, and jesus fuck, you were so *damned* protective. Controlling and bossy and stubborn...I think that was your way of saying you care. You need to work on that."

Leaning onto the bed, I took Reagan's hand. It was warm against my palm, which I supposed meant something. It was also rough and still stained with dried blood. All of us were. We'd yet to change or shower after all.

"Such a grumpy bastard. *The* grumpiest. When did things change? When did you go from the asshole who never let me do anything to one of my two favorite people on the planet?"

A choked sob left me, and I tried to breathe around it. Edward's thumb shifted back and forth across my skin, a soothing gesture that solidified how much he cared. My lungs filled comfortably again, and I shook my head, sniffling up the signs of the emotion breakdown in place.

"It wasn't just sleeping with you. Over the years...I've grown to rely on you. You've always been there, orders or no. So, I need you to be okay. I need you to wake up and be that grumpy asshole again."

I pulled my eyes away from Reagan to look at Edward. "We *both* need you."

When I shifted my gaze back to my godfather, one of the two men I'd fallen in love with, I let the tears slide down my cheeks, not bothering to wipe them up.

"And I love Edward, too, so you better be cool with that."

Edward chuckled behind me, and I felt his lips pressing into the top of my head as he leaned over, closing my eyes to drink it all in. The sensation felt right, necessary. And I knew without a shadow of a doubt that it was these two men. I was choosing them, and that was that.

They were mine.

"I can't believe you love that stuffy asshole."

My eyes flew open, Edward's kiss leaving me abruptly. Reagan's voice was raspy and quiet, but it was him. It was that same attitude—the same penchant for sarcasm.

"Reagan!"

Leaping out of my chair, I jumped up onto the bed and threw my arms around his neck. Reagan flinched, hissing as I jostled him. I knew that it probably stung. Hell, it could hurt like a bitch, but I didn't care. I needed to feel him against me.

Edward laughed behind me, then circled the bed to the other side. When I looked up at him with a huge fucking grin, he smiled back and then turned his hazel stare on Reagan.

Planting his hands on Reagan's face, Edward pulled him forward, planting a kiss right on his mouth.

A little yelp of surprise left me, and my godfather's eyes blew wide, his pupils dilating. The kiss was profound, and when Edward finally released him, Reagan was gaping up at the man in utter shock.

"I hadn't done that yet." He smiled, very satisfied with himself. "You owed me one."

It took a good ten seconds before Reagan could do anything

but lie there nonplussed, and I giggled at him, giving him a kiss of my own since it certainly did seem like the thing to do. Edward got one, too. It was only fair.

"I…Jesus." Reagan shook himself. "This has been a fucking day, hasn't it?" We laughed at him, but his expression shifted, focusing on both Edward and me so intently, his brows knitting together. "Edward hit me with a similar brick before we got you out of that warehouse. And after thinking I was dead, I wake up to hear you doing the same."

My cheeks heated, but there was no way in hell I was taking any of it back.

"Apparently, it's the day for fucking confessions all around." Reagan tried to scoot up on the bed, hissing when his shoulder kicked up a jolt of pain. "Stupid fucking bullet wound. I'm so ready for this thing to be gone."

"Reagan, it's been three hours." Edward glared playfully at him, cocking a brow.

"Three hours too many. Ugh," he sighed, pinning us down with those stern, deep brown eyes of his, "I suppose I do owe you. But you should know I'm not fucking good at this shit. I've never said any of what I'm about to say to you to anyone. *An-y-one.*"

"Get on with it, Daddy." I winked at him, chewing my lip as Reagan's stare darkened all the more.

"I've been looking after you for years, Lila. I don't know when the switch flipped either, but it did. I…I can't think about my life without you in it. You're a brat and pain in the ass—"

"Hey!" I wacked his good shoulder.

"But you're *my* pain in the ass. *My* brat." He looked up to Edward. "*Ours.*"

The tears were stinging my eyes again, but I didn't say anything, letting Reagan finally get out all the things he probably thought he might not get the chance to say.

Reagan's stare flicked between the two of us. "I want nothing more than to be with the two of you for the rest of my days. I'll do whatever it takes to keep both of you safe." Now, his eyes focused on Edward. "As for you, I knew you were a problem the moment I saw you. The connection was instant, and when it started to become more...I'll admit that scared the shit out of me. But something about almost dying puts things into perspective."

Edward and I laughed, my tears spilling over as Edward settled himself on the bed, creating a little sandwich with Reagan right in the middle.

Sucking in a deep breath, Reagan shut his eyes, lingering there for a moment before he open them again, a glassy coating shimmering in the soft lightning. He looked so beautiful like that, open, expressive, and I reached up, tucking a strand of his long hair behind his ear.

"I love you both, which is some kind of fucking miracle."

Again, we were laughing, and I crashed my lips into his again. Edward was right there after me, kissing us both as we overflowed with emotion and gratitude.

"You both already know I love you," Edward whispered. "But I'll say it as many times as either of you likes. I love you. I love you."

"I'm sorry I couldn't tell you at the same time as Edward, but your dumb ass was unconscious." Reagan narrowed his eyes on me, pinching my chin as his hungry stare ate me up. "But I love you, Reagan. And I want that, too. I want this."

I hugged them both against me, and for a time, who knew how long, we all just lay there in the bed holding each other. When the door to Reagan's room opened and Sloane came in, we all glanced back at him. His eyes were wide, but for once, he didn't open that big fat mouth and make some comment about things.

"Good." Reagan glanced between Edward and me, then

up at Sloane. "Because this Family is going to be a lot of changing."

"Get your fucking clothes off. *Now.*"

Reagan hadn't let any of them get more than a foot into their shared room before shoving me down to my knees and making Edward sit on the edge of the bed.

We'd all moved into my room, knocking down a few walls to make room, and the "master suite" had been converted into a proper medical bay. It had only been about a month, but everything in the house had changed.

Not the least of which was who was in charge.

"You're so bossy." I smirked up at Reagan, chewing on my bottom lip. "You sure you're *up* for this, Daddy?"

Dragging my eyes down his body, I could very well see that he was, but Reagan and Edward had been edging me for thirty days now, and if we were finally going to do this, I was pulling my brat card out and not putting it away.

A low growl rumbled out from Reagan's chest, and he took a step closer. Pinching my chin between his forefinger and thumb, he squeezed, eyeing me hard.

"We've established some new ground rules, Lila. If you don't think you can handle any of them, speak now or forever hold your peace."

We had. In fact, we'd all added quite a number of things to our list of yeses and maybes, and there was no way in hell I was punking out on any of them. I was desperate.

Plus, Edward refused to fuck me until Reagan could join in. A show of solidarity.

Asshole.

"Absolutely not."

I adjusted my position, becoming the picture of the perfect

submissive for him as I spread my knees wide and arched forward, putting my hands behind my back because I knew he liked it.

But not without flipping Reagan off first.

Edward's fist found my hair behind me, gripping the curls at the root and craning my head back.

"You're such a little brat." He kissed me as I was forced into the awkward position, nearly toppling over. "I'm sure we're *both* going to have a lot of fun with that."

Reagan and Edward had decided that during this next scene, this first one since Reagan had been shot, they would both be acting as Dom. It was an unspoken understanding that my men needed to feel what it was like to have this level of power, but I'd made one addendum.

"As long as I get to see you choke on Daddy's cock, right, Boss Man?"

Yeah, this was going to be fucking fun.

Edward yanked on my head again before tossing it forward. As I righted myself, looking up at Reagan, I realized he'd gotten much closer to me, his cock freed through his downed zipper.

My pussy clenched hard, already dripping at the sight of him. I hadn't been allowed to touch myself at all, and even though both Reagan and Edward could tease me, they never took it to completion.

I was fucking *frantic* for an orgasm. Or fifty.

Instinctively, I reached up for Reagan's cock, but he slapped my hand away and then dealt another to my cheek. The burn was so quick that I actually gasped, and I had to remind myself that I'd said yes to this—*emphatically*.

"Ah, ah." Reagan shook his head, clucking with his tongue in that demeaning way I absolutely adored. "I'll take care of this while you do a few things for me, princess."

"Like what?"

I sneered at him, and Reagan was quick to change his expression, his face becoming this imposing image of someone who was *not* amused.

"You still have clothes on. So does Edward." He leaned over me, stroking his cock inches from my mouth, which fucking watered. "Fix it."

Like lightning, I got naked, flinging the tiny black panties and bra I'd been wearing somewhere in the room. Edward was next, and he absolutely didn't help me as I struggled to undo his buckle and get his pants off.

"Struggling, princess?" He smirked, his eyes sparkling. "Come on, get those little fingers to work faster."

I did everything I could to do just that, fumbling and managing to stab myself in the finger with the pin on Edward's belt. But his pants were off, and his shirt was next. That was an easier prospect.

Gripping the two halves of his button-down, I found the midpoint and wrenched the fabric apart. Buttons flew everywhere as I tore Edward's shirt open. All I could do was smile. I'd been training to get strong just so I could do this very thing.

Checked off the bucket list.

"Whoops."

Edward looked down at me, and the expression he wore was like nothing I'd ever seen before. Reagan chuckled—all dark and menacing—and then Edward was bucking me off his lap and back down onto the floor.

"This was an expensive shirt, princess."

I smiled, so ready for this next part. "I'll buy you another one."

His eyes lit up, and damn, it felt so fucking good to say that. I was golden. These two incredible men could do whatever the hell they wanted to me now, because I was on cloud fucking nine.

Because *I* got to use *their* line.

Then suddenly, I was dragged across the floor, presumably by Reagan, and then flipped over so I was looking up into my handsome godfather's face. Goddamn, he was pretty, and I told his as much often enough that I didn't think he needed to hear it right now.

"Can I help you?"

Reagan was clearly done with my shenanigans because he just eyed me, pointing at the floor. I knew he wanted me to get into the kneeling position again, and I obliged, flipping him another bird, of course.

His eyes narrowed, and I had to admit that the level of intensity that was radiating off him was enough to get me swallowing hard. It was possible that I'd gone just a hair too far.

Too late now.

Reagan walked up to me, putting his patent leather shoe between my knees. I had my hands clasped behind me again, but he ran his eyes across my arms and shook his head.

"Hands behind your head, brat."

I did as told, not pushing it this time.

"Good girl." He leaned forward, putting his face in mine so there was no way to ignore him. "For once. Now…"

The silence hung, and I knew he was testing me. God, I wanted to say something, but dammit, I was already in trouble. I knew that well enough.

"…lick my shoe, slut."

My mouth fell open. "What?"

"Did I fucking stutter?" Reagan grabbed me by the hair, forcing me to bend over so that my lips pressed against the leather. "Lick. My. Fucking. Shoe."

I trembled, my traitorous pussy pulsing. I was such a whore for Reagan's brutal commands, the way he used me, made me do whatever he wanted. Arousal dripped from me.

Trepidatiously, I extended my tongue and dragged it across the shiny leather of Reagan's shoe. It was pretty clean, a lot if you considered it was a fucking shoe, but there was still the lingering taste of sweat.

"Good girl."

The praise lit me up, and I cursed that damn part of me for being so easy to manipulate—but not much.

"Now, ride it. Ride my fucking shoe like the desperate whore you are."

My cunt clamped down, and I shifted without dropping my arms from behind my head. I knew I was supposed to keep them there, and I was aching for some contact. I'd been so pent-up, I didn't care if I looked like a wanton hussy for being this damn excited to straddle Reagan's fucking loafer.

Crawling over the top of the toe, I lowered myself down until my lips split over the rounded edge of Reagan's shoe. I rubbed myself across it, the sensation so goddamn good for how starved for it I was. It was several seconds of thrusting against his foot before Reagan hummed to himself, satisfied.

"That's enough."

Reluctantly, I pulled back, a tiny whimper leaving me as I had to stop the build-up of pleasure that was coursing through my veins.

"Oh, look at that. The little slut got my shoe all dirty. Better clean it up, princess."

"You're such a dick." I glared up at him, but it was hardly at full strength, the need and enjoyment swirling with the irritation and humiliation.

Reagan leaned forward again, taking my chin in his hand and squeezing. He upped the power until I was whining, and then chuckled.

"You love it."

God, I fucking did.

His thumbs found the hollows of my cheeks, and Reagan

forced my mouth open.

"Hold out your tongue."

I did as asked, having a feeling I knew what was coming and buzzing from it all the same.

With a smirk, Reagan spat on my outstretched tongue, his saliva mixing with my own and smearing over my chin.

"In case you need help getting my shoe clean."

With that he shoved my head down, and I diligently went to work licking my cum off the leather. The taste of myself was a drug, making my nerves fire wildly with need.

The noise of stroking nearly pulled my eyes up to Reagan, but I wasn't tempting him to stop by not finishing my work. He *was* a dick, and Daddy wouldn't hesitate to pull me away and stuff me somewhere. And I needed to come too badly. Hell, doing this to his fucking shoe was getting me pretty damn close—the degradation intense but undeniably hot.

"Do you think our princess is being a good girl, slave?" Reagan spoke above me like I wasn't even there, adding to the hot burn in my cheeks.

"I do, Master." Edward moved behind me, the sound of the bed adjusting so loud in my oversensitive ears. "And she's *dripping* for us, too."

"Oh, is she now?" I could hear the smile in Reagan's voice. "Well then, why don't you give yourself a treat. You've been such a good boy waiting to fuck her until I could join you."

Without any further prompting, Edward's hands found my ass and spread me wide, his tongue plunging into my soaking folds. I gasped, reeling back before I had the sense to get my tongue back on that leather.

Even still, I groaned against it, rubbing myself up and down over Edward's mouth. Needles of sensation—spearing and potent—tingled through my clit. I whimpered, digging my fingers into the fluffy cream carpet beneath me.

"*Please*," I begged, the word muffled by Reagan's shoe.

Reagan threaded his fingers through my hair, yanking me up to look at him.

"Please, what? Daddy's little princess needs to use her words."

I was fucking tearing up. Who the fuck was I? But the ache between my legs was too goddamn much. I was going to explode if I didn't come soon. I wasn't even sure I could stop it if Edward let me get too close.

"Please let me come, Daddy. I *need* to."

His sadistic smile was a thing of beauty, and god, I was trembling from head to toe.

"Do you? Do you really need to *that* bad?" He gripped my locks tighter.

"Yes!" I sobbed, Edward's tongue swirling as his fingers probed my pussy and asshole, stretching both so that I would be ready for them.

We'd talked about this after all. I was going to take both their cocks, and even just thinking about it while Edward was teasingly eating me out was almost enough to shove me over the edge.

"Oh, princess." Reagan craned my head back farther, making my hands come up off the ground. "How about this? I'll make a deal with you."

"Ugh!" Squeeled, trying to hold back the orgasm as Edward sucked my clit into his mouth and my irritation flared brighter. "What!"

"Haha." That damned chuckle again. "You suck Daddy's cock, you make it so damn good, and I'll let you come. Not only that, I'll give you a present."

I nodded before the hungry words came out, only half hearing Reagan mention a gift afterward. He was a crafty asshole and that could be any number of things including what all sane people might consider punishment.

But I loved me some good punishment.

Going for his cock, I took it from Reagan's hand, stuffing the entire thing into my mouth roughly. I sucked. I sucked like my damn life depended on it, pulling out all the stops. Toying with the head, running my tongue along the underside of his shaft, taking his balls between my lips, and humming as I ran my hand up and down the length.

He groaned, fucking into my fist, and Edward—savior that he was—turned up the attention on my pussy. He slipped to fingers inside me as his tongue swirled around my clit. Then, as if that weren't enough, he used his other hand to shove two fingers into my ass.

My leg was craned up over his shoulder, and I could hardly keep my balance, but oh god, it was incredible.

"Shit, shit, shit!"

The words tumbled out as Edward furiously devoured me, and I stroked Reagan's cock clumsily as the pleasure ratcheted up higher and higher.

"Don't you dare come without my cock in your mouth, little slut."

I was forced onto his shaft roughly, taking Reagan until he hit the back of my throat.

Fuuuuck.

Everything blurred, and I swallowed his inches with everything I had, bobbing my head. Edward's fingers thrust into me in time with my strokes, and the world dropped away. All that there was were the sensations drilling through me like a hot poker.

I was right there. I was right on the damn edge, and then Reagan's cock twitched against my tongue, thickening even more so that I was good and choked on his massive erection.

Edward was observant in all things, and in the bedroom, that only doubled down. He noticed how I tensed up, how Reagan's face must have changed in the few seconds Edward had gone up for air, and he returned to my clit, sucking it hard while he hooked his fingers into my G-spot.

I gushed, coming and squirting all over his mouth.

It was the first time I'd ever actually squirted, not just a gentle trickle that oozed out of me. Apparently, being that worked up was one hell of a motivator.

Flying over the cliff, I came so hard I saw stars, and then warmth gushed down my throat, Reagan's spend coating my tongue. He tasted so good, so much more so since it had been so long since I'd had him.

Sure, to other people, a few weeks was probably nothing. But I'd almost lost him. I'd nearly lost both of them—the men I loved—and I had needed to feel them both like this as much as I needed air.

I'd been suffocating for too long, and now, I could finally breathe.

"Ugh, fuuuck." Reagan pumped into me, spilling more of his cum across my tongue before he pulled back and painted my lips. "That's such a good little slut. So good for Daddy."

The praise was the cherry on the cake, letting my own climax last for several moments. When the moment did slow down, Reagan released my hair and patted my cheek. My leg was next, Edward setting it down gently.

Crawling around in front of me, Edward stole my face, pressing his lips to mine. The bit of Reagan's cum that I hadn't swallowed mixed with my own as Edward entwined his tongue with mine. The taste was pure sinful delight, and I knew we were only beginning.

"Get on the bed. Both of you." Reagan smiled through his hungry glare, starting to shuck his clothes and leaving them in a pile on the floor.

The three of us wound together in a tangle of limbs, naked and nibbling and kissing any inch of skin we could get at. I could just picture us, this mass of rutting bodies too high on sex to care about anything else.

It was so *fucking* amazing.

"Are you ready, princess?" Edward crooned in my ear, his cock rubbing against my thigh. "Are you ready to take us both?"

"Yess," I hissed, groaning when Edward reached between my legs and found my clit, rubbing it briskly.

I was so sensitive, so previously starved for touch, that even though I'd just climaxed, I was already barreling toward another one.

"Suck Edward's cock, princess. Make my slave feel so good as I get your ass good and slick."

Oh. So that's who was going where.

A part of me wanted to giggle. I knew Reagan was a fan of my ass, of asses in general, so it made sense, and damn, I *was* going to need to be slick if I was going to take his thick cock there.

Leaning on my elbows, I reached for Edward's dick, opening my mouth and sliding him in until I couldn't take another inch. His head kicked back, his fingers lacing in my hair and gripping tightly. He groaned slowly pumping into me, and then I felt Reagan's tongue teasing my asshole.

He held my cheeks apart with his hands, using his thumb to stretch me and smear his saliva across my skin. My flesh was on fire. I was going to come from just this wicked delight alone.

"Oh, fuuuck. Daddy...*please*," I whined, begging with everything I had.

"Oh, ho, ho," he chuckled, "and now Daddy's princess is begging for my cock in her ass? Where'd my little brat go?"

He continued teasing me, and Edward held my mouth clamped around his dick, not letting me up to answer. I groaned, whimpering and screaming muffled complaints as I bounced my hips on the bed in some vain attempt to get more sensation.

"There she is." Reagan shoved his thick fingers into my ass, and I yelped before it melted into a grateful moan. "Fuck my fingers, baby girl. Fuck them so good while I lube you up."

I heard the flick of a bottle, completely unaware of when Reagan had grabbed it. It didn't matter, though. I was fucking myself on his fingers like my life depended on it, swallowing Edward's cock until I tasted the tell-tale salt of his precum.

Reagan worked me through a *brutal* climax just as Edward came, shooting his spend down my throat. Both my men had mastered going back to back, and I knew this was the lead-up to taking them both inside me.

In a flash, I was yanked away from Edward and hauled up so that I was being held in Reagan's hands like they were a seat. Edward grinned like a drunk fool as he crawled up to me immediately, taking my legs so that they hung right at the crook of his elbows.

My thighs were split wide like this, my ass and pussy up for grabs. Edward's blunt head rubbed against my seam, and I whimpered, unable to do anything but take it. Between the two of them, it was as good as being bound in ropes, the ability to move utterly stolen from me as Edward notched his cock at my entrance. At the same time, Reagan wrapped a massive hand around my throat and restricted my breathing.

"You're going to take everything we give you, little slut. You're going to look Edward dead in the eyes as he stuffs his cock into that tight pussy, and you're not going to say a damn word."

Reagan was truly back, and my heart soared even though anyone else might think we were insane. I knew all of this came from his intense desire, from both of theirs, and I wanted nothing more than to give myself over to it.

I nodded.

Still grinning at me, though now his eyes sparkled with sadistic delight, Edward sheated himself deep into my cunt, thrusting in until he bottomed out. I wanted to scream, but between the order and the hold on my neck, all I could do was suck in a sharp intake of air.

"Oh, princess," Edward groaned, pumping in and out, "you're squeezing my cock so fucking good."

The dance continued for a few moments more before Reagan growled low, the feeling of it in his chest rumbling through the skin of my back.

"Stop, slave. Stay right there as I fill our princess completely."

His face contorting from the effort, Edward forced himself to hold still. I whined, rocking myself as little as I could because I wanted more, so much more. He gritted his teeth, his brow furrowing as he reached up for my face and crashed his lips on mine.

"You're such a naughty thing, making it so hard for me to obey." Edward nibbled on my lip, reaching down to tweak a nipple hard enough to get me gasping again.

My brain was a mess, struggling to process all the incredible sensations as my body still cried out for more. Edward kissed me hard, and then I felt Reagan's hand massaging my ass. He slipped a finger inside, then two, stretching me until his cock nudged against me.

Like I was made for him—for them—Reagan thrust himself home, and suddenly, both of them were seated inside me. I squirmed and stretched and reeled, silently yelling before, at once, Reagan let go of my throat.

The scream tore free in an instant, and I was sure the entire house could hear me. Maybe China, too.

But as soon as I was sucking in air to either scream again or moan uncontrollably, Reagan clamped down on my neck once more, silencing me.

"That was so very pretty. But I like to see you suffer, unable to yell like you so desperately want to."

Edward and Reagan were moving in tandem inside me,

their cocks fucking my pussy and asshole until I was ready to explode into a thousand tiny bits. It was everything to feel them inside me like that, the way I was so filled, the way Reagan held me so I could scarcely breathe, it was utter bliss.

Leaning toward me, Edward brushed his lips against mine, and I instinctively moved for him, kissing him as his cock reached up to my G-spot and made me see stars. Reagan was right there with him, rubbing nerves inside me that we typically neglected. Every thrust and pull and swirl fed off the next, and I orgasmed harder than I ever had, gushing around the cock buried in my cunt.

"Our filthy little slut, coming all over like that," Reagan admonished, the tease going straight to me clit. "You're soaking our bed, and you're just going to have to clean it all up when we're done."

He was definitely saying words, but I was too fucking gone to care.

Cocks thickened inside me, harder and harder, and just when I thought they would crack me in half—a wonderful way to go if it felt this damn good—both Reagan and Edward came inside me.

Warmth poured from them as they filled me up until it was dripping down my skin, adding to the mess I'd made of the covers. The release drove through me, and I clamped down around them, my holes fluttering as I orgasmed yet again.

"That's it, baby. Come so much. Come until you can't stand it."

Edward was still pumping into me, somehow still hard as he drew out every last drop of cum he could give.

"One more, princess." Reagan released my throat, and I cried out while he pushed deeper.

"I…I can't. It's…" I whimpered, my clit on fire as my walls gripped them both tightly. "It's too much."

Reagan yanked on my hair, craning my head back. "I said

come, slut. And you do what your Daddy tells you."

And fuck, when he put it like that.

A jolt of electricity zinged through me as one more climax blew me to smithereens. I wasn't sure what happened after that because I'd left this earth. Victim to the best goddamn sex of my life.

"That has definitely earned you your gift." Reagan smiled, looking over at Edward and me as we lay in the disheveled bed. "Both of you."

"Both of us?" Edward sat up, idly dragging his hand up and down my arm as I continued to come down from that incredible session. "What have you been up to?"

Reagan only smirked, stepping away from me and Edward and sauntering over to his dresser, so very proud of himself. We hadn't gotten everything in the house fixed. It had only been two weeks, after all, but the bedroom was so much better now.

It was a good start, which was exactly what we all needed.

Well, right now I need snacks and a bath, but whatever.

As Reagan reached inside his drawer, he cleared his throat and then turned around with twin velvet boxes. They looked large to be something like a bracelet or a ring, and we'd already talked about not really caring about getting married.

Not that we wouldn't. It just wasn't top priority.

"When exactly did you have the time to go out and shop?" Edward asked, smiling up at Reagan as he and I maneuvered to the edge of the bed, much to my chagrin, I might add.

"We have people for that kind of thing, Edward. I just submitted the order and had *them* fetch it."

"You made Val do it, didn't you?" I smiled, teasing Reagan about his own unique form of hazing for the new don's number two.

"I did. He was *not* happy, which of course, was precisely what I wanted."

We all laughed at that one, but then Reagan was sitting on the bed, forcing Edward and me to get down on the floor at his feet so we could look up at him. We did, taking up our kneeling positions, even if I still flavored mine with flipping him off.

It was my thing.

"Brat. Which…" Reagan looked closely at the boxes, switching them around in his hands and then presenting one to each of us. "…should make this perfect for you."

I took the velvet box, running my fingers along the smooth surface. Exchanging a glance with Edward, we silently agreed to open them together. We each took a deep breath and then nodded, cracking the lids.

Two gasps sounded simultaneously, and then I forgot there was anyone else there.

Inside my jewelry box was a necklace of sorts—if you could consider a collar a necklace. Still, this one wasn't clunky or too large. It was delicate but purposeful.

A necklace. A collar. For me.

Dragging my fingers across its strands, I admired how it was made from both chain and leather. The thin metal was linked with such small pieces that it looked downright fragile, and that contrasted with the thin strips of black leather that would be the pieces that sat flush to my skin.

In the center was a traditional O-ring, but mine was shaped like a heart, and dangling from the point at the bottom was a little red gem.

"Turn it over, Lila."

Flicking my eyes up to Reagan, I had to admit that they were teary again, but for an entirely different reason. I took the collar out of the box, which had a tiny lock at the back, ensuring it wouldn't be removed.

As I turned it around, I saw that on the back of the red gem was an inscription, "Daddy's Brat."

I fucking beamed.

"I love it!"

Breaking our protocol, I leaped up off the floor and through myself into Reagan's arms. I would gladly accept punishment if it meant I could show him how much this meant to me, and yeah, I was a brat anyway, so listening to the rules unprovoked wasn't really my thing.

He chuckled, the sensation rumbling against me as I hugged him. It only took a moment for Reagan to pull me up and crash his lips on mine in a hungry kiss. It went on, too, and when he'd thoroughly kissed the hell out of me, I looked up at Reagan all dreamy and thrilled.

"Oh!" I spun around in Reagan's lap. "What's yours?"

Edward smiled up at us, getting up from the floor and sitting down in the bed next to Reagan. He showed me his collar, and I gasped again, taken aback by how perfect it was for Edward.

The thin black straps were tooled with etchings of intricate designs, subtle from a distance but mesmerizing when you looked at them up close. He had an O-ring, too, but his was the classic O shape, set perfectly into the center of the collar. It was simple and lovely, even the metal had a black hue.

"Does yours say anything?"

Turning down the corners of his mouth, Edward looked to Reagan. Our dom smiled again and twirled his finger, miming that Edward should turn the collar over. He did, and hot damn, if Reagan didn't make Boss Man a little teary, too.

"What does it say?" I demanded excitedly.

Edward cleared his throat, smiling as he met Reagan's eyes. As he held up the collar, turning it over so that I could see the charred phrase imprinted on the back of the leather, I understood why, putting my hands to my mouth as I too got a little choked up.

No pun intended.

Reagan cocked his head, smiling at Edward. "Find me after hours…forever."

He yanked Edward to his lips, pulling in over the top of me so that we made a tangle of limbs.

"And I mean it." He looked between us, his eyes shining. "I love you both, forever."

"I love you, Reagan." Edward kissed him again, then tilted his head down toward me. "And I love you, Lila."

Putting a hand on both their cheeks, I grinned so fucking big. "I love you both. My two overprotective assholes. All to myself."

"Hmm," Edward hummed, "funny you should mention that."

29
The New Roles

Edward

"**F**unny I should mention which part?" Lila furrowed her brow as she asked, her Spidey Sense tingling.

I had to laugh. She had always been quite good at reading people, and those skills seemed to only improve after everything that happened with her father, likely because Lila was even more confident in herself and was listening to her instincts.

"Overprotective." I smiled at her. We were cuddled into our shared bed, a thing I never thought I'd have, let alone with someone like Reagan *and* Lila, and the truth was that was about as much sharing as I was comfortable doing on the long term.

"Oh, I see."

Raising her eyebrows, Lila turned down the corners of her mouth and patted my cheek. Our little brat was such a delicious tease even now. I'd never tried coming three times, but I could certainly be motivated to practice.

"So, let me guess." She put on a serious face, and I chuckled, Reagan joining in when he craned over the top of her and saw for himself. "I'm fired."

Nodding to myself, I sighed, so utterly called out. "Not exactly. I'd like to offer you a different position at the club.

Bartender."

Lila's eyes flared wide. "I'm sorry, what? I know nothing about bartending."

"You knew nothing about blow jobs or sex, and you figured that out okay."

"Edward!" She smacked my arm, but the mock fury was short-lived. "Jesus, bartending? Are you sure?"

"I am. I think you'll be fine. And to be very, *very* honest," I pulled Lila closer, scooping my hands around her to grab her ass, "I don't want you servicing anyone else but us."

Squealing, Lila grinned, a charming laugh echoing through our room. Reagan leaned over her, piling on top of both of us, and I was utterly crushed. Laughter filled the room until we all settled back down into the bed again.

Jesus, I feel like a teenager again.

"So I can add jealous and possessive to the list, huh?" Lila eyed me and then Reagan.

Reagan and I exchanged glances, and then both of us nodded purposefully, simultaneously answering, "Yes."

Lila laughed again, her eyes closing as she settled into the bed between us, the peanut butter to our tasty little sandwich. *Sandwich? Christ, Edward who even are you?*

Still, I couldn't bring myself to be annoyed with my sudden affinity for Hallmark. Lila brought it out in me, and it was as pleasant a surprise as finding out that Reagan had a heart under all that baggage.

"I guess. It can't be that hard to bartend, right? You're not expecting me to do that bottle flipping thing, are you?"

"Not unless you feel really compelled to do so. I'll set you up with the staff for training, and you'll be good to go."

Reagan sat up, leaning back against the headboard. "And what will you be telling your staff about *why* she's moving to the bar?"

We'd talked about Lila avoiding clients. We'd talked about

Reagan's sudden and inevitable promotion to don. But we hadn't discussed the potential of anyone knowing the inside details.

I had come up with my own answer, though.

"I'm going to tell them the truth. If they ask, of course. They can stew in their own juices all they want, but if someone approaches me, I won't be lying."

Lila shot up, her eyes finding mine as they glossed over with unshed tears. I grinned, knowing I'd never get tired of that expression.

"You're going to tell them about me?"

"Tell the world that Lila is mine? Ours? Yes, princess. I want everyone to know exactly who you belong to."

A tear slipped free just as she launched herself at me, getting right against my chest and kissing the fuck out of me. I laughed against her lips, smiling as she squished me.

When she sat back, Lila turned toward Reagan. "And what about you, Daddy? Am I a secret or—"

"Ugh," Reagan narrowed his eyes at me, his jaw tense as he silently communicated his annoyance, "well, I think I fucking *have* to tell people now. Little slave set a fucking precedence."

Lila was all giddy delight, proud that we'd both managed to get Reagan into a situation where he was forced to do what we wanted. Reagan was a private person, but this was the "time of change," as we were calling it, and I knew both Lila and I wanted the secrecy to be among the traditions that were left behind.

"I would have thought the collars were enough to make my point," Reagan said, his stare dancing between us, "but to use our princess's word, 'duh.' You're *both* mine, and the entire fucking *universe* will never hear the end of it."

"Well, I *guess* I'm fine with it then." Lila was going to milk this for all that it was worth, I just knew it. "But I'm putting in my own request."

"Which is?" Reagan asked, only just beating me to it.

"I'd like you each to cook me dinner once a week."

My jaw dropped, and Reagan's brows shot to his hairline. It took us both a solid ten seconds before either of us could speak.

"Princess," I began, "are you trying to kill yourself? I'm a terrible cook."

"Yeah," she was still all grins, "but Reagan's not. He's incredible at it. He can teach you."

She was arranging date nights for us. Time to be just the two of us while still getting something out of it. Goddamn it. That was impressive.

Reagan furrowed his brow, pinching Lila's chin between his fingers. "You are a crafty little minx. You know that?"

"I do." Lila kissed the tip of his nose, turning to plant one on my cheek. "It's one of my core personality traits."

"Well, I guess it's settled then." I reached out to shake Lila's hand.

She took it, crossing over with her other one to shake Reagan's. "Gentlemen, you have yourselves a deal."

Emilio's office, his *old* office, was organized in such a particular manner that it was like cracking some sort of code to get through all his shit. We'd allowed ourselves a moment to be happy after everything that had gone down—last night being a particular favorite of mine—but now it was time to get to work.

I needed to figure out the extend of his networks. Emilio hadn't just started this trafficking bullshit, and putting a quick fucking end to all of it was top priority. I'd already had to perform a few "lay-offs" because a handful of the Family still believed the fucker had had a point.

Good thing there was no shortage of new recruits to replace them. Even better than Val was among them. I'd done myself a fucking favor bringing him in, and after what he did during the showdown, he'd earned himself the position of consigliere.

"This is wild. How much fucking shit was my dad into? Ugh, I am so glad I killed him."

Lila groaned from where she sat in one of the oversized club chairs. We'd been going through his files, digital and hard copies, for hours now, and even I had to admit that it was becoming mind-numbing.

"Too goddamn much." I looked up from the computer, still feeling odd to be sitting in the don's chair. "Val, I need to arrange a full Family meeting again. There is more in these files, and I want a sweep conducted of every 'contact' Emilio set up. We're severing ties, and I know that'll come with some angry assholes looking to strong arm us. I won't have it."

Val nodded from his seat across the room, standing up and closing the folder of print-outs he'd been reading.

"That sounds a lot fucking better than looking at this shit. I'm on it." He turned to Edward. "We good to use the club as a meet location?"

Edward sighed. "Yes, for the initial meeting. Don't kill anyone in my fucking basement."

Smirking, Val winked. "No promises."

He was out of the office like a shot after that, leaving the three of us alone. Lila immediately seized the opportunity, hurrying over and sitting in my lap.

"Daddy, you look so stressed."

She was teasing, using that fucking voice on me because she knew it got me thinking with my cock.

"Yes, but we do not have the time right now. The renovation team will be here soon. We've already delayed meeting with them twice."

Looking affronted, she put a hand to her chest. "That wasn't *my* fault!"

I cocked an accusing brow at her, and Lila blushed, chewing on her lip. "Mostly."

"Come on, both of you." Edward stood from his chair. "We're about to knock down the first wall. We should call everyone in."

I nodded, still not looking forward to this part. Getting up, I walked to the intercom system I'd had installed almost immediately after I was patched up and called for a "house meeting."

It didn't take long for the twenty-seven members of La Famiglia de Carpinelli to arrive and gather round my desk.

"Thank you all for coming. As you know, things have changed. Your former don is dead, and I've stepped up into the role. I've already dealt with the most vocal dissenters, but I want things to be crystal fucking clear. This Family is mine to run. I will not tolerate disloyalty or betrayal. You fuck with me and mine? You're dead."

The room remained silent, but I felt Lila and Edward's presence behind me, lending silent support.

"We do not traffic in humans—end of story. Furthermore, I will not hear shit about my relationship with my partners. Do and you're dead. You are welcome to pursue relationships within the Family and out. You fuck up, and I think you can all guess the consequences. Come to me with any chatter about dissent, issues affecting the Family, and prospects. We need to keep ourselves afloat. I'm not looking for landmark numbers, but don't bring in what we need to thrive, and you're out."

The people in front of me nodded, men and women I'd known for years, and new faces all the same.

"Now, we have a renovator to meet with because this ostentatious bullshit is gone. Deliver any questions or concerns to Val. He'll see them back to me."

Without waiting for anyone to speak or move, I turned to the door and headed out, Lila and Edward hot on my heels. As I walked out of the room, Edward put a hand on my shoulder, leaning in enough to whisper.

"I forgot to mention, my rates for silence have quadrupled."

I smirked, not bothering to look at him as I let out a tiny growl. "Well, I'll be taking it out of your ass, so keep that in mind."

"Ooh, I love that idea!" Lila giggled, linking her fingers through mine as we made our way downstairs. "I offer mine as a bonus."

"Hmm, I think I can make that work." I glanced over, offering my princess a tiny smile.

Just then, Edward's phone rang. He answered as we rounded the corner and jogged down the main staircase.

"Yeah?" A brief pause. "Hey, Drake. What's up?" Another pause, and Lila looked across me to eye him. "Oh, really? That's excellent. God, we've been desperate for a new sub since that bitch tried to kill Lila."

A predictable frown creased Lila's forehead, and I smoothed my thumb back and forth across her hand.

"Yeah, let's bring her in. Name?" We reached the foyer just as the doorbell rang. "Gabriella. Perfect."

As one of the newer members stepped up to answer the ring, I smiled. Yeah, everything was pretty damn perfect.

Epilogue
The New Routine

Lila

Six months later...

"**O**h fuck, oh fuck, oh fuck!" My pussy was going to explode. I was going to fucking die, expire off this earth and into the goddamn heavens.

Everything burned in the best possible way, the stretch so damned intense that I was utterly unable to focus on anything else.

"That's it, princess. Fall apart for us." Reagan's voice was straight to my clit, and I tipped over the edge—again.

Their cocks were grinding inside me at the same time, and being stuffed full of them like this was better than I could have ever imagined. Hell, I didn't think it was possible at first. They were both so big, but my cunt was happily accepting both of them like it was the perfect drug.

"Daddy! It's…Fuck!"

I was just a bundle of orgasming nerves at this point, and Edward circled his hand around to my throat, his chest pressed against my back as he fucked me in time with Reagan.

"Shhh, baby. Clench around our cocks like our good little slut."

And boy, did I.

Reality was a blur as I began to come down from another perfect evening with my men, and they'd filled me so damn full of their cum that it was gong to be leaking out of me for days. *Ah, this is the life.*

"Alright, princess. I'm leaving you in good hands."

Edward had gotten dressed again at some point, but I couldn't remember when. I was still riding the high, trying to work out the drop after being so consumed by sub-space. Plus, my body ached from all the wax and flogging, and I needed to pass out for a while. He landed a kiss on my forehead, and I turned into it, wanting more of the grounding contact.

"Baby, I have to go to work." He helped to face me toward Reagan. "Daddy's going to take good care of you."

"I hate you leaving," I grumbled.

"I know. But the new sub is still getting acclimated to the club, and I feel a little protective of her."

Cracking a lid, I frowned at him as Reagan ran his hand up and down my arm.

"Do I need to be jealous?"

Edward's laugh was annoying and comforting. "No, never. It's just…"

Reagan was actually the first to check in after that non-answer from Edward. He'd become a bit more curious about how the club worked after things settled down in the Family.

"That sounds fucking ominous. What's that about?"

A sigh left Edward, and I watched only slightly more coherent as he straightened his tie.

"You know that feeling you get when you can tell someone is unhappy? Well, that's Gabriella. She won't open up about it, but I can tell that something is eating her at home. It's none of my business, but—"

"I'm in tomorrow when she's working. I'll see what I can do." I smiled up at him, my eyes closing as exhaustion pulled at me.

"You're amazing, princess."

Snuggling into Reagan, I pulled his head down toward mine so he'd put his weight on me, his lips coming to my head in a constant, comforting kiss.

"I know."

Edward's chuckle was nice, and I knew he appreciated it when I checked in on the girls. Between me and Elle, Boss Man knew he had a team of people he could trust with them.

"Ugh, I don't want to leave, but I'll be back early. I'm not staying for that second meeting. Drake can handle it."

Reagan laughed this time, and it rumbled through me as everything slowed way down in my head.

"Yeah, I saw that coming." He laughed again. "Just like you did, in fact."

"Fucker," Edward smirked. "Okay, I'll be back. Reagan's going to get you up out of the dungeon when you're ready, and then I'm coming home for cuddles and more sex as soon as I can. Deal?"

I smiled, my eyes still closed, as I appreciated more and more how I'd been very *particular* about our home remodel. Less gold. More chains and wall mounts.

"Deal."

Acknowledgements

Thank you to everyone who continues to support me on the wild journey, not the least of which is my wonderful friend, Tori, who encouraged me to go after a contemporary pen name—even if it was just so she could write books with me. I adore you.

To the patrons who have given the Scarlett Oleander world their love. I'm so glad that Westley and Andi spoke to you so that I could go on to tell the stories of everyone at the club and beyond. A special shout-out to— Brittany, Cheyanne, Samantha, and Denis. You all rock.

As always, this book wouldn't have come to fruition without the support of some truly amazing people: my author friends for sharing their resources with me, my first-look readers, and, of course, my team of helpers that gets the word out.

To my ride-or-dies, Ally and Rachel, I thank you for every book you continue to read from me. Your support is incredible. To family and buddies who have helped me form a support system I know I can count on.

And to the one and only Ryan. You've been my rock when life gets lifing, and I am so grateful. You've been there to help entertain the kiddos when I've needed to write, and you never once told me to stop pursuing my dreams. I love you more than anything.

About Liz

In the world of Liz Highland, you are encouraged to embrace the dark side of romance.

Author of dark contemporary romance novels and novellas, Liz Highland tells tales that revolve around intimacy, lust, love, and every way that a heart can both break and grow. Focusing on characters who all flaunt their red flags proudly, you'll find stories fit for fans of the darkest of the dark and the spiciest of the spicy.

During their off time, Liz can be found enjoying a cold cup of coffee that's been microwaved at least six times at this point because their tiny goblins keep interrupting them and reading all the delicious dark romance they can get their hands on.

Check out everything Liz has to offer by following them on social media under @lizhighlandauthor, and be on the lookout for more stories coming from the world of the Scarlett Oleander, including Edged & Ensnared featuring a new sub who's in a hell of a lot of trouble, and more.

Also By Liz

Fallow Trilogy

Hunted- Fallow Trilogy Book One
Wanted- Fallow Trilogy Book Two
Trapped- Fallow Trilogy Book Three

Dark Haven Universe

Mutual Interests- A FemDom Standalone (2025)

The Scarlett Oleander Series

Bought & Bound- Scarlett Oleander Series Book One
Traded & Teased- Scarlett Oleander Series Book Two
Edged & Ensnared- Scarlett Oleander Series Book Three
(TBA In Progress)
Masked & Manipulated- Scarlett Oleander Series Book Four
(TBA)
Stalked & Saved- Scarlett Oleander Series Book Five (TBA)

Anthologies

Drama Queen Anthology- Royal Debts (Full Novel coming
2025)
Violence & Virtues Vol. 2- After Hours (A Traded & Teased
Prequel)

Check it all out at linktr.ee/lizhighlandauthor

Stalk Liz

For the latest updates from Liz Highland, be sure to follow them on all their social media under @lizhighlandauthor.

Follow them on Facebook
Follow them on Instagram
Follow them on TikTok
Follow them on Threads
Join The Demon Club- Reader Group for RE Johnson & Liz Highland on Facebook

You can find all links at linktr.ee/lizhighlandauthor.

Are You Looking For More?
Such a Brat.

Well, since you asked so nicely, be sure to check out the link below for a After Hours- A Traded & Teased Prequel. It shows all the deciousness of how Reagan and Edward started hooking up.

Talk soon!

(And be on the look out for Edged & Ensnared, featuring the aforementioned Gabriella, whose new to the club and in a heaping dose of trouble.)

https://tinyurl.com/AfterHoursClaim